FIGHTING THE MACHINES

Book 1. Escape

D0890792

by
David Geoffrey Adams

Grosvenor House
Publishing Limited

This book is published by
Grosvenor House Publishing Ltd
Link House
140 The Broadway, Tolworth, Surrey, KT6 7HT.
www.grosvenorhousepublishing.co.uk

This book is a work of fiction. Any resemblance to
people or events, past or present, is purely coincidental.

A CIP record for this book
is available from the British Library

ISBN 978-1-83975-052-6

Dedication

This work is dedicated to my darling wife, Marion, without whose support and encouragement I would never have finished it.

Contents

Prologue   xi

New Orders   xi

One hundred years before.   xi

Chapter

1	Cambridge	1
2	Geneva	7
3	Eureka	13
4	Exotics Harnessed	30
5	Houston	36
6	Three Years On	44
7	Discovery on the Red Planet	55
8	Buried	70
9	Fuelling the Warp Drive	84
10	Interstellar Probe	95
11	Now for the Stars	113
12	A Change of Plan	125
13	*And a Change of Course*	129
14	This is Why	130
15	*Urgency*	151
16	On the Way	152
17	To Warp	156

18	*Alarm*	163
19	Onward	164
20	In the Void	166
21	Centauri	176
22	Solar System - First Contact	193
23	Amongst the Stars	202
24	Personal Concerns	220
25	Horror in the sky	228
26	Danger in Hyades	247
27	Dissension	259
28	Eden lost – again	268
29	Land Ahoy!	278
30	*A Watcher Awakes*	297

Acknowledgements

There are a number of people whom I should thank. My Creative Writing tutor, Dave Copson, who gave me the confidence to believe that I could write a book. Those many authors over the years whose books helped me. The greats H G Wells, Arthur C Clarke, Isaac Asimov and John Wyndham to name but a few.

The characters in the story are, of course, completely fictional but the brilliant work of two real scientists gave me the idea for the Einstein and its fellow ships. Mexican theoretical physicist, Miguel Alcubierre, whose design, adapted by the NASA scientist Dr Harold White forms the structure for the ships in this story.

Professor Stephen Hawking has been an inspiration to many people. The references to him are, again, fictional and there is, as yet, no such award as the Hawking Medal.

Finally, my granddaughter Megan who produced the painting that forms the cover.

Preface

This book was ten years in the making. An avid science fiction fan myself, I have read hundreds of books over the years. When thinking that I had a book in me to write the ideas were many though most centred on what might happen if we could build a starship. After retirement from the full-time job I still struggled to work out how to proceed. Then a local adult education class in Creative Writing caught my attention. Two years on the first book is done. Other authors have been quoted saying the characters took over. Well they did and the story line developed well beyond the original idea as well.

It is a story of success tinged with sadness at times. To quote one character "Why me?" well you will need to read on and, I trust, enjoy.

Prologue

New Orders

Ellen sat in her quarters gazing at, but no longer seeing, the visage of Titan below. Her entire world had been turned upside down with the new orders from Earth.

"Why me?" she thought. "Captain of a starship, yes. But responsible for the survival of our species?"

One hundred years earlier.

The fleet continued to follow its course powering ahead at three quarters of light speed seeking another target. Sensors alerted the outliers to primitive radio noise emanating from a system almost eighty light years to the right of its course. The command craft recognised evidence of an intelligent civilisation. Instructions flowed and one hundred ships started a turn towards the system leaving the rest of the fleet to continue on its original track.

1. Cambridge

Not for the first time Megan struggled to sleep. This time it was not the regular student party. Her mind was still operating at full speed after the morning's events when she had learnt that her dissertation had met the standard required by her college and that she had achieved her degree with first class honours.

As she waited for sleep to claim her, she let her mind drift back to the first time she had heard about particle physics.

She had still been at primary school when the Large Hadron Collider had been scheduled to be downgraded to a slipway for the new, one hundred kilometres long, accelerator. The LHC, as it was known, had led to the discovery of the Higgs Boson which had been the fundamental issue first targeted by the early researchers and evidence of its existence had been found in 2012 shortly before she was born.

"What's a God's particle, Daddy?" she had asked her father, after seeing news reports about that earlier discovery.

"I don't really know." He answered. "It's something very small but it must have been important because lots of clever people called physicists were searching for it for a long time."

"I think I want to be one of them." She said with all the confidence of a bright youngster aged just ten.

"You will have to work very hard at school to do that." Her father replied with a smile.

As time passed, she had become more and more interested in the science of physics and eleven years after that earlier conversation she had now completed her degree course. During that period the LHC had delivered some amazing results even if there seemed to be more mysteries and unanswered questions than could have been thought of back in 2010 when the first near light speed collisions had been instigated.

LHC's replacement had been due to start operating at the same time that she completed her A-Levels and obtained, to her delight, a place at Gonville and Caius College, Cambridge. While studying for her degree in Theoretical Physics, she had kept a close watch on the results of the research being carried out at CERN. The scientists there, however, were struggling with frequent difficulties in the mechanical operation of the new particle accelerator and new steps forward in their research were lacking.

By 2033 there was still one "event" which had been seen on multiple occasions in LHC runs and on a few of the early runs of the new accelerator. The latter was continuing to suffer repeated mechanical failures so new data was still severely limited. Despite that, the event could not be, or at least had not been, explained. The particle which caused the events, did not fit with any existing theory and was in danger of being consigned to the status of an unexplainable error in the data.

Megan had an intuitive ability to think outside the box which had, at times, led to, it must be said, heated discussions with her tutors and professors. As she looked for a subject for her dissertation in the particle area which was unexplained, the experiences at CERN kept her attention. After spending some time considering the options she settled on the new particle – what might it be or what was causing its all too brief existence?

She reviewed the research papers which had been written in the early days of the discovery including two papers by Stephen Hawking himself. One paper, written in the 1990s before the LHC had been completed, had considered how energy and particles might be able to escape a black hole and it had been this which provided Megan with an idea for her own paper.

The idea of parallel universes remained an unproven if not largely fictional idea but at the same time her fellow students studying mathematics and or theoretical physics were quite ready to argue that the idea of multiple dimensions and thus other universes could not be denied as a part of the solution to some of the more esoteric research problems.

Megan wondered, was there a process occurring at the temperatures in the collider which weakened the "space" between such parallel universes so that a particle from another domain might, briefly, break through only to return nanoseconds later? If so, what implications did it have for future particle accelerators then being built to accelerate not just particles but light weight molecules such as hydrogen and helium to close to light speed?

Then she had had a sudden premonition – had the particle event been examined to see if it was possible to identify any structure? A swift search of the various papers written in the early days of the occurrence of the events had indicated that the particle had not existed long enough to be examined, even via the recordings which had shown it to occur.

She was unhappy that it was, in her view, necessary to leave open such uncertainty and had decided to review and then to simply, to the initial horror of her tutor, change her approach midway through her paper – scrapping it and starting again from scratch.

In her new paper she surmised that the event and/or particle in question might be tied to an application of string theory - supersymmetry. This theory required that different particles, bosons and fermions, had to be matched on a one to one basis, but that it had not been possible to find the additional particles needed. The accepted theory was that their existence required such heat and energy that they would have decayed almost immediately after the Big Bang had occurred.

Her paper concentrated on two points. First that the LHC had, possibly, for a few nanoseconds replicated the local conditions of the Big Bang and that the larger more powerful accelerator would, she theorised, produce further events similar in nature but that the particles would also not disappear so quickly. Secondly, and when writing this part, she held her breath, if and it was a big "if" the energy contained within the particles, as predicted, could be harnessed then immense clean power might be available. As a postscript to the main paper she suggested that such research would be enhanced if heavier atoms or molecules could be used.

Now she knew that her college considered that such an outcome of her paper warranted high enough marks to allow her to achieve her degree with first class honours. It had not occurred to her that refusing to lay down a definitive outcome was that essential part of winning the argument.

A few days later the email invitation she received was so totally unexpected that her first thoughts were that it must be an elaborate hoax. As she considered how to question its validity without looking a fool, she received a call asking her to attend the Chancellor's office urgently.

The Chancellor's PA showed her into his office as soon as she arrived with a beaming smile, which was in itself a little unnerving. "Miss Newcombe to see you, Chancellor, as you requested." The two men present rose to greet her.

"Megan, thank you for coming so quickly. I did fear you might have gone home for a break before Thursday's ceremony." the Chancellor said, "I believe you will remember Professor Lawrence from your first-year studies?"

"Yes Chancellor, of course. Professor – welcome back to Cambridge."

The tall scientist and scholar shook her hand. "I am glad to be back if only for a few days and even more pleased to hear the news regarding your success."

"Sorry?"

The Chancellor interrupted. "Take a seat Megan. Geoff, Miss Newcombe is not yet aware of what is to occur at the graduation ceremony. I wanted you to be present when we told her."

Megan's mind was in a whirl – how could they know about the invitation – unless? "Sir, I received an email this morning that purports to be from CERN – is that what you mean? And may I ask how you might know? Especially as I had not applied to them." She felt forced to be honest enough to add "Yet anyway."

Geoff Lawrence laughed. "Tony, it seems the CERN bureaucracy has worked quickly for once!"

"I suspect that, once you and your colleagues had concurred with our thoughts, the back office felt they needed to move quickly to ensure that Megan did not accept any of the other invitations I am sure she will receive after Thursday."

Megan struggled to breathe – just what were the two men referring to?

Three days later her success hit the headlines as the first recipient of a new award, the Hawking Medal, awarded for "exceptional and thought-provoking work in theoretical physics" by an undergraduate.

2. Geneva

Megan had aimed high and now she was in Geneva.

The physical size of the new particle accelerator was invisible from inside the operations room deep under the Alps. Yet here was one of the world's most expensive scientific experiments and nobody who entered that room could fail to be affected by the nature of such a human venture. And if they were there as newly graduated physicists, then they had often made it through an exhausting and highly selective process which reduced the hundreds of applicants from across the globe to a handful. Only a very select few received a direct invitation such as Megan's.

"You didn't think I would make it here, Dad, did you?" thought Megan as she entered the room before coming to a sudden halt as the importance of the location to her sank in.

"What am I doing here? Among so many real scientists?" She almost panicked with the realisation that she really would be working at CERN.

"M'selle." The greeting startled her and she realised that, to her chagrin, she had daydreamed her way across the room. She recognised the person immediately and her face reddened as it always did. "Professor, I am so sorry – it is so overwhelming...."

Her new boss grinned "It gets any serious individual in exactly the same way. If you weren't overwhelmed then we would have been wrong to invite you to join us! Even Professor Hawking admitted to a highly emotional response when he visited the site in the days of the LHC."

"Sadly, he passed away while I was at infant school and I never had the chance to meet him but he was my inspiration to study Physics. That and the discovery of the Higgs Boson!" she admitted.

"Stephen always kept in touch with me and my predecessors on a private level rather than official. Most of us attended symposia at which he spoke and met with him out of the public view. I was in London earlier this year and I met his successor who passed on the final draft of your dissertation. He made a quiet suggestion that we would benefit from your ability to think outside the box or, as he put it, outside of the circle."

Megan gasped. "B-but" she stammered, "he never said a word to me and certainly did not suggest my dissertation was anything but a bit above average! I know it was published within the Cambridge group and thought that someone here must have seen it there. But the direct invitation was a complete shock."

Yuri Lentenov laughed again. "He and his colleagues hold you in very high esteem, not least because you were prepared to put forward a logically argued process that, even if it seemed close to science fiction to others, touched legitimately on mathematical research and recurrent theories and elements of the Big Bang. And that, naturally, led to you being awarded the Hawking Medal. That also, in his view, supported the idea that you have the courage often needed in our research areas to put up fresh ideas in front of your peers and argue their validity against sceptical responses. Tomorrow I shall enjoy hearing your thoughts on these indefinable particles. As an invited newcomer we ask that you make a presentation of your paper to an audience made up of the rest of the team."

Later in her room Megan's thoughts went back to the past few years of her degree studies and the frequent need to argue her views on the current state of research into particle physics. Now it would be her chance to air her theories, in her presentation the next day, directly to experienced scientists, who lived with that research every day, and she expected to have to justify her views to the full.

After a restless night she was up early walking over to the main building for breakfast receiving a friendly welcome from those people who were in the staff restaurant. She was glad to be able to sit with one of the still relatively few female researchers present who introduced herself as Elena Gallo, an Italian from Milan. After the self-introductions the conversation moved on to Megan's presentation.

"Nervous?" Elena said, continuing as Megan nodded. "I shouldn't worry too much. Most of the team will have read a synopsis, if not the full paper, already. I am sure they will want to challenge your views, after all your ideas cover an area most had "filed" as not worth spending time on. But you will have faced that sort of challenge back at Cambridge I am sure."

"True," said Megan, "But that was quite a protective environment."

"Don't worry. They will give you a fair hearing, as I said, while wanting to challenge you. Now I must go. The latest test run is due in an hour and I need to be in place."

Megan finished her meal and returned to her room to complete her presentation notes before walking over to the auditorium in time to set up before the 11am start. To her amazement the room was already almost full. With more than 500 people present it meant that the audience included members of other research teams.

At 11 o'clock sharp Yuri Lentenov, as leader of the new accelerator operations team, opened the session with the announcement that the test run had been completed successfully. He then turned to Megan, introducing her to the audience and reminding them, to warm applause, of her exceptional award.

Megan then commenced her presentation outlining why she had chosen this particular aspect of the LHC data. She touched on how her initial thoughts had changed to the idea that the particles might be a super-symmetry solution. At this point, there was an outburst from the audience.

"Herr Lentenov, is it necessary that we waste time on this rubbish? This poppycock? We know that these particles are almost certainly random muons! This... this...science fiction approach to our research will simply make us look fools to the outside world!"

Professor Lentenov responded. "Grigor, I am well aware of your views on the issue and still await some supporting research from you and your colleagues. In the meantime, please give Miss Newcombe the courtesy of hearing her full presentation."

However, Megan herself also responded directly to the challenge recognising the man in question. "Herr Professor, I understand your concerns and you are not the first to suggest that my work sounds like science fiction."

"It is. Rarely have I heard such propositions within the science community. Perhaps you should write a book!"

Unused to such harsh and venomous criticism Megan paused for breath. Then she decided to take the bull by the horns. "Herr Sokolov, I am prepared to have my theories disproved if they are wrong. Are you prepared for yours to be wrong? Would you be ready to work with me to find the correct answer?"

There was a stunned silence amongst the onlookers.

Her challenger stuttered. "You have only just graduated. You have no experience. Do you really believe that we could work on equal terms?"

The silence was replaced by a murmur of disapproval from the audience which buoyed Megan as she realised that they did not all agree with the Professor's attack.

"You work with other graduates as part of your team. How would this be different?"

Yuri Lentenov rose to his feet. "Professor, we have limited time here today. Please allow Miss Newcombe to complete her presentation and to answer other questions. We can follow up on this conversation later."

Sokolov subsided grumbling quietly to himself. It would not be the end of this Megan realised but she would just have to fight her corner more than ever before.

The next day a meeting between the two professors and Megan resulted in an agreement that she and Grigor Sokolov would jointly investigate the issue of the particles, if they did occur, using the data provided by the operations team. Sokolov agreed with as much good grace as possible following the reaction of the rest of his team to the idea of having Megan join them.

As a part of the discussion Megan also found out that plans were already afoot to take up her suggestion of using heavier atoms, in the first case ferric oxide molecules were to be tried.

3. Eureka

Several months of hard work, mixed with frustration, followed as the accelerator runs were frequently cut short due to various equipment failures. It did not seem that it mattered which starting molecules were used. There was some data but rarely did the runs reach the planned peak velocities needed for Megan's theory to be tested. After a month of zero data the teams met for a brainstorming session to try and identify the causes.

Grigor commented. "These issues seem to keep happening at around seventy per cent of the planned run times. What is it that is affecting the magnetic fields?"

It was, as Megan called it later, a eureka moment. Suddenly, turning to the operations team, she asked "Do we have records of the changes in temperature as each operation progresses?"

"Why might that be important?" asked both of the Professors.

"We believed, or expected, that if we were able to run the accelerator to its full extent we might, for the last 50 nanoseconds or so, replicate the velocities of particles believed to have occurred in the aftermath of the Big Bang."

"And?" Grigor interrupted.

"Those conditions must have involved ultrahigh, though cooling, temperatures." Megan continued. "But the projections of temperature growth have always suggested a steady state until the very end and then a rapid, short term, peak. Are we seeing this peak reached much earlier and could that be triggering the shutdowns?"

"Yuri, can we adapt if that is the case?" Grigor asked of Professor Lentenov.

"I'm sure we can but it won't be easy. We will need to amend the cut-off levels, adjust the magnetic field strengths and look at how maintaining those temperatures for longer periods might affect the structural integrity. This will not be a swift fix I'm afraid."

"Sounds like we may have been too successful in achieving the velocities we thought were hard." Another member of the team commented.

"That's a good problem though." Megan said, to herself, as the meeting broke up.

***   ***   ***

By now the relationship between Megan and Grigor had mellowed over the months and while it would be too much to suggest they were close friends they had developed mutual respect and it was no surprise that they could now be found trying to interpret the data they did have.

On their third coffee of the session Grigor sat back with a sigh. "I can't help but feel that we are missing something important."

"I agree," replied Megan, "but what it is escapes me for the moment. Perhaps we should run a comparison between the last several runs – see if there are direct similarities? Not identical, of course, but looking for similar changes in conditions?"

Grigor shrugged. "That is certainly thinking outside the box as Yuri told me you would. I take it you are not looking for matching collisions but to see if the general state of flux is doing something odd?"

"We'll need the rest of the team to help but that's right."

Grigor called in the rest of their colleagues and after a short briefing as to what was needed, they all set to running the data and film recordings. Those particle collisions, in the moments before shutdowns, were the primary target.

As had already been identified the local temperature had started to rise quickly in every case and was accompanied by an explosion of new particle trace lines.

"That's it! That's what we were missing." cried Megan.

"The temperature and increased particle reactions are linked? Of course, but how? And how on earth did we miss it?" Grigor responded.

You'll think I'm off on my sci-fi route again thought Megan hesitating.

"Spit it out" said Grigor, "even if it seems crazy to the rest of us." He smiled. "I haven't worked with you for these past months not to realise I was wrong that day you arrived."

"All right, I think we may be replicating the expansion period post big bang."

There was silence in the room and then everyone starting speaking at once. Grigor sat with a bemused look.

"Now that is pushing the edge of the book." He said, grimacing as he felt that his English was failing a little. "But that implies immense energy production at higher temperatures if we allow the planned runs to complete. We need to work out just what the impact will be before they restart the accelerator."

One of the other trainees interrupted. "Professor, did you not know? They started a test run twenty odd minutes ago."

"We must tell them to abort. Now! Go!"

Megan grabbed her mobile and started calling Yuri. When he answered Megan quickly passed the message to abort and then added "Kill the containment fields below the air vents and clear those areas fast."

Lentenov, to his credit did not question why, and Megan could hear him yelling to his team to carry out her instructions. She also heard a cry of "The temperatures are off the scale."

Moments later the building shook to the sound of metal shrieking under immense pressure. Then just as suddenly, and more disturbingly, silence fell. Megan and Grigor led a rush from their research desks towards the control room. Half way there they were stopped by an incredible sight. The corridor had been severed by a force which had left a large hole in the floor with a matching hole in the ceiling. The holes were, to the naked eye, identical and smooth circles.

Grigor and Megan exchanged looks of amazement before, without a word, they turned back to the last exit from the corridor to find a way around the obstacle and reach the control room as quickly as they could. Even as they went around a corner radiation alarms started going off. Megan checked her radiation monitor finding it to be, if anything, below normal background reading levels. Thinking it might be faulty she asked Grigor whose reply sounded perplexed.

"Either it is faulty or there is something very odd going on. Yours is the same?"

"It is, so why the alarms?" she replied equally unsure.

At that moment members of the operations team hurtled around the corner at the end of the passage almost knocking them over. Immediately there was a chorus of voices checking people were OK and asking what had happened.

Grigor's voice suddenly cut through the pandemonium. "One at a time, please! First, can we get to the operations room safely? Second, the passageway behind us needs closing off, at least until we understand what has really happened. It is Pierre, yes? Then please inform us as to the state of play."

The young man, seemingly startled at being recognised by the Professor, explained that the accelerator's torus had been fractured in two places. The radiation alarms were an automatic response to the breaches. A minor breach had occurred first, seconds before Megan's warning. The major fracture had been at one of the spots where they had killed the containment field. The operations room was naturally in uproar but no-one had been badly hurt, just a few bruises where the individual was off balance when the breech occurred and the building had shaken.

Grigor despatched two of his team for equipment to measure the holes in the ceiling and floor of the corridor emphasising the care needed, as they could not be sure how deep the hole in the floor might be. In the meantime, he and Megan would be in the operations room trying to get initial views as to what had happened and how bad the damage was.

In the operations room Yuri Lentenov and his team were desperately working to ensure that no data had been lost while running backup programs to share the details of the test run with scientists around the world. He took Megan and Grigor to a side office to outline the first reactions while thanking Megan for her swift intervention which he advised might well have avoided a major disaster with temperatures in the accelerator having first spiked and then rapidly risen further. Unfortunately, the relevant sensors had burnt out as the temperature had passed ten thousand degrees.

"How high?" gasped Megan. "How could that have occurred?"

"We don't know but two possibilities are the added velocities beyond previous accelerator runs and the fact that we included heavier atoms in the source particles."

Yuri's mobile rang.

Answering he listened for a moment then his face paled. "We will move to our nearest video conference room and will call you back."

Turning to the others he indicated that they should move to the conference room. "That call was from the NASA operations centre in Houston. They want to show us pictures recorded by one or more of their orbital satellites, I think anyway."

"What could they have seen which requires such urgency?" asked Grigor.

In the conference room a technician had just completed the connection and the screen was showing another operations room with several individuals. One turned to face the screen and introduced himself as director James Edwin, before asking for confirmation of the identities of those present at the Geneva end. He clearly recognised Yuri and Grigor but seemed perplexed by the presence of Megan and questioned the appropriateness of her being a part of the call. Grigor was swift to respond beating Yuri to the gun.

"I assume that your call has something to do with the events here in the past couple of hours. In which case Miss Newcombe is very much the right person to be involved. Not least because her swift reactions enabled us to limit the effects of extreme plasma heat."

"I see. I wonder if you realise just how this event has impacted the outside world?"

What followed left them speechless. The director showed three clips of film recorded and downloaded in live time from two satellites in geostationary orbit and then from a lunar orbiter. The first showed a bright light rising from the area close to Geneva before apparently being cut off, the second from a different angle showed a bright oblate object speeding past its orbital station. But it was the sight of the same object with little apparent change smashing into the lunar surface and leaving a glowing crater behind that brought gasps from everyone including some of those in Houston.

The director provided some background data. "That object actually cooled and slowed as it moved. It nearly hit the first satellite which measured its speed at over ten thousand kilometres per second with a temperature higher than forty thousand degrees. The film stops because the sensors and camera were, we assume, burnt out. The second film from around a thousand kilometres away confirmed those measurements."

"And when it hit the lunar surface?" Megan could not hide her amazement but Yuri could see that she was already putting together an idea of what had happened.

"Five hundred klicks per second and around ten thousand degrees. First estimates are that the impact crater is half a kilometre across but not as deep. The impact was more like a water balloon hitting, rather than a solid object. Just what were we seeing?" The director's voice underlined his confusion.

Yuri turned to the others. "Your first observations or guesses, please."

Grigor's comment surprised him. "Don't ask me. I have no real idea. Though I suspect Megan might have."

Megan took her time before answering. "I can suggest a possible solution but, and I mean but, it will need a lot of work to confirm."

"Go on." The others demanded in unison.

"We were considering the results of earlier aborted accelerator runs when it happened. My thoughts were that we might be close to replicating the conditions that are surmised to have existed at or about the time of the post big bang expansion period of the universe. On a small scale, of course."

In the stunned silence that followed, she went on to explain that they had tried to stop the test run and attempted to avoid a complete ground disaster within the accelerator.

"I wasn't sure what exactly was happening but the indications were that providing an "escape route" for the plasma that was forming seemed a good idea. The actual extremes were beyond anything I could have imagined but it now seems that killing the confinement field on one side of the accelerator not only provided an outlet but we may have provided the plasma field with a directional push from the continuing fields. What you saw was pure energy."

She paused and then continued. "At the moment we don't have the systems in place to contain this energy but if we could…." She let the sentence end unfinished.

With the image of the energy plasma striking the lunar surface difficult to erase and Megan's suggestion, as to the cause, ringing in their ears, the listeners stayed silent for a long time before the director closed the session with a request that he be kept informed of progress in their analysis of the events and promising support from NASA and its associates in the space programme. "You understand the implications for the planet and, dare I say it, space flight, if we could produce and use this energy in a controlled manner." He finished.

With the video conference at an end, the trio sat looking at the empty screen for several minutes before Yuri said. "We all have a lot of work to do. You both need to lead the analysis and investigation while I must look to see how much damage to the machinery has happened and how long before we can try to run the system again. I suspect you will have a few weeks before we can provide you with new data."

* * *　　* * *　　* * *

That evening the team really relaxed for the first time in some weeks and the party went on into the early hours but, for Megan, the idea that her own theories might have been supported in such emphatic fashion seemed unbelievable, despite the evidence and she found that sleep did not come easily, as she wondered if they would be able to repeat the experiment.

In fact, it would be almost four months, after the events of that day, before the accelerator was ready for use again but Grigor and Megan were far from idle during that time. The vast amount of data took them and their team many days to analyse and, eventually, reach conclusions that supported Megan's initial thoughts on that fateful day. Both were then invited to present their results to NASA and, to Megan's delight, to the science community back at Cambridge.

At both presentations her closing remarks preceded massive applause. "We believe that it should be possible to repeat the process once we can run the accelerator again. That means that we can generate an energy source for the future. We must turn to our engineering colleagues to find a way to allow us to keep it under control."

At NASA there were other meetings outside the public's eye in which the question was always what might be needed to answer the challenge of Megan's closing remarks. The general agreement was that the problem would be being able to generate a strong enough electromagnetic field in a relatively small container and how to direct the plasma into the container. The presumption was that once contained the plasma would retain its energy but, as Megan kept reminding herself, they were dealing with energies and issues beyond any previous experience.

Returning to Cambridge for the first time since her graduation presented different challenges. She was however unready for the warmth of her reception. After her first chat with old colleagues in the physics centre, she found herself invited to another meeting in the Chancellor's rooms.

"Megan, a delight to see you again. As ever you are making the headlines for all the best reasons."

"My pleasure to be back, Chancellor." she responded before turning to the third person in the room. "It's Alan isn't it?"

"You know each other?" the chancellor interrupted.

Smiling, Alan Piper responded. "We were classmates during our first year here. An overlap between our degree courses."

"But both of you following on with more success, of course."

"Well, I'm not sure mine is in the same class but we have made some progress with materials and propulsion research at Bristol." Alan replied with a modest grin.

"And is that research why you've brought us together, Chancellor?" asked Megan also smiling.

It was, of course, exactly the reason although, as the chancellor freely admitted, he was only acting as a go-between on behalf of the aerospace company. Their head of research had been present at the NASA conference and on returning to the UK had drawn together his team with the aim of being the first to successfully develop the necessary kit to enable Megan and her colleagues to capture the plasma and hold it in place long enough to analyse just exactly what was developing so as to refine its production, if that were found to be possible.

"I've agreed to accept a secondment to your team, Megan, if that is acceptable to you."

Megan thought hard and while having no objection herself had to point out that it would not be her decision. That would fall, she considered, to either Yuri or Grigor, if not both, as she explained to the others.

"We can check with Grigor later. He will be joining us for this afternoon's session. I don't see a problem but I wouldn't want to prejudge any decision."

There was a knock on the door and they were invited to the dining room for a light lunch at which Megan took the opportunity to quiz Alan about his work. It proved interesting and very much at the forefront of material developments for the aerospace industry with applications in both aircraft, satellite manufacture and other space technology.

"I understand about the strength of graphene but how does that interface with buckypaper?" she asked.

"We are looking at ways in which the nanotechnology used to produce buckypaper might be used to improve the various forms of graphene. Basically, to improve the heat tolerance of the combined product and its absolute strength. Both areas would have the potential to assist in meeting your requirements."

A waiter came to the table. "A Professor Sokolov to see you, Chancellor."

Grigor joined them at the table but refused any food, settling for an orange juice. The issue of who needed to approve Alan joining the team on a secondment was raised. "I have no problem with that but you are right, Megan, final sign off will need to be by Yuri."

They agreed that it would be best to have a conference call with Yuri Lentenov after the presentation.

"To the auditorium then." The chancellor led the way and they joined a stream of people from not only Megan's former college but from other colleges across the university and, she understood, there were also members of similar faculties from Oxford and Warwick.

Continuing the chancellor added, "Just to warn you – there will be members of the press present. That means you may get questions that are not purely academic or scientific. Such as why are we spending such large sums of money on scientific research when the issue of climate change is so much more important."

"That might be easier than you expect, Tony." replied Grigor. "If we could find a way to control the plasma in question it is a very clean form of renewable power. Without that research we would not have this as a possible source of energy."

As expected, the presentation was well received and, yes, the press raised questions in line with the Chancellor's warning. Grigor took the lead with careful but understandable answers to some exacting queries.

Afterwards a cocktail party enabled invited members of the university the chance to discuss the potential of the project and to talk more privately with Megan and Grigor. The conference call with Yuri went as they had anticipated and Alan was confirmed as a future member of the team. Yuri's welcome to Alan was candid. "Alan, your background and the support of the aerospace industries in both Europe and the USA, in particular, is exactly what we will need if we are to be successful in utilising this energy. I look forward to meeting you in person."

The following day Alan returned to his home in Bristol to pack and Megan took the chance to visit her family in the Midlands for a rare few days back with her parents and her sister, Marion, who was in the final year of her own degree, in medicine.

Grigor stayed on in Cambridge to meet with the particle physics department teams and learn how their theoretical research was going. He had always supported such contacts as the best way to transfer knowledge between practice and theory and enjoyed many a conversation with various lecturers and their students.

Time waits for no man, or woman, and two weeks later the three were back at CERN headquarters to find out when they might be able to attempt a repeat performance. To their surprise the serious damage to the accelerator had been limited to a single focussed column which was already in process of repair, again Megan's swift thinking at the time was shown to have saved the day. Now they looked forward to understanding more about the actual plasma content and maybe why it formed. Controlling it would ultimately need the input of Alan and his colleagues back in England and other engineers around the world.

Having been briefed, it was Alan who caused a little uproar with the suggestion that the repairs be changed to provide a deliberate option to open a channel to allow the plasma to escape. At the same time, he suggested that for safety a no-fly zone should be organised when each run was made. Geostationary satellites were already being checked to ensure that a repeat of the damage caused to the NASA satellite was not repeated.

In the following weeks there was extensive testing but with each run being deliberately aborted before the events of that initial incident could recur. Finally, it was decided to take a run to the last stage but aiming to restrain the event by capping the "escape column" with a sphere that could be jettisoned if necessary. It was hoped that this would allow sensors more time to record information.

On the day the team gathered in the operations room. There was a nervous anticipation in the air as, despite the aborted tests, they were not sure that there would be a repeat performance. As zero hour approached Megan found herself almost shaking with nervousness. If they couldn't repeat the experiment then her theory would be in tatters. As she waited Alan moved next to her.

"Don't worry," he said, "it'll be fine. That first event cannot be a one-off, it was too major a reaction."

Megan smiled a little, "I hope you're right."

He gave her shoulder a gentle squeeze and made a promise. "When it's done, whatever. I'll take you out for dinner tonight."

Her smile widened, "Are you inviting me on a date?"

"If you like!" he grinned.

Yuri interrupted their private thoughts with the announcement that the run was about to commence. The warning siren, sounded at every accelerator run, could be heard with an added urgency on this occasion, it seemed.

As the minutes crawled past very little happened. Only the normal particle collisions seen on hundreds of runs of the LHC over the years were appearing on the monitors showing live pictures of the results. Megan started to despair, why was nothing happening?

Then there was a change. The temperature in the accelerator started to rise. Slowly at first but then more rapidly. Within the room there was a collective drawing of breath.

"Ready everyone. At eight thousand degrees we will need to open the outer fields, ready for the escape of energy if we are to avoid a repeat of last time."

As they watched, the plasma began to form. Cameras and sensors reported energy excesses that did not seem to be generated as a direct result of any of the collisions being seen separately. Finally, Yuri threw the switch and the energy ball of plasma started to escape its restraints of the primary magnetic field into the column within which a secondary field aimed to keep the plasma to a specific path. Despite this the temperature of the plasma continued to rise and a pressure front started to grow – within seconds it became clear that not only was the original event being repeated but the extremes were being exceeded.

"Unlock the cap," called Alan, "it won't be able to hold this without a risk of major rupture."

As planned the technicians operated the magnets to loosen the bolts holding the cap. Moments later a ball of plasma was climbing through the air at a phenomenal rate. Various satellites targeted it with instruments in line with plans set up in advance of the run. To Megan's delight, and her amazement, they tracked the plasma ball out of the atmosphere and past lunar orbit in barely three hours. Long range cameras lost sight shortly after, possibly because the plasma had finally dissipated.

Grigor seemed to hesitate and then asked if any ground-based telescopes might have been focused on the area or perhaps one of the near-earth orbit monitors. He explained that he felt it odd that the energy field should vanish so quickly.

Yuri agreed to set enquiries in motion before turning to Alan. "Hopefully we will have enough data for you to start work. It is a good time, I think, to let you all know that the Security Council of the UN has unanimously agreed that all the information should be shared and joint co-operation between the various aerospace and energy industries should be encouraged, with the aim of finding ways to control this seemingly unlimited but also clean source of power."

"That is unprecedented surely." said Alan, "It must be being seen as a major step forward in countering climate change. Maybe there is some hope for future generations after all. I've often wondered if our work, any of our work, would ever have a positive input in that way. Now it feels like time to celebrate."

"Hopefully we aren't being too optimistic," replied Grigor, "but I agree this is unprecedented. How the UN managed to convince the likes of the US and Russia to work freely together is still a mystery to me."

"Megan, we have a date," smiled Alan, "see you later."

"I, I, well, sure, OK," stuttered Megan.

4. Exotics Harnessed

The observations from the near-earth orbit telescopes added nothing to the satellite images. It was only some weeks later that an image downloaded from the Hubble telescope added to the mystery. An observation aimed towards Andromeda was not as clear as expected. The astronomers were initially mystified by this and concerned that the space telescope had suffered some damage. But other images were clear. Then they realised that what the telescope had recorded was a fast-moving gaseous object. By back tracking its estimated path they calculated that it had emanated from Earth. It then took a little added time before they recognised the CERN based origin. The shocking information passed to the scientists in Switzerland came in two pieces. Size now thirty times larger than at the start and velocity still around twenty thousand kilometres an hour. As Yuri commented – they were faced with even more questions to answer.

Over the following months the various teams worked without success to identify individual particles within the plasma field or to find a means of control. Increasingly Megan's theory of replicating that period shortly after the Big Bang gained credence even if, as she said herself, it might never be possible to prove.

In their leisure time Megan and Alan found themselves spending more and more time together. From that first date to regular walks and gradually they became inseparable. It was no surprise when they moved in together. One success that met with support from their colleagues.

Eventually, Alan was recalled to Bristol to provide more direct input to the materials research programme. The night before he was due to leave was emotional. It would be their first time apart in almost a year. After an enjoyable meal they headed back to their apartment. It was in the early hours that Megan woke with a start. "Alan, wake up, wake up. I think I have the answer to the containment problem."

Alan, still sleepy, responded "Say again, how?"

It took some time but eventually Megan managed to explain that she had had a brainwave in two parts. Firstly, they should repeat some test runs using lighter atoms than the iron ones to see if they could generate a less powerful plasma result. They'd need to make sure that they were still heavier than any used in the LHC runs but it might work, she surmised. The second idea, she admitted fell very much in Alan's field. Would it be possible to construct a torus shaped container which might allow the plasma to circulate within a containment field? It might need to be contained within a larger torus or maybe a sphere full of liquid nitrogen? Was it possible, she wondered aloud, to use carbon nanotubes to surround a graphene surface?

By this point Alan was wide awake and scribbling furiously on the notepad he always kept by the bed for recording ideas that surfaced, on occasion, in the middle of the night. While noting Megan's ideas he was himself thinking rapidly.

"Not sure about the nanotubes but carbon fibres might work. They aren't as strong but might prove more heat resistant for our needs. You talk to the team about playing with the atomic weights. I will look into the container ideas. Now perhaps we should try to rest – we need to be up early after all."

Megan's answer was definitely more physical than verbal and sleep was a little while coming. The next morning, they made their farewells and Alan headed back to the UK with a renewed vigour - determined to find a solution as suggested by his love.

* * *   * * *   * * *

The next morning, Megan took her usual walk to the CERN offices carrying Alan's notes as a reminder of the brainstorming thoughts from the early hours. As she walked, she called ahead asking Yuri and Grigor for an early meeting. That in itself was unusual so there was a sense of anticipation as she entered the room.

Her opening question caused a stir and both the Professors took time to respond. "Why did we stop using the same particle mix as that used in the LHC? We weren't repeating identical experiments after all because the end results would be happening at much higher speeds."

It was Grigor who replied first. "It's a valid question and I'm not wholly sure that we really considered lighter starting points than iron but the first test runs did only use helium and hydrogen. There was a wish to test the heavier atoms and, I guess, we always felt we could move back down the scale. And to be fair, you did suggest that was a route to try in your dissertation, even if I did consider it science fiction then."

Yuri agreed with a smile "Your paper did encourage us to move up the scale. And we did, of course, obtain interesting results. Am I right in thinking you want to move that way? And if so, perhaps you can explain?"

"I got to wondering what might happen. Not as low as the LHC levels but say around four fifths the current starting point. Could we produce a more controllable result?" Megan's confidence was starting to drain, it had seemed so obvious in the early hours, now she was questioning her own ideas with an unusual doubt. Could she have sent Alan on a wild goose chase? Should she call him and tell him not to bother as she was wrong?

Yuri had been thinking before he answered the original question. "So rather than using iron atoms you would be looking at, perhaps, scandium?"

"I had thought of titanium," replied Megan, "but scandium would be closer if we can get an appropriate oxide to split. Do you think that this might work?"

"We can only try it," came the joint reply amidst laughs.

And try it they did. Six weeks later scandium atoms were generated and fired around the accelerator. As their velocity approached light speed the on-lookers held their breaths as the temperature started to rise. Unfortunately, it rapidly plateaued and, although the resultant collisions proved highly interesting for later analysis, the hoped-for outcome was missing.

In the post mortem discussion later it was acknowledged that the one positive to be taken was that there was now a lower limit to the production of the energy. Whether or not it meant that iron was the lowest point could only be tested by using atoms with mass falling between scandium and iron. The next run would use titanium, as it had already been prepared, to be followed by chromium if necessary.

During this time the reports from Bristol and NASA's materials teams were positive – progress was being made in producing the containers that would be needed. For the moment however there was still a problem. No-one had managed to come up with an external material that had both strength and flexibility adequate to meet the expected pressures of the plasma. It might be some time before a breakthrough would occur and, unfortunately, the other research teams around the world had had no success either. For Megan, and her colleagues, it was a case of using what they had and being watchful that any escape could be targeted at a safe route.

The tests using titanium and chromium both failed to generate a plasma effect and the final run, involving manganese as the original substance, was to take place the following week.

Megan and Alan had been in constant touch but even so his call that Friday morning came as unexpected. "Megan," his voice demonstrating his excitement, "we've done it!"

"Go on" Megan almost yelled her response.

"When is your next run? Next week? We'll be asking Yuri and Grigor to delay, so that we can bring a new substance into the containment field but I wanted you to know first."

"You mean we could be ready to hold the plasma in place? Oh, I love you!" she gasped with a grin spreading across the video screen.

"Me too," Alan laughed, "and I'll be home tomorrow!"

The next run was delayed a week but its result only provided a final confirmation that the plasma effect could not be produced with atoms lighter than iron. Alan's new material was not tested but, as he commented, it would give them time to understand a little more about his invention.

"Your invention?" cried Megan.

"Well, it was my idea and followed up our midnight chat." he grinned. "It took some time to devise the structure itself and then even longer to convince the guys that it could be done in quantities sufficient to make the "bottle". Anyway, they managed it and now I'm back to stay. At least for the moment."

In due course they completed a fresh test run using iron atoms and, as before, the plasma formed. This time, though, the escape containment field diverted the plasma into its own torus. The run was aborted as soon as it filled and the scientists went into analysis mode as fast as they could, not knowing how long the container would hold. It was then that Alan's additional work came to the fore. A single narrow cable allowed a small amount of plasma to be extracted without forming a pressure point causing the equipment to break away from its holding brackets. That single stream could be analysed in detail and it produced some amazing results.

It would take time but from the first set of data it was clear that the power could be controlled and might be inexhaustible. The resultant analysis generated confirmation that it would be possible to provide clean energy with a positive impact on climate change.

The future for the planet now looked more promising than for many years. For the CERN team and the aerospace teams at NASA and Bristol, in particular, the future was assured.

5. Houston

"SP5 you are cleared for take-off. Bon voyage."

The space plane started rolling down the runway accelerating as the pilot increased power from its plasma fuelled engine. As it left the ground its nose rose to start the climb towards space and low earth orbit before transferring to the newly enlarged international space station.

Alan watched still awestruck that he had been the person who had led the development of the new engines for both the space plane and ISS1, the craft now being completed in orbit that would carry the first manned mission to Mars.

Four years had passed since the first plasma energy had been captured. Time that had seen his relationship with Megan develop despite periods of separation as she continued research into how the energy was formed and why. That research was soon to bear fruit in a way that neither of them might have thought possible.

Megan was now heading for Houston to join him in a new project using plasma energies even greater than the first – discovered by using atoms heavier than iron. He left the viewing room and headed outside down to the limo that would take him to the airport to meet her.

His driver turned on to the freeway, much clearer in these days with vehicles restricted unless, like their saloon, they were all-electric. Alan still marvelled at the speed with which the US had adapted to the need to deal with climate change, from a major emitter of greenhouse gases with a president in denial, to a country which had switched to a carbon neutral economy in little more than a decade. Although the process had started before the plasma energy had been found it had accelerated reducing the target period for change to a few years rather than decades. Now most of the population used trams and bicycles in the cities and electric buses in the more rural areas. It was a shame, he thought, that it had taken the super hurricane's destruction of most of southern Florida and the loss of almost twenty thousand lives to waken the nation to the situation. Weather extremes were still dangerous but, with the worldwide reduction in greenhouse gas emissions, they already seemed to be easing. It might be possible that the changes had been curtailed before they became unstoppable.

"Should be there in plenty of time," the driver commented, "Miss Newcombe's flight is on schedule."

"Dr Newcombe these days," Alan corrected. Megan having finally completed her PhD on the Big Bang expansion period and supersymmetry. She had been presented with her formal doctorate by Grigor Sokolov. From a serious critic of her approach and theories he had become completely convinced that Megan was the "Einstein" of her time and considered it an honour to be a part of her success. Alan was, of course, delighted but, in truth, had always expected her to cross that hurdle with ease. That she still wanted to be with him amazed him as he had difficulty in realising that from her viewpoint, he was her counterparty. The person who could convert her ideas into reality.

In due course they met and headed downtown to their hotel where, after settling in, Megan asked where they would be eating. Alan's selection of restaurant had been based on two thoughts, Megan's jetlag and the fact that they would have very little private time together in the following weeks. As a result, after changing, Megan found herself walking into one of the finest eateries that Houston could offer. Classic Italian food with superb Californian wine provided for a relaxing evening with the only person she truly wanted to be with.

Even so, she was totally unprepared for Alan's actions. After the main course had been completed and deserts were still awaited, to her surprise and momentary embarrassment, he stopped the waiters and leaving his seat dropped to one knee in a motion that had changed little in the previous hundred and fifty years and proffered a small box.

"Megan, will you honour me by being my bride?"

"Oh, Alan, you are a romantic fool! Of course, I will. What took you so long?"

After applause from the restaurant staff and other guests and a bottle of complimentary champagne, Alan explained that it had taken him some time to pluck up the courage. Their relationship being as wonderful as it was, he feared that he might break the magic spell. Megan's response had finally dissipated that fear and they moved rapidly on to when and where for the wedding.

*** *** ***

The next day brought them back down to earth with several long meetings, with senior NASA directors, to discuss the new projects which would involve teams of the world's top design engineers, sourced from around the world working alongside a smaller team of physicists equally well known for their expertise in energy matters and, to their surprise, aerospace developments. Their combined aim was to develop particle accelerators capable of generating the plasma while being much smaller than that of CERN. That would allow for the energy to be available around the world and in particular to the old third world so that it could follow the major economies in eliminating the remaining fossil fuel usage.

The final discussion of the day involved talking through the list of the candidates for the two teams. Starting with the engineers they worked their way down a long list which it turned out did not, to Megan's amazement, include Alan. Her angry muttering was nothing compared to his shock at his fiancée equally not being in the list of physicists. His angry question addressed to the NASA directors, produced an unexpected laugh from a man who, they had been told, was present only as an observer.

"Perhaps I should introduce myself. Gordon Drake." The rest of the group turned towards him.

"I have to explain," he continued, "I am not from NASA as you may have thought. My role is to represent the President in certain matters of deemed national importance. You will not be surprised that these projects fall under that definition even as international collaborations."

"So, are you the reason we weren't listed as participants?" demanded Megan. "Aren't we good enough? Or aren't there enough Americans?"

Drake laughed out loud. "Not good enough? Are you serious?"

"So why? Mr President's man. Why?"

"Megan, easy does it. Give Mr Drake the chance to answer." Alan broke in.

"Megan, Alan, there is a reason I am here. You are that reason. As I said these projects are considered of national importance and the President wants to know why it is proposed that neither of them be led by Americans."

"Sorry? We haven't covered those choices yet."

"She tasked me with reviewing the nominees and confirming those appointments on her behalf, if I concurred. You are both missing from those two lists as NASA has nominated you both as the joint project leaders. Having researched your backgrounds and seen you in action, I am pleased to add our backing to your appointments, which will be formally confirmed at the United Nations next week. Assuming that you agree, of course." Drake finished with a smile. "A second reason for congratulations, I understand."

"Thank you, sorry I shouted at you." said Megan as she tried to regain her composure. "But, look. We know that seeking a way to produce the energy plasma with smaller accelerators is one element of the project but it would be useful to know what else we are expected to do. All we know is that it will bring together the top people in their roles from across the world, Germany, China, Japan, Russia, India, America and Britain – to name but a few of the countries represented. These teams will be unprecedented in an international sense but we can only make educated guesses that it will involve the expansion energy and some development in aerospace technology."

Drake sat back. "I think you had better grab a drink and settle down. I need to tell you a story."

Over the next hour or so Drake explained that as long ago as the early 1990s NASA had been researching how a spacecraft capable of crossing interstellar space might be built. In 1994 a Mexican theoretical physicist, called Miguel Alcubierre, had designed a theoretical engine capable of warping spacetime. The drawback was that it required immense amounts of energy far beyond anything that neither the then current, nor even future technology as envisaged at the time, could supply. Despite that difficulty the research continued until around 2010 when a NASA scientist, Dr Harold White, of the Advanced Propulsion Team announced a new development that reduced the required energy by a significant factor. Originally the energy required would be that generated by converting the mass of Jupiter. The new development reduced the energy requirement to that of converting the mass of a NASA probe. Still, of course, impossible. An artist's impression of the craft had been released by NASA in 2012 and Drake handed round copies to the company.

"This is all very well," said Alan, "and I'm sure that I have seen this picture before. But unless I'm mistaken the limiting factor is still the speed of light."

"True and I'm not sure I fully understand it." Drake continued, "I can only say that the engines work by warping spacetime. The ship itself wouldn't exceed the speed of light but would be transported across space in a bubble of its own spacetime."

"And you want us to complete the design of the ship and power it with exotic energy?" Megan sounded as awestruck as she felt at the sheer scale of the project.

"What I don't pretend to understand is why the USA isn't going it alone? Surely it could afford it?" Alan asked.

Drake responded. "The powers that be have recognised that the original work happened in Geneva and was developed by international co-operation. For once they saw that the skills set needs input from across the globe. So, while we might be called upon to lead the projects, we don't feel that we can or should exclude other countries. Now let's be clear no-one expects this to be an overnight job. I suspect that you and your teams will need to make major advances in material technology. Dr Newcombe, your energy source is already powering manned craft around the solar system with the Mars mission ready to leave orbit imminently. Now is the time for the next step – from interplanetary to interstellar. Are you up for it?"

"I am, of course we are. But I will still need to take some time out. I do have a wedding to organise!"

* * *   * * *   * * *

Drake was completely correct – designing and building an unmanned probe would take more than ten years, a period that included frustration and many false starts as different aspects of the technological requirements produced a need for new ideas and changes to various design formats. Nevertheless, the teams were encouraged to keep working on the project not least by the successes in the development of spacecraft within the Solar System.

Despite the difficulties it was a time of much joy and promise. Alan and Megan duly married a year later back in Cambridge in Trinity Church. Having settled into a new home close to Houston they had the perfect place to relax away from work and twelve months later Judy, the first of two daughters, was born, followed a year later by Molly.

The development of improvements to the engines to be used by interplanetary shuttles meant that Alan frequently found himself on the international space station which had been expanded to include ship-building.

Already manned craft were visiting the asteroid belt seeking out metals and other ores now rarely found in sufficient quantities back on Earth. Settlements were also being expanded on the Moon and more recently on Mars where Megan's sister Marion, having completed her medical training and having specialised in off-Earth medicine, had been posted.

The plasma engines allowed craft to use constant thrust and journey times across the system were shortened from months to weeks in some cases. Powering a starship would need a much higher energy level and a more secure structure for the containment fields that would, probably, be under greater stresses than the interplanetary craft. The particle physicists, led by Megan, had made progress in finding a way to generate the higher energy levels, at least in theory. In practice there was simply not enough of iridium, the source metal, and could only refine their calculations until one of the ships in the asteroid belt was lucky enough to make a find.

6. Three years on

"Shuttle Denver, you are cleared for landing." Mars control out.

"Roger, Mars control. Leaving orbit.... Now."

The Denver's side burners lit up cutting their orbital speed enough to start the descent – "Commander would you like to take over?" the shuttle's pilot asked the new deputy commander of the Mars settlement.

"No Jeff – you're the expert. I've only visited Mars once before on the second mission." Bjork Linden replied.

"No problem just thought you should have the chance." continued Jeff Brasher as he deftly adjusted the shuttle's attitude to reduce the bumpiness of the ride his gaze moved steadily across the readouts and dials of the control panel checking for any anomaly that might signal trouble.

"All in the green, Ellen?" he asked his co-pilot.

"Yes, sir" Ellen Bayman responded. "We are clear to descend. Thirty minutes to ......" the proximity alarms went off in the middle of her sentence.

"What the...? Incoming! Everyone, brace! Prepare for decompression." Jeff shouted as radar indicated an object closing rapidly. With no time to take avoiding action the meteor smashed into the shuttle throwing it off course and into a deadly dive. As it did, he slumped forward in his seat, blood oozing from a head wound.

"Jeff? Jeff!" Ellen's voice rose as she realised that the pilot had been hit, "Damn it. Come on controls! Give me something."

"Mayday, mayday. This is the Denver. Meteor strike." Bjork took over the radio. "Losing altitude and power – estimate crash landing." He turned to Ellen who was struggling to regain a degree of control using what power she had left. "Ellen, how far short?"

"At least thirty kilometres, if there is nothing in the way."

"Mars control, thirty kilometres to your north."

"Roger that Denver – rescue teams on their way." There was no need to say how fast – the teams had practised for all sorts of emergencies though a shuttle crash was not at the top of the list.

"Sir," came a series of voices. Good people thought the commander noting the lack of emotion apparent, "fire in the rear, sir, may be out of control."

"Commander," Bjork turned his head at Ellen's voice, "sorry about this but this is going to be a hard landing. I'm not sure that we will be able to clear the hills. Or at least I think I have one burn left which could lift us enough but it will mean no control at the landing point."

"Do your best, Ellen, we are out of other options. How long?"

"Fifteen to twenty minutes – damn!" her voice died behind the explosion in the rear of the shuttle. "Make that ten minutes, all power gone. Port attitude wing gone."

The shuttle started to spin – "jettisoning starboard wing." Further explosions indicated the bolts being sheared on the starboard side.

For the next life time it seemed, she struggled with the shuttle's attitude trying to slow the speed of their descent. Without its wings the craft had minimal gliding capacity but by some means or another Ellen managed to succeed in flattening their approach.

The planet's surface was still approaching at a frightening rate but at least the angle of approach was no longer vertical. At the last second the craft heaved as she used the last attitude fuel at the front of the shuttle to reduce the impact a little. The crash that followed included several bounces before the craft came to a rest after what seemed like kilometres of screeching destruction.

"Everyone out!" Ellen's yell started some movement but, as she looked back to the rear, she realised that not everyone was going to able to make it. "Commander, are you mobile?"

"Thanks to you, Ellen, yes. Bruised but no more. Now I suggest we get moving. Thankfully the fire has been smothered, so we can take time to check on everyone."

"Sir, Jeff isn't going to be one of them." Ellen's voice cracked. "Jeff was a friend as well as my boss. Why didn't I spot the warnings quicker?" A few tears started.

Bjork put his hand out gently. "Ellen, no-one could have reacted quicker. You've done as much if not more than most. That was a fantastic piece of flying. I do know about the capability of these shuttles. After we lost power we should have dropped like a stone. You managed to land us with forward speed. Everyone who's made it owes their life to your brilliance."

"I wish it was everyone."

"That was never in your control, Ellen. It could have been none of us that made it but for you."

As they talked and made the injured as comfortable as possible Bjork took the lead as the senior officer but allowed Ellen to tend to as many as possible helping her to push her grief to the back of her mind. They were occupied for the next hour before the rescue teams arrived and they were both able to step back and take some rest.

On their arrival at the settlement, now known as Schiaparelli Town, the medical unit were quickly in action checking all the survivors for less obvious damage. In the end, of the sixteen people on board, miraculously there were only two deaths and three serious injuries.

It would take a month for the shuttle's replacement to arrive from Earth which meant that Bjork had time to learn more about how Ellen had reached Mars and before that an astronaut. As she would have to say many times in the coming months.

"My parents were British, Dad a Scot and Mum English, but I was born in Houston and my father worked in the spaceplane development and design, even before we had the new plasma engines. I can't remember a time when I didn't want to be an astronaut and it was the best day of my life when I got my astronaut's "wings". I never did think that I would be happy that we were still using an older design of shuttle when we crashed. It was due to be replaced with the latest ships within a few months but if the plasma core had been our power source and exploded" usually with a wry smile, "landing would not have been a problem."

Shortly before the next interplanetary ship arrived, Ellen learnt that she was being recalled to Earth. The timing which cut her term of duty on the Mars space station by half was, to her, not surprising. She had failed her shuttle commander by not spotting the intruder until too late and she waited for her transport with a heavy heart.

She was caught by surprise when Bjork and his colleagues threw a farewell party for her and made it clear that they knew she was not being recalled for any bad or negative reason.

Shortly after the party began the Mars commander called for the attention of those present.

"I realise that we are here to wish Ellen farewell but it would be remiss of me not to firstly ask you to raise a glass to absent friends."

As the group stilled and came to a mutual silence, Ellen's spirits fell with the loss of her friend and the new arrival, Jenny Whitfield, hitting hard. Several of her fellows spotted her distress and moved to reassure her. But before they could speak, Avy Patel raised her voice.

"Sorry but your attention again please. We lost two people in that crash but we should never forget that sixteen survived and they owe their lives to a display of outstanding flying skill. Ellen Bayman heads home still feeling not about that but more of the losses."

Turning to Ellen she continued. "Ellen, you cannot forget the loss but you must remember that you saved everyone that you could. As you head home remember that you go with our thanks and best wishes."

It was not an easy journey despite the best efforts of the crew of the interplanetary craft and the others on board. Ellen could not help but fear the worst, that her career as an astronaut was over. Even if she was exonerated of fault the crash must have an adverse effect on her future.

Having finally reached the Moon Ellen found herself being summoned to a meeting of the Committee of Enquiry. She was not surprised. In the past several years no other accident had claimed as many lives in space. Its chairman spoke first.

"Ensign Bayman, thank you for coming. Please note that this is not a Court of any type. Our job is to examine the evidence and decide what actions might be taken to avoid a repeat. I am sorry that we need to ask this of you but please tell us, in your words, exactly what happened."

Ellen had prepared herself for this ordeal, knowing it would be asked of her. Nevertheless, although she was able to speak clearly it was not without a degree of emotion. The committee allowed her to speak without interruption but there were a number of questions afterwards. She realised later that none of these were antagonistic but simply seeking factual confirmation of certain points.

At the end of the session, the Chairman thanked Ellen for her input and acknowledged that the events must have been traumatic for her. "But," he finished, "without your skill they would have been much worse, you are to be congratulated on your performance at the wheel, so to speak. We wish you well.

A week later Ellen, having had a little time to rest, took a shuttle home to Houston where she was amazed to be welcomed back as a hero. She was due to take leave, not least to allow her to adjust to the higher gravity of the Earth, but found herself being immediately summoned to Space Command Headquarters for a meeting with the officers responsible for space operations on behalf of NASA and the world's other space teams who were overseen by the UN space corp.

On entering the room, she was amazed to find a table at which four senior commanders and a fifth man, whom she did not recognise, sat. It seemed incredible that so much seniority was needed to deal with a mere Ensign and her first reaction was that she had gotten the room number wrong. As she snapped even straighter to attention and began to apologise for interrupting, the unknown man stopped her.

"Ellen, if I may be so informal, you are in the right room. Gentlemen, I think Miss Bayman has not been given enough information about our purpose here today."

"So, it would seem, Mr Drake." The senior officer replied. "Ensign Bayman, please sit. This will not take long and, just to reassure you, it is a pleasure to meet you."

"I don't understand sir." Ellen stuttered. "I thought I was to meet with Commander Evans."

"A small subterfuge, for which I apologise, but we thought it might be best if you were not warned of the purpose of this meeting in advance. Please would you take us through your actions during the incident, I know that you have told this story many times and I doubt that you find it easy but, for reasons that will become clear, it is necessary. Mr Drake may ask a question or two."

Over the next hour Ellen repeated the details of the crash, the time extended by Gordon Drake's questions which centred on clarifying technical points rather than any suspicion of inaccuracies. At the end, as she sat waiting to be dismissed, she saw the generals look at each other with mutual nods. "Was that of approval?" she thought with surprise.

The senior officer turned to her. "Ensign, please stand."

Ellen rose to her feet and stood to attention, her spirits falling.

"Ensign Ellen Bayman," he continued, "it has been a pleasure and privilege to finally meet you. Your actions were outstanding and in the highest traditions of the astronaut service, and its associated parties around the world. We are pleased to confirm your promotion to Lieutenant, to take place with effect from the date of the crash."

"Sir." Ellen started. "Thank you, sir."

"I believe, Mr Drake has something to add."

"Ellen, I can only add my congratulations. Except that you should take the opportunity to rest up here in Houston for the next few days. I have reason to believe that you will be called upon to take a journey and you will need to be more acclimatised to Earth's gravity."

"Lieutenant Bayman, you are free to take some of that leave you are due." With which the officers all rose and took the opportunity to shake Ellen's hand before formally raising their hands in a salute that Ellen just managed to return, before leaving the room in a daze.

That state of mind had barely left her, when a couple of days later she received a call from Gordon with a request that she join him in Washington bringing with her, her new dress uniform. Somehow, he knew that this had reached her earlier that day and, not fully understanding why she was taking the request as an order, she caught a flight the next morning.

On arrival in Washington, she found herself being met by a limousine and whisked direct to a hotel she could never have afforded, even on her new pay level. Gordon was actually waiting for her in the lobby and taking her to one side advised her that she would be dining that evening and should be in dress uniform. He would collect her in good time but refused to answer her questions as to what purpose she was in the capital for.

That evening Gordon duly collected Ellen and they left the hotel in a limousine. After a few minutes, to Ellen's surprise, the driver turned into Pennsylvania Avenue.

With a slight stammer she asked. "Gordon, where exactly are we going?"

"Ellen, I can't hide it anymore," smiled Gordon. "The President is hosting a dinner party and you will be the guest of honour. She wishes to meet you and I believe she has other reasons."

Ellen fell silent as they turned into the grounds of the White House, then. "Gordon, who are you?"

"Your cousin's wife, Megan, once called me "Mr President's man" and I guess that is not wholly incorrect. There are times when the president needs to make or confirm decisions but needs someone closer to the action that she trusts to act on her behalf. That is sometimes myself. Now we are here."

A few minutes later Ellen entered a reception room to find a group of people enjoying a drink. As she came to a halt, uncertain which way to go, there was a sound from the other side of the room and the President also entered the room and came towards her. Ellen came to a sharp attention and saluted. The president smiled and returned the salute.

"Lieutenant Bayman, welcome. Now please relax and join us in a drink before dinner. I think you might recognise a few people tonight but I am also sure that most of the party will wish to chat with you. So, I will let you mingle for the moment. We will have time over dinner to talk."

The president was, of course, correct and the time passed quickly before dinner was called at which point Ellen found herself sitting next to her commander-in-chief. For once though, she was not expected to tell the story of the crash again and was able to enjoy the experience and the food. At the end of dinner, the president raised a hand and silence fell.

"Ladies and Gentlemen, thank you for coming this evening. As you are all aware there is an underlying reason and I would ask you first to raise your glasses to salute our guest of honour, Lieutenant Ellen Bayman, one of our brave astronauts and an exceptional pilot. Ellen."

The group responded accordingly before falling silent again as the President continued. "Lieutenant, please stand." Ellen quickly stood, a little nervously.

Standing herself the president took a more formal stance.

"Lieutenant Bayman, you showed exceptional ability and calmness in circumstances that might have led to a terrible tragedy. It is my pleasure to advise you that your actions have been acknowledged to be in the finest traditions and I am delighted to announce the award, to you, of the Congressional Silver Medal in recognition of that fact."

The room erupted in applause as Ellen gasped and blushed with shock. "Madam President, thank you, I don't know what to say."

"Ellen, there is nothing to say, you earned this. I wish you well in your future career in space. Now enjoy the rest of the evening."

The party lasted into the early hours by which time Ellen was struggling with gravity fatigue and Gordon appeared by her side to help extract her and arrange her return to the hotel. As they parted Ellen said.

"Gordon, I'm sure you had something to do with this and I'm equally sure that I don't deserve it but thank you."

"Ellen, I had little to do with it except to confirm that the president's other advisers were correct. You do deserve it and I, too, look forward to following your career in the future."

The next day Ellen flew back to Houston to receive her new orders now with more confidence than she had had for some time. Having received a superb welcome back, she did, in due course, find herself transferred to interplanetary operations based on the Moon. For the moment the future was hers.

7. Discovery on the Red Planet

The breakthrough came some nine years after the first Mars landing. The settlement was growing steadily and exploration trips from the base were moving further with each year. It had become clear that much of the redness was iron based but not all. Explorers focussed on areas that were identified from the air by automated drones as being of interest. Then one spot proved to be extraordinary. The message sent back to Earth was directed straight to Megan's desk and then to the space station where Alan was on one of his trips.

The various team members convened a conference call during which it was agreed, not to Megan's delight, that a team of three including Alan should be despatched on the next Earth/Mars supply run. Alan returned to Houston the next day to prepare for the Mars trip. His welcome home was as warm as ever with all three females happy to see him if only for a short time. Later, with the two girls in bed, Megan and Alan had a blazing row.

"Why you? This is one that you could have delegated." raged Megan.

"Because my knowledge of what is needed is the driver and I have some astronautical experience already."

"So do Tom and Aki! That's not an answer."

"Megs, please. I know you don't want me to go but how could I turn down the chance to travel to another planet? And it's not like it's the first mission. The risks are very small now. After all Marion is there."

"And I always said she was mad! Small risks! I don't want to take any risk of losing you. And the girls will miss you!" Her eyes filled with tears. "I know you're going to go but how I wish you wouldn't."

Of course, the decision had been made and in due course Alan and his team boarded the interplanetary shuttle the IP Deimos for the five-week trip to Mars. After transferring from the Deimos to the Mars space station, the team boarded a landing shuttle for the final step down to the Red Planet.

The shuttle started its entry into the atmosphere – a gentle process which would take almost a full orbit as it used the minimal air resistance to slow its descent before the final glide into Schiaparelli Town.

The Captain turned to Alan. "I know we could land under power but this approach is still the easiest and you get a good look at a number of features."

It was not long before they could feel the shuttle shudder as it dropped lower and the black of space was rapidly replaced by the reflected redness of the planet below. Soon their view of the surface below improved as their flightpath took them south past the imposing bulk of Mons Olympus. The highest mountain in the Solar System dominated the skyline across the Terra Sirenum and was easily visible from the growing settlement. As they made their first pass the multiple domes of the settlement could be clearly seen.

Fifty minutes later having completed its drop through the red skies the shuttle glided into a smooth landing, rolling the final 200 metres towards the nearby dome.

The crew and passengers sealed their environment suits before disembarking and crossing to the dome's airlock. Spacesuits were no longer needed but protection from the carbon dioxide dominated atmosphere was essential even for the short walk to the safety of the dome. Even with heated suits the cold could be felt and though it was a summer day near the equator the temperature was still below freezing shortly after sunrise though that was a long way from the pre-dawn low of minus eighty degrees.

Those of the passengers who were now on the planet for the first time - slowed to turn and view the landscape. The area was a largely flat plain and almost entirely red, the view broken in one direction by the immense solar panels gathering energy from the light of a paler sun now much further away than on Earth.

As they passed through the airlock the settlement's commanding officer was waiting to greet them with a hug for Alan. "It's been a long time my friend."

"Siobhan it really is you! How did you make it out here?"

"It's a long story but, after John was killed in that accident, I didn't feel there was anything left on Earth for me. With his friends and my background in project management, it wasn't too difficult."

"I should have guessed but your surname isn't one I recognise."

"It was my mother's maiden name."

Understanding their wish to discuss the finding with the team that had made the discovery she did not waste time beyond a swift introduction to her senior officers including Marion. Alan was delighted to see that she was clearly enjoying her role. Then Siobhan took them to a meeting room where three men were waiting.

"Gentlemen, this is Alan Piper, Adrien Bernard and Laurent Martin. Alan this is the team who checked out the anomaly – George Rodriguex, Naoko Sato and, their leader, Miro Benter."

After mutual introductions were complete, Siobhan continued, "Miro this is your baby, fire away."

Miro started a video. "This film was taken by one of our drones. As you can see at this point the surface is the standard red dust probably iron based as is most of the plain. At this point we are just over two hundred klicks from the base."

He stopped talking and a moment later the landscape changed to a darker shade at first of red and then they could see spots of white or silver.

"The drone is flying at fifty to sixty metres on auto pilot so we didn't get to see these until the film was reviewed back here at base. We do have software which looks for inconsistencies in the surface and that allows for a high-speed scan, as a first check. You won't be surprised that these pictures had the software "screaming" at us."

Adrien interrupted "Do you mean that spotting anomalies is only based on colour?"

Naoko responded, "Not really, this is a first scan of the material but the sensors are also using spectrographic imaging and the scan can identify variances in the apparent make-up of the rocks and sand. It was those results that were exciting in this case. Such that it was considered that we should treat that area as a priority on the next expedition."

"And what was identified as warranting such urgency?" Alan could hardly hide his excitement.

"The silver spots seemed to match the spectrum of iridium, something that we did not believe could exist on Mars." Miro answered. "and an element we have been asked to keep high on the priority list. Though I don't really understand why."

"To be truthful neither did I but if we could find a reasonable amount it would be useful in the production of a new fuel and maybe a part of the vessel we are researching. But those specks don't look as if there is a viable source here? Or have you found other lodes?" Alan still felt excited but wary.

Miro continued with an explanation of the investigative process. "Well firstly we sent a second drone to examine the site. Following confirmatory data, we three then set off overland – a two-week round trip. We got back last month. and sent the message to NASA HQ which landed, I guess, on your desk. What didn't get sent was this."

He handed over three lumps of, what appeared to be, metallic ore to Alan and his team. "Be careful they are quite heavy."

Alan decided not to let on that an earlier message had been sent which the team back on Earth had reacted to without waiting for confirmation from the expedition.

It was Laurent who was first to speak after examining his sample. "I guess you have already carried out some analysis. While I am not a chemist this does not seem to be iridium, it doesn't seem quite right."

"That is the biggest understatement you may ever make." Miro's wry comment brought them to the edge of their seats. "These samples had to be cut from a single deposit of an alloy or compound that we have still not managed to identify. What we appear to have is a large deposit of a pure alloy. And it is large at around five hundred metres in diameter. We don't know for certain how deep but best estimates using x-ray and ultrasound scans is at least the same. We seem to have a sphere, roughly speaking, of around 65 million cubic metres. It might have been a meteor strike except there is no apparent crater of the size that would have been created by such an impact."

"As I understand it then," said an amazed Alan, "we have a spherical deposit of a pure alloy made with elements, one of which is iridium. That seems an almost impossible discovery. How could that have occurred naturally?"

George answered with a grin, "The best we can say is that there is no record of any such ore being found in a structure like this and" he emphasised, "without any apparent imperfections. The main constituents appear to include an iridium carbide and lead. There may be other elements that we have not been able to identify yet. But the astounding thing is that though there may be such elements they form an alloy that is constant in each of the samples. Chemically you could not separate them. I don't believe that this deposit can possibly be natural. Despite the implications I cannot but believe that it has an artificial origin."

"That suggests that an alien species visited Mars at some time in the past, presumably before intelligent life had developed on Earth. You are sure that this could not be from the impact of a meteor?"

"As I said," responded Miro, "we considered that as a possibility but the local geology does not support that theory. Even if it had happened so far in the past for the resultant crater to have worn away it does not answer the main question – how could it have formed naturally? Iridium as a separate metal is hard but brittle – this alloy is not only dense but hard to drill which implies that the carbon is countering the brittleness."

Alan came to a decision. He would have to visit the site and with his colleagues consider how the iridium might be mined. He had already concluded that it could source the fuel for energy production sufficient to power a warp drive but that assumed that it could be moved from the planet.

It was agreed that they would set out the next day. In the meantime, Alan sent word back to Earth and asked for the engineering teams on the ISS to look at what equipment could be shipped out to Mars and landed at the site in question. A direct personal and private message to Megan went via a secure and encrypted route direct to Earth.

The next day two vehicles left the settlement with the teams on board. Faced with almost five days of travel, there would be no side trips on this journey, Alan settled down to watch Mars pass by much as a tourist might back on Earth. He wanted to make the experience worthwhile although he had been warned that boredom was the most likely outcome of what was an often-unchanging red landscape, and the most dangerous! The settlers were, of course, consummate professionals and they reached the location for the anomalous substance late on day four without mishap.

Alan had to admit that using drones was clearly preferable to ground level observations for, as the vehicle rolled to a halt, it was not at all clear that they were in the right place.

Miro explained. "As you can see, from here it's not immediately obvious that this place is any different to anywhere else. On our first trip we almost came away empty handed. Then we realised that the top surface layer was looser than normal and very thin but not dust. You know, of course, that past experience has suggested that the top layer is either dust or at least a metre thick."

"Anyway," Naoko interrupted, "we decided to brush the top aside and that's when we found the deposit. What the drone saw were small areas where the top surface had drifted in the wind. There had been a major dust-storm a few days earlier which had crossed this area and that must have been strong enough to expose the underlying strata. That's not unusual but it's the first time anything like this has been found."

The visitors looked around, "Based on the film we should be able to see at least some evidence of silver contrasting against the red but I'm afraid I can see nothing," said Adrien.

"Which shows how lucky that the drone, which was deliberately sent to cover the storm trail after it had dissipated, crossed this area when it did." Miro commented. "Since the first landings on Mars it has become apparent that, although the atmospheric pressure is very low, the air, for want of a better description, is rarely still. A flypast by the drone even a day later might not have had anything to see and even our dig spot has now been covered over. It is too late to start working outside now. We will need to wait until morning."

Despite his urgent need to investigate further Alan and his colleagues were forced to accept Miro's comments. With external temperatures likely to fall close to a hundred degrees below zero even their environment suits would struggle to protect them in the open at night.

The next morning, as soon as the temperature had risen into the minus forties, they left their vehicles and walked across the site. Naoko produced spades and offered them around. Alan made the first tentative move and found the top surface to be as described. Within a few minutes he had exposed an area of what looked like nickel silver – completely incongruous against the red landscape. Having succeeded in that he attempted to penetrate the exposed surface only to find that the spade could barely make a mark. He looked up to see Miro smiling and holding, with George's help, a powered drill.

"I thought you would appreciate the chance to find out how hard this substance is. We may have forgotten to tell you that those samples we took back cost us a diamond bit each. It really is a tough material."

They spent the day confirming the size of the deposit at ground level and managed to measure the slope at several points to confirm that, based on the x-ray images, they were dealing with a spherical object, if not a perfect sphere.

The following day they headed back towards the settlement. On the third day the settlement warned that they needed to find shelter as another storm would cross their path, before they could reach the settlement in safety. Miro changed course towards an outcrop of low hills near the edge of the plain and they set up camp in their lee. The two vehicles were linked to each other using their airlocks and, for added security, steel "ropes" were fixed to the ground with climbing pitons. With their precautions all complete they settled down to wait out the storm.

***　　***　　***

Back on Earth the teams were working hard to see if they could replicate the Mars substance based on the first analysis received which had led to Alan and his team leaving for Mars. The heavy workload had the benefit, for Megan, of taking her mind off worrying about her husband but meant regular late nights at her computer screen, after her daughters had gone to bed.

A few weeks after Alan's departure, Megan left her office early to collect the girls from school. Eight-year-old Judy, bursting with excitement, rushed out to find her Mother. "Mom, Mom, guess who came to school today?"

Megan grinned at her daughter's delight. "And who was that, little one?"

"I think that was me," came a voice from behind her. She turned to find a familiar face smiling at her confusion.

"Ellen! When did you arrive in Houston?"

"Mom, you know her? She's an astronaut like Pop!"

Megan studied the other woman for a moment, "Not quite like your Pop, Judy. Ellen, or perhaps I should say Lieutenant Ellen Bayman, is a real astronaut and a hero. She has been working at the Lunar settlement for the last four years. More importantly she is your cousin."

"My cousin? What's that mean?"

Ellen smiled at Judy. "Your grandad's sister was my mother, they moved to the United States to work on the first spaceplanes and I was born here. We had fallen out of touch with the rest of the family until your Dad became well known for leading the team that made the spacecraft engines we use today and my mother recognised him."

"Judy, we need to get you and your sister home." Megan intervened. "Ellen, where are you staying? We'd be happy to have you stay with us."

"Oh, please, cousin Ellen. Please come and stay." Judy was dancing around them. Molly was quieter not having been in the class which Ellen had been talking to.

"That would be great if you can manage it, I just need to pick up my stuff from the hotel."

As they waited, Judy asked her Mom. "What did you mean Ellen is a hero?"

"She is. Judy, when you get home have a search on the web for "Shuttle Crash on Mars" that will tell you why she received a medal."

That evening Ellen found herself cornered by Judy who wanted to hear more about what an astronaut did. Molly appeared less interested but still curled up to listen with her mother while playing on her tablet. Megan soon realised that Ellen was very tired and gently despatched the two girls to bed with a promise that they would see Ellen the next night.

"You do look exhausted, an early night or can you manage a drink first?" Megan said.

"I am tired but a drink would be nice. It's the higher gravity, although we get back to Earth at least four times a year, the first couple of days are quite a drain." Ellen gave a wry grin. "You never get used to it but where is Alan?"

"Half way to Mars!" Megan could not hide her anxiety very well. "And I wish he wasn't. He's going to be away for three or four months and I miss him. Sometimes I wish we hadn't managed to find the new energy sources." To her double dismay her emotions welled up and she had to brush away tears in front of Ellen, who she believed would never feel like that.

"Megan, you really are missing him aren't you." Ellen gave Megan a hug and continued. "Let's have that drink and you can tell me all."

The rest of the evening passed quickly as they worked their way through a bottle of wine before Ellen was forced to concede defeat to her fatigue but not before Megan had let out all her emotions. Ellen worked hard to reassure her that just because she was a very important and respected person in her field having private emotions was perfectly okay and, frankly, what made her real.

The next few days passed quickly as Ellen continued her tour of the local schools making presentations on why the space program was even more important in the drive to control climate change than ever before. At their school both Judy and Molly became the centre of attention when they revealed that "the astronaut" was a relative. In the end Ellen gave up her day off to go back to their school for a second set of presentations to more classes before her brief stay on Earth came to an end and she returned to space and then the moon.

That evening Megan suffered a sense of déjà vu when Judy said to her "Mom, I want to be an astronaut. How do I do that? Ellen just said work hard."

"Judy, little one, Ellen was quite right. You will have to work very hard at school and then, probably at university. And science subjects will be those at which you need to be best."

"OK, Mom. Oh, Mom. Molly says not to tell you that she wants to do that too."

Megan groaned knowing that her daughters were very like their mother and, having set their minds on something, would very probably succeed. She could see a day in the future when they might very well have left Earth and headed to other planets, if not the stars. At that moment it did not occur to her that there might be circumstances where she would be glad to see them go and would be wishing them god speed.

The next few weeks continued to be hard, with messages to and from Alan becoming disjointed as he first neared and then landed on Mars. The struggle to replicate the molecular structure of the deposit continued without much success. Although they could produce an iridium carbide chemical structure the rest of the alloy defeated the teams and they could not even be sure that that formula was correct.

It became clear that they would need physical samples to make any further progress and the scarcity of iridium on Earth supported the view that mining equipment capable of lifting large scale volumes of the actual Mars alloy would prove essential in any case. If they were to be able to develop the fuel and energy for a working warp drive the quantity on Earth would always have been insufficient.

It was Grigor, who had been appointed Megan's deputy, who finally admitted defeat and agreed to handle the mining project from the Earth end. The biggest problem would be lifting the heavy gear into orbit before loading it on to the largest existing space craft capable not only of making the trip to Mars but also of landing on the planet close to the required location.

His message to the team on Mars outlining his proposal crossed with another message from Schiaparelli to Houston. It contained distressing news.

Alan's team, caught by the storm on the way back, were still out of contact even though the storm had crossed over their camp site three days earlier. Even if all their radios had been damaged meaning they were unable to update their progress, they were still a day overdue. Search drones had been despatched but no sign of the party could be found at their last known location or on their expected route back to the town from there. A rescue party had been despatched but would need to go slowly so as to ensure they did not miss the incoming teams.

That night Megan did not sleep. She had not told the girls that their father was missing but realised that the news was likely to break the next day and she feared that she would not be able to hide the situation beyond breakfast.

Breakfast was the usual process of disorganisation with the girls not ready for school but starving as ever. As they finally settled over their food and drink, Megan broke the news that their father was missing. She tried, to no avail, to soften the news by trying to emphasise that the rescue process was underway and how safe the vehicles the expedition was using were. Both Judy and Molly dissolved in tears knowing that their Mom was in her own state of terror that their Pop might not return. In the end Megan was forced to call their school and give the head the news that the girls could not attend for the next few days. Megan refused to explain why and the head was not too pleased, making it clear that she did not agree with pupils missing classes for no good reason.

Later that morning Ellen called to say that she was delaying her return to orbit so that she could be with them while they waited for news. She also suggested that they would need help when the news of the missing group broke.

"You can expect reporters and TV cameras to camp outside and even going out will mean running a gauntlet."

Later that day her words were proved only too true. The inevitability of discovery meant that NASA was forced to release the news. In the maelstrom that followed Megan was to really remember only one specific telephone call. The school head calling to apologise for berating her over the girls' absence, only wishing she had felt able to confide in her.

8. Buried

As the storm approached the team's communication with Schiaparelli became intermittent and then failed. Miro was comfortable with this, explaining that the dust contained sufficient metallic particles to cause radio signals to fade and then be blocked, a bit like the communications blackouts suffered by the early Apollo missions on returning to Earth.

"I guess we might as well use the time to write up our notes on the substance and look to head back to Earth with the samples as soon as we can." commented Alan. "How long will the storm keep us in camp?"

"Satellite images suggested it's not a big one, so probably a day and a half before we can head on back." replied Miro. "We can expect to feel the winds in the next hour or so."

Dust storms had been seen from orbiting probes back in the last century but it was only after the first manned landings and the beginnings of the settlement that their frequency and size could be really recorded. What had been believed to be no more than an irritant from orbit proved to be more serious than that and something to be wary of. Hence the original warning to the team to find shelter. The shelter they had found was not perfect but, as the Mars part of the team were forced to acknowledge, ideal shelter was rarely available.

As the storm hit it became clear that it was much stronger than indicated from the satellite transmissions. A surprising amount of larger debris was soon bombarding the camp site as the hills provided an opportunity for lulls in the wind force as it passed over.

With the vehicles rocking more than a little and crashes of debris against the outside increasing, Miro ordered everyone into full environmental suits. "Let's not risk a seal fracture. You can leave helmets open for the moment. George, you and Naoko best move into the other vehicle and we'll seal the airlocks. In a worst case," he said to Alan and his team, "we might lose one vehicle. If we did lose air in one, we would still have the oxygen supplies of the other."

The sky had darkened as the storm hit but there was still a red haze. Gradually the haze faded into a virtual blackout as night itself fell. With the constant noise, it was no longer possible to work or sleep. All they could do was to wait and rest.

About four hours after the storm hit, the shaking stopped abruptly and the noise lessened to little more than a background murmur.

"The eye of the storm?" asked Alan.

"These storms don't normally have an eye. They aren't of hurricane strength. I'm not sure what's happening." was Miro's worried response.

"George, any ideas?" he asked over a comm line linked to the other vehicle. There was no reply. "George, please respond."

The silence continued. Alan decided action needed to be taken quickly. "Miro, we need to check on them. I suggest we button up and try the airlock link."

Miro nodded. "Seal helmets guys. Closing the vehicle's oxygen feeds. That way if there has been any reduction in atmospheric pressure, we will only lose the current air. Having said that if there is a pressure imbalance the airlock shouldn't open without an override."

Moving to the airlock he started the process. Sensors indicated a slight difference in the pressure but not enough to stop the airlock from opening. As it did there was a brief light breeze as pressures equalised – to their surprise it blew from the second vehicle. George and Naoko were apparently asleep but did not stir at the noise. A flashing light on the control panel indicated a warning of high carbon dioxide levels but there was no additional warning sound. The team reacted quickly. Alan and Laurent swiftly pulled oxygen tanks from their storage and started to feed the contents direct to the two unconscious team members.

Adrien moved to help Miro check the instruments to try and find an answer to what was causing the problem. It became apparent that one of the absorption cylinders was fractured and not filtering the air correctly. Miro took the decision to switch the process to a backup and gradually the carbon dioxide level began to fall. It took a little longer but Naoko slowly responded to the oxygen feeds and became aware of the others being present.

"Miro, George isn't responding." Alan's tone voiced real concern that the man was still unconscious despite the oxygen. "His pulse is steady and he is breathing but there is no change in awareness."

"Keep trying, Alan. Feed the oxygen through his face mask. Laurent with me. We need to find out why it is still dark outside. Adrien, see if you can raise the base. If you can't from here you had best try from the other vehicle, in case we have a local failure beyond the CO2 issue. Explain the issue with George and tell them we need emergency recovery."

The two men moved to the airlock. "Alan," Miro added, "we are going to seal this airlock and then move vehicle one a few feet away to enable us to go outside and see what the situation is."

They followed through the actions, as Miro had decided, only to find that vehicle one refused to move despite its engine being at full throttle. Miro shut down to avoid the engine overheating and stopped to think. Then he moved to switch on all the external lights. They could see that these were on through the reflected glow but beyond that nothing was visible. It was Laurent who first voiced the thought both men had had.

"It seems we have been buried by the storm and, I guess, that means no comms and no exit since the airlocks are our normal exit point from the vehicles."

Miro nodded. "Seems the most likely reason." Then he continued. "But not our only way out, if we are lucky. There is a hatch in the roof. Problem is that it is not an airlock. If we try that we will lose the air in whichever vehicle we use."

"Perhaps we should try vehicle two's engines first see if they have any success in moving against the sand. If that works, we could use both vehicles in tandem, with vehicle one in reverse." replied Laurent.

Returning to the other vehicle they found that Adrien had not been able to raise the settlement. After briefing the rest, they tried the engines. Although the vehicle shuddered a little it seemed to be sliding sideways rather than forwards and Miro aborted the attempt.

George was still unconscious so the team carried him into the other vehicle. Naoko was still a little groggy and complaining of a headache so Mori asked Adrien to join him in the effort to extricate themselves from vehicle two leaving Alan and Laurent to watch over the injured pair.

After sealing the airlock and sealing their suits they switched off the oxygen tanks and Mori moved to blow the hatch. Adrien stopped him.

"Where are the spades, we used to dig around the deposit?"

Mori responded "On the roof. If we can get through the hatch, we can reach them."

"Then that should be our first aim," Adrien stated, "which may help if we need to do any digging."

Mori nodded and activated the explosive bolts. "Get back!"

There was a loud thud as the bolts blew. The hatch itself became loose but did not move upwards as designed, a shower of dust fell from around the edges. The two men looked at each other and then moved to pull the hatch down. It came easily followed by a cloud of red dust and lumps of the same substance. By the time the debris stopped falling they could climb it back to the ceiling of the vehicle and the open hatchway. The hatchway was blocked but they dug with their hands shifting more sandy material into the vehicle. Eventually they managed to push a panel into the gap, stop the inflow and gain access to the near part of the roof sufficient to get two spades down.

As they explained when back in the other vehicle. "There must be tons of the stuff up there. We've got two spades but how we can get out, I don't know. Any ideas welcome." Mori was glum.

Alan asked the question. "How long can we survive down here?"

"Two weeks if we cannibalise the supplies from two for oxygen. We have plenty of water and food if we don't binge out!" Naoko's smile softened the atmosphere a little. "The problem will be if the drones can't see the vehicles, they may question our location data. That storm is like nothing we have seen since the first Mars landing."

Alan, thought for a moment. "Miro, when you tried vehicle two you said that it seemed to slip sideways? I think we need to try again. We need to split the airlocks apart so that we can get outside so the vehicle going sideways needn't be bad news. Or have I missed something?"

"I don't think it can do anything to hurt us as long as we have disconnected the locks. But we should make sure that there are enough supplies in both vehicles in case we succeed in splitting them apart but still can't get out."

The preparation took a while but once completed they did not waste time. Naoko suggested and it was agreed that one thing to try, if they could not get out, would be to try pushing a cable through the dust that could then be used as an aerial.

They decided that Miro and Laurent were best suited to the task and they switched to the other vehicle. With airlocks sealed vehicle two's engines were restarted, slowly at first then with increased power. The vehicle started to vibrate but the earlier movement was absent. Laurent watched Miro start to ease back and suggested that they try short bursts of full power both forward and in reverse.

"If we can get her rocking. It might help."

Miro agreed and started short bursts of power. After a few moments they felt the vehicle start to move – slowly at first but then they could feel it pushing through the sandy cover at an increasing rate away from the other vehicle. Then to their relief external light started to filter through the windscreen.

"Keep going – we need to be sure we are in the clear before we stop."

Once they were clear they halted and then looked back. To their dismay the tunnel or gap the vehicle had pushed through had collapsed and the other vehicle remained totally buried. It was clear that they did not have the tools to manage a rescue without help nor did they appear to have a working radio link.

An examination of the outside of the vehicle showed significant damage to the power links and indicated that the backup power from solar panels had been completely destroyed. A decision to head back to base was not difficult until they realised that the landscape had been changed by the storm and there was only one way that they could move and that was not in the direction of Schiaparelli in so far as they could see.

It was Mori who decided their next series of actions. "I think that we should try that exit and see how far we will be off the expected route before we can turn for home. If it is too far then we need to return here. We are already overdue to report back and I expect that they will send drones to our last reported position before deciding if a rescue party is needed. If we are not on the drone's flight path, they may miss us entirely."

"Shouldn't we wait for the drone then?" asked Laurent.

"We should have another ten or twelve hours before that's a problem for us. I suggest we head out for four hours. If there has been no opportunity to change direction, we can return here in time for a drone sighting."

They set off and for two hours made good progress but without any opportunity to turn towards home. As they took a rest, they reviewed what was known of the geography of the area and came to the conclusion that, based on satellite mapping, they should already have found a valley in the right direction.

"There was something very odd about that storm," commented Laurent, "it did not seem to reflect the norm."

"I can't agree more," replied Mori, "let's head back. I'm no longer confident that we will find an escape route from here."

Half way back disaster struck again – their path was blocked by a landslide. With no alternative the two men climbed out and started to try and dig a way through. After a few minutes they changed tack and started to move the sand onto two slopes in the hope that they could ride over the blockage.

Back in vehicle one most of the attention was focussed on George who remained unconscious with shallow breathing despite being given an oxygen enriched feed via his facemask. Alan, his face pale with worry, turned to Naoko.

"We know the others have made some progress but if they can't contact base when can we expect a rescue team?"

"I suspect it will depend on what they do when we are really overdue. Probably they will send a drone as soon as the storm has passed and we have not been in contact. If the drone cannot see us then they will despatch a party. All in all, I'd guess four days before anyone can reach us unless there is a shuttlecraft on approach, in which case they might divert it towards the plain we were on."

* * *   * * *   * * *

"Why wasn't I told sooner?" the settlement commander raged.

"The storm effects seemed to last much longer. It was only when other communications had returned to normal that we realised that they had not checked in." Siobhan's deputy caught his breath, not being used to his boss acting in that way.

"What have you done?"

"We launched two drones on parallel flightpaths direct to the site where they took cover. They should be overflying that spot in about an hour."

"And?"

"Rescue party are prepping now, just awaiting a briefing on what the drones see."

"Right," growled Siobhan, "we'll discuss communications later. For now, what do we know about this storm? What was so unusual?"

"Apart from its speed, it moved quicker than is usual, and its density, the opacity of the storm centre was much darker, again compared with other storms we have seen. The guys are investigating and looking at orbital scans to see if they can find anything odd."

"Good, now make sure I am kept informed as soon as we learn anything." Siobhan's tone made it quite clear that she was still not happy.

Ninety minutes later she had more reasons to be unhappy. The drones, using their own internal systems, had reached the spot where the expedition should have been only for nothing to be seen. Acting on their own initiative the operators had sent one on to the site of the anomaly before routing it back along the route the returning vehicles would have taken. Having tried to identify the spot based on historic satellite images and failed they sent the second drone along a valley which appeared to have some tyre tracks.

Siobhan asked the question on everyone's lips. "Are you saying that we can't confirm the location of their camp? That the landscape has been so affected by the storm so as to be unrecognisable?"

The response was not without hope despite confirming that Siobhan was correct. "We have identified some landmarks which are helping us to get a fix on that position. Our best guess at the moment is that their site has been buried by sand/dust and debris. It may be that they are stuck but there are what appear to be tracks leading up a valley from the site. One drone is tracking that way but we only have about half an hour left before we will need to recall it to refuel."

Siobhan thought briefly and then made a decision. "Unless the tracks cease or there is a physical block you do not recall the drone. We need maximum coverage. The drone can be recovered later if necessary. When will the second drone have completed its track to the anomaly and back to the camp site?"

"It is due back imminently."

"Does it have the kit to carry out an ultrasound probe or similar?"

"Of course." was the reply. "We can search across the spot using dead reckoning."

"Then get to it." Turning to the rescue party, Siobhan continued. "You need to get on your way and take digging equipment. Good luck. Wait, Marion, are you really needed?"

Marion's response was much as Siobhan expected.

"I am. We don't know what state we will find them in. William is just prepping the rest of our gear and, let's be clear, that is my sister's husband out there. I couldn't face Megan if things went wrong because I wasn't on the spot."

As the various personnel moved to carry out their roles Siobhan returned to her office. Helpless to do anything else, other than worry, she started to review the various reports that as ever littered her desk. Containing little of urgency, the reports, nevertheless, would occupy her while she waited for news. She started to deal with them in a lethargic manner until some thirty minutes later she jerked into full alertness when she saw the headline attached to a routine report from the orbital survey team based on the Mars space station. "Meteor Strike."

The report noted that an orbital survey satellite had recorded a meteor striking the ground about five hundred kilometres west of the settlement three days before. The report noted that a large volume of surface material had been blown into the air by the impact which had generated a directional wind due to its very shallow angle of trajectory. The wind had then been funnelled by the local geography increasing its focus.

Leaving her office, she almost knocked her deputy over.

"Gordon, I think we have identified the cause of the storm."

Her deputy's expression of concern mixed with bemusement was suddenly changed by her brief explanation.

"That explains why the vehicles are buried so deep."

"Pardon? Are you saying we have found them?" Siobhan's voice cracked.

"I was on my way in to tell you. We've located one vehicle which appears to be buried by some ten metres of sand and other debris. The second vehicle appears to have forced its way out and followed a valley exit from the area. We're still trying to find it."

A few hours later the second vehicle was finally spotted twenty kilometres away, close to the landslide which had cut it off from returning. With no sign of life apparent, the drone had been dropped to ground level before being landed next to the vehicle. With insufficient power to reach base it was left with enough to allow the occupants of the vehicle to communicate with their rescuers.

In the circumstances, Siobhan instructed her team in the space station to despatch a shuttle with a targeted landing point as close to the first vehicle as possible and then instructed one half of the rescue team to change course to reach the second vehicle.

With everything done that could be, there was nothing to do but wait. The rescue teams would take the best part of twenty hours to reach their target areas and although the shuttle could land closer it would still only be a few hours ahead of them.

First news came from the shuttle team. Without the digging equipment coming overland they could not start to excavate the site but having found the spot where the second vehicle had dug itself out, they managed to get a line through the loosened sand to the first vehicle and communicated with the men inside. The good news that Alan, Naoko and Adrien were fit and well was tempered by the fact that George remained in a coma.

The arrival of the rescue teams at both sites was almost simultaneous and work on digging out the first vehicle started urgently. At the second location the news was not good. The vehicle was empty and there was no sign of Miro and Laurent. Shortly after that came word that their bodies had been found. It seemed that as they dug into the landslide there had been a further collapse of the valley wall which had partly buried them. It had also caused their suits to be damaged beyond any repair capability.

It was a sombre group who were welcomed back to the base the next day following a brief flight in the shuttle. Relief for the three uninjured men, concern over George who was rushed to the infirmary, and sorrow for the loss of Miro, who was a well-liked member of the community, and Laurent, who would now not be returning to Earth.

The success of the mission to the anomaly was not to be downgraded but, as Alan said, it had come at a high price.

Back on Earth the message of his impending departure on the trip back was received by his family with unimaginable relief and joy. That Laurent's family was in mourning was not lost by Megan who caught a flight to France to be present at a private memorial service for Alan's colleague. There would be a second more public one in Houston, once Alan and Adrien had returned, to celebrate the lives of all the men who had lost their lives. George had suffered brain damage from the carbon dioxide poisoning and remained in a coma.

9. Fuelling the Warp Drive

As soon as they were landed on Earth, the iridium alloy samples were rapidly sent to a number of different locations for analysis. While this took time, the lead teams back in Houston decided that, whatever the final results of that effort were, it was the sheer amount of iridium that counted.

A month later heavy lifting craft were launched into orbit carrying mining equipment for transfer to Mars. At the same time a team of mining experts was recruited to carry out the excavation of the anomalous deposit. While the work would not require permanent transfer to the Mars settlement the recruitment team found that the idea of becoming a true member of the settlement was the most common reason for the applicants.

Three months after that the first mining work began and, from then on, the regular supply craft headed back from Mars with holds full rather than empty.

Back in the research laboratories there was little success in handling the alloy. The separation of pure iridium from it should have been straightforward. Using a heated centrifuge, the extraction of the target element should have been a routine process but despite varying the process across a range of trials only small amounts of the metal could be obtained.

Pressure began to build on Megan and her colleagues to generate the fuel for the interstellar probe which was, by now, being constructed in orbit. Larger than the space station from which the construction crews were based it was almost the largest mobile craft to be built in space. Only almost. Being constructed in parallel was a new interplanetary craft designed to take a complete space station out to Titan and allow a survey team to study that unusual moon, Enceladus and the rest of the Saturnian system from close up.

Megan and Alan called a conference to be attended by all the researchers and others involved with the project. Their main aim being to have a series of brainstorming sessions in an effort to find an answer. After three days of tiring work there was one idea that had not been considered before. Megan summarised the result in just a few words

"We are going to try a new idea – to vaporise the alloy and use the resultant particles."

Setting up a working vaporisation process took longer than expected but later that year the particle accelerators had the opportunity to test the practical outcome of the associated theoretical analysis which indicated that the fuel produced would contain adequate power to fuel the warp drives of the probe.

Megan and Grigor were back in CERN to watch the first test run and to the delight of the Swiss based team two new faces were present. Judy and Molly had made the trip with their mother as a holiday treat.

As the accelerator started up so did the vaporising process and the gaseous outflow was directed into the target zone. The teams of technicians started their recording of the increasing activity as the particles approached a measurable percentage of light speed. As hoped for, temperatures rose in a manner similar to those that had occurred when ferrous particles had been used. Then the process appeared to stall just short of the original energy expansion. Despite this the containment fields still filled with pressure as exotic particles formed.

"I don't understand," said Grigor as they watched, "if those figures are correct, we have a fuel that is lower pressured but might be more powerful. I can't see how."

"More to the point how can we test it at this level?" replied Megan. "I don't think we have enough."

As the accelerator was wound down, they received a second surprise. The generation of exotic particles continued for some time, despite the alloy particles being fully closed off and the vaporisation hub being cooled down. In the end the containment field was at full pressure and stable.

"Right," said Yuri, "everyone, go home. We'll reconvene tomorrow and try and see if we can make any sense of these inconsistencies."

*** *** ***

Grigor turned to the two youngsters, "Judy, Molly, what would you like to do this evening?"

Judy turned and answered, "Can I see a piece of the alloy? Pop didn't bring any home and it sounds wonderful."

Megan started with surprise, "There still isn't that much of it, sunshine."

"But I think we can manage a look," replied Grigor.

Grigor led the way through a door into a second room in which was a display cabinet with one of the original samples inside.

"Oh wow!" said Molly, "can we touch it?"

"Sorry, we have to keep it in a sterile environment, for the moment." said Yuri.

Judy was leaning on the cabinet's support and rubbed her hand across the glass. She looked surprised and looked up.

"What is it?" asked Megan.

"The cabinet is warm and its vibrating."

"Pardon?" Both the adults were startled by her comment.

"Feel it. Shouldn't it be warm?"

"No!" cried Grigor. "Everyone out of the room. NOW!"

As they went through the door Megan looked back and to her horror saw the sample starting to glow. Throwing the girls to the floor she hit the fire alarm before dropping down herself. Grigor, too, looked back and dropped on top of the girls. Seconds later there was a flash and an intense screaming sound as the sample, according to CCTV pictures reviewed later, launched itself in a straight line. The buildings rocked to the impact of the object as it smashed through walls and then roofs. Apparently immune to the gravitational pull of the Earth its line stayed straight as it gained height due to the curvature of the planet below and accelerated towards the sun.

Megan slowly rose to her feet and then screamed. Grigor was still lying on top of her daughters. His clothes were smouldering and there was a dark line across his back. In protecting the two youngsters he had left himself in the line followed by the sample.

"Get the medics, get the medics." She yelled at the men rushing into the room as she gently moved Grigor's unconscious body off her girls. To her total relief both were no more than shaken.

It was Molly who asked, "Is he OK?"

"I don't know." answered Megan as the medical team arrived and started work.

"He saved us, Mom, didn't he?" said Judy. "I hope he's going to be all right."

"He did, Judy. Now we need to move away and let the right people do their work."

Yuri Lentenov appeared looking as agitated as Megan had ever seen him. "What happened?" he asked Megan.

"I wish I knew. Judy told us that the sample case was warm and humming. Then all hell let loose. Yuri, we need to warn the other sites with samples and then work out what was different about the structure of this sample."

"We're on it, Megan. Now get your girls back to the hotel. We'll let you know about Grigor as soon as we have news. I'll see you in the morning."

Later that evening Megan got a call with news of Grigor. In the event his burns had proven to not be too serious and he would make a complete recovery. With that good news she and her daughters were able to get a good night's sleep after all.

*** *** ***

The next day Megan left her daughters with one of Yuri's researchers who had agreed to show them the sights in Geneva. Judy was not that happy at not being able to return to the CERN operations but was told that she would have another chance, provided she helped with her sister.

Arriving at the operations centre Megan found that Yuri's entire team had been at their desks all night trying to understand the event. Most had not actually left for home and had willingly stayed on. By now they were showing the effects of no sleep but the room was still buzzing with the knowledge that they had an answer for Megan and, via video conferencing, Alan and the team still in the USA.

Yuri introduced one of his team.

"This is Jean-Paul Boivin. He joined us just after you left for the States, Megan. I'd like him to lead on the report as it was his thinking that led us to a realistic answer. Even if we don't understand how, he can tell you what happened and why, we think, it happened."

Jean-Paul stood up, slightly nervously, and turned on a video screen. "We don't have a full record of the event but internal CCTV picked up the sample as it crossed a number of areas within the building before breaking out through the wall on the first floor in section 9. As you can see the tail is glowing almost white with heat producing a jet of superheated air as a, for want of a better term, propellant."

He continued, "The film shows that it is only the rear quarter, or so, of the sample, that appears to have been directly affected. We are agreed that the way the sample moved was a logical result of one part changing temperature while the rest did not. Our difficulty was that we couldn't understand why until someone asked if there was a reason that the sample might differ in cross section."

Yuri interrupted at this point. "Jean-Paul is being a little modest in his presentation and has not told you how we made the leap to the answer you have before you. Jean-Paul?"

"Thank you, Professor. Yes, I did wonder if we could have done anything to the original sample that might have affected its balance. It was lucky that we had kept a series of records which showed it at different stages. Apparently when we took shavings from the sample, to run tests on the alloy's structure, they were all taken from one end. It seems that this must have caused an imbalance in the residual material."

It became apparent that the young man had led a fast and highly successful investigation. The shavings had, it proved, included more iridium in proportion to the complex compound which made up the rest of the sample. The properties of that part of the alloy had still not been identified but an imbalance must have allowed it to act as an extreme exothermic source. Radar tracking suggested that the sample had reached Mach Five while still in the lower atmosphere.

"What about other samples? And what about the mined amounts being transported back?" Megan's concern was obvious.

One of Alan's team responded. "This seems to have been a unique occurrence. Everyone has been warned and all cargos will now be monitored."

"What was different about that piece? Do we know yet?" asked Alan.

It was Yuri who provided the answer.

"It appears that we were the only location to have taken thin slices of alloy to produce the iridium. As a result, the balance of substance was out of alignment with our slices being underweight in the non-iridium part. We are still analysing the event but the last sighting showed the "sample" coasting on a path that may lead to it falling into a cometary type orbit of the sun. That suggests the chemical make-up is back in balance."

Alan turned to someone off camera and was heard to ask if there was a spacecraft close enough to complete an intercept and recovery. The answer was non-committal but the Houston team would start investigating the possibilities.

The meeting was ended and the two team leaders moved on to other matters. Megan met with members of Yuri's team to discuss the results of the previous days production run of the accelerator.

"I'm calling it a production run now as we have definitely made a new fuel with significant power." She said. "The question is how much power and how much fuel would we need to handle a six-month round trip for the robotic probe?"

Jean-Paul spoke up. The formerly shy individual had found confidence suddenly from the earlier presentation.

"Strictly, we don't know yet. But everything suggests that, if we can produce perhaps fifty times the current amount, we will have sufficient fuel for a six-month trip. We still need to carry out testing to see if the actual power generated is going to be enough to start the warp drive."

"How do you plan that testing?" asked Megan.

"We have started working on it. My gut feeling is that we may need to do this off planet, there is potential for something going very wrong, if we don't get it right. After all we are dealing with energy production that seems to break the law of the conservation of energy."

Megan thought for a moment. "Post Big Bang I wonder if the expansion period had the same inconsistency? There have always been theories that suggest that current physical laws only developed in the aftermath of the Big Bang. We will need to review that in due course. Let me and Alan know when your planning is ready. Thanks all. I head back to the States later but first stop is the hospital."

As she had said, Megan and her daughters visited Grigor in his hospital bed to make sure he was on the mend. He was clearly still in some pain but managed a welcoming smile for the two girls who would have hugged him if Megan had not held them back.

"Careful, girls. I suspect your hero will be a little sensitive to pressure."

"A little," smiled Grigor, "but I'm just glad you are all OK."

"Thank you," said Molly, "please get better soon."

"Me too," said Judy.

After a few moments Megan asked the girls to say goodbye and then motioned them out of the room. Turning back to the bedside she bent down and gently kissed Grigor on the cheek. "I cannot thank you enough, my friend. You made sure the girls were safe, at a cost that might have been your life. They called you a hero and they were right."

*** *** ***

Back in Houston the next morning, over breakfast, Alan and Megan discussed the latest progress in the search for the warp fuel.

They concluded the new fuel could reasonably be expected to generate the needed power levels but that the final proof could only be obtained by using the star probe itself. If the warp drive operated as designed for a short trip, they would be able to refine the fuel to allow longer interstellar flights.

"One thing, aside from those recommendations," said Megan, "I feel we should arrange for Jean-Paul to be transferred to the team over here. I sense he has an instinctive ability to cross fertilise theory and practice."

"He reminds me of someone else around here," grinned Alan, "I agree though, that he appears to be another thinker outside the box."

A few days later, Jean-Paul was invited to join the team in Houston, a little to Yuri's chagrin. At the same time came the news that George had not recovered consciousness and had died as a result of brain damage caused by the carbon dioxide poisoning.

*** *** ***

The idea that construction of the star probe should carry on with some adjustments to its fuel core storage was proposed to the NASA team responsible for the international development of the probe. This was not accepted without extensive challenge – not, as it happened, the idea to continue the build but that the design should undergo such a major change from the structure that Alan's team had originally driven through. In the end the probe team accepted that the changes would not affect the engine power with either fuel.

Jean-Paul duly arrived in the States and brought with him a warning. With Yuri's consent, he and a small team had done additional research into the potential side effects of the warp drive operations. The results were quite startling with two elements that would need to be taken into account.

In the first case the modelling suggested that far from being limited to the starship itself, as had been assumed, the spacetime impact would cover a larger volume, up to five hundred kilometres in diameter outside of the ship's own structure.

In addition, and from an operational point of view it was clearly the more important, Jean-Paul outlined a threat to the ship.

"The problem is. If we start the warp drive too close to a significant gravity well, such as the sun. There is a high probability that the drive could implode due to the distortion of the spacetime caused by the warp drive overlapping that of the local gravity well itself."

"That is something we had thought about before." said Alan. "We had concluded that we should be some distance from the Earth/Lunar system. Are you saying that that is not enough?"

"Not enough by a long way. Our calculations suggest that we should not activate the drive inside the orbit of Saturn. It is possible that that is a conservative location but I believe that it would be best to be safe rather than sorry."

"We will need to review your analysis but assuming it is correct, then Saturn's orbit it must be. Though I doubt NASA will be happy!"

And NASA and the international group of developers were not happy but, in the end, accepted that such a risk could not be ignored. Their next step would be to appoint a new crew for the Saturn mission craft. That ship, also in construction, would be able to complete two missions at the same time, but would need a crew with an understanding of the warp capable ship. It would also need to remain on station for the expected four months of the probe's trip until it returned.

10. Interstellar Probe

A press conference in Houston, later that year, would clash with a second in New York. In the United Nations building the UN Secretary General took the chair to announce that the Security Council had unanimously agreed that funding would be made available to complete a robotic probe which would attempt to use a warp drive to make the trip to Alpha Centauri.

This was the first time that the existence of such a probe was announced in a public domain and reception was mixed. There were those that were excited by the idea that such a trip was a possibility. Many others asked the question often used to question any space expenditure "why?" and then made comparisons as to what the funds could be used for in the continuing fight against climate change.

There was no doubt that the Secretary General had been properly briefed and was able to make the point that one of the biggest moves to countering the effect of fossil fuel usage had come from the same research that had made the prospect of a working warp drive possible.

Meanwhile fourteen hundred miles south, NASA was holding a conference on behalf of the international space group at which the captain of the ship, that had now been re-named the ISP Monitor was named. To the surprise of many Americans the captain would not be an American, or even Russian, but was a man born in Marseilles.

Gerald Pasternak had extensive experience in interplanetary craft, having made nine trips to Mars as well as spending time on the moon helping develop the Lunar settlement. When asked how he felt about being given the command of the largest ship ever built, his answer was simple.

"I am honoured to have been chosen but I will not be alone – there will be a team supporting me. We will lead the way. Saturn beckons."

The rest of the crew was appointed not in secrecy but not in front of the same public gaze. Captain Pasternak was called on to make his own recommendations the first of which was his first officer to be Fran Hawkins. Her history included Mars trips as well and she had also commanded interplanetary craft. As they both knew each other and this was a craft with a difference – the largest ever built, she did not see it as demotion but like him an opportunity.

They spent some days looking at options for the rest of the crew before settling on their choices.

A week later, Judy received a video call from the Moon.

"Hello, Judy."

"Is that you, Ellen? Where are you? We haven't seen you for ages." Judy's excitement at receiving such a call was overheard by her sister and her mother who came into the room.

"I'm sorry about that but I've been here for most of the time and, sorry again, but this call has to be short as I'm due to leave for my new posting."

"New posting?"

"Yes. Megan, I hope you are pleased but I will be on the Monitor!"

"The Monitor?" Molly squealed.

"Yes, youngster. I am heading for Saturn and we will be escorting the star probe to its launch point. But I wanted to call now because I will be away for over a year and we won't be able to talk in that time."

"Oh wow!"

Megan interposed. "I hope we can talk again before you depart. In the meantime, bon voyage, cousin. Jean-Paul will be our on-board expert for the probe, if he can finish his astronaut basic training in time, that is!"

"I'll look after him. Got to go now. Bye all."

For Gerald Pasternak, and his crew, the following weeks were extremely busy as they bedded down the new craft and completed the extra training that was needed for such a large ship. There was also the need to understand how the process of towing the Titan space station would affect the performance of the kilometre-long ship, given that the station itself was almost as big.

"It is a good thing that the probe has its own interplanetary propulsion capability. Even with the power of the Monitor I don't think we could have managed to tow both." Fran commented during the daily officer's meeting three months after arriving, in her case, from the Phobos station.

"If the new fuel being promised for the probe lives up to expectations it could probably tow us both!" responded Gerald. "Ellen, have you heard anything from your cousin?" That Ellen and Megan were related was well known but Gerald did not normally need to seek an inside line in that way, since as captain of the Monitor he did have direct contact with the Earth based teams.

"I haven't spoken to her for some weeks. What with everything going on here and with the teams working on fuel preparation and storage, having little or no time for relaxation, there hasn't been the time."

"Well, my own update is that the star fuel is living up to the expected parameters and will power the warp drives. Not sure that we could use it for interplanetary journeys yet. Our containment fields aren't strong enough. Ultimately the only guarantee that it will work will be the sight of the star probe disappearing from our vision."

"Will we have to learn the detail behind the warp drive and how the probe's AI will control it?" asked Fran.

"Fortunately, not in detail," Gerald grinned, "the last member of the crew will be an expert, to the extent that anyone can really be. After all, this mission is as near the cutting edge as it gets."

"He's a young man who Megan and Alan think very highly of." Interposed Ellen.

"So, the jungle drums have been beating," responded Fran, "tell us more."

"You must have some details already. At least a summary of his time at CERN."

Gerald commented drily, "True, but it's pretty thin. So, if you can add anything?"

"As I understand it, he graduated from Harvard three years ago – impressive in itself for a Belgian student to be accepted in the first place and with a scholarship. After a break, he went to CERN where, Megan told me, he helped her team answer some difficult questions using a degree of intuition that led us to the current developments. She told me that we could blame him for having to go to Saturn before we can engage the probe's warp engines. To use her words, she shipped him back to Houston as fast as she could."

"He should be near to finishing basic astronaut training now and I suspect will be joining us early next month. Now, we need to move on to discuss Titan station in a little detail." Gerald moved the conversation on.

The station was only half the size that the international space station had grown to over the years, as space travel had expanded with the new plasma engines. Because it had been purpose designed from scratch, though, it looked even smaller. It was still capable of supporting a team of twenty including crew and scientists for about a year without supply replenishment. There were already ships being built that could make automated supply runs in two to three months depending on the variable Earth-Saturn distance. Although close to the size of the Monitor the station did not have engines capable of interplanetary distances only for ensuring that its orbit around Titan was maintained safely.

The team were led through the tow process by a senior engineer, Scott Bailey.

"In short, immediately before we leave orbit, we will lock the ship to the station using their own extendable arms. Early acceleration will be lower than we could handle alone but the combined tonnage will add structural stresses to both parts of the combined vehicle."

Fran's first question was simple "Why wait until the last minute?"

"Just to limit the orbital stress of such a large vehicle in Earth orbit – we aren't or won't be as stable as the space station by itself. Our aim should be to leave orbit within three hours of the lock being completed."

With the early restriction on acceleration not being an issue for the star probe it was decided that it would leave after the Monitor and its cargo. A second craft would then escort it until it had caught up with the Monitor.

Two months later spaceplanes took off from Houston, the Baikonur Cosmodrome and from Geneva each with the same mission – to deliver the new fuel for the star probe's warp drives and additional stocks of fuel for the Monitor and the probe's interplanetary engines. With them came the final members of the Titan station's research team and Jean-Paul Boivin, who would act as an observer on the Monitor and provide on-the-spot advice, should there be any difficulties with the probe.

Within a few days the space-station was moved alongside the Monitor and the two craft were locked together. As planned a few hours later Gerald Pasternak gave the order to start engines. Slowly the huge combined mass moved outwards away from the Earth heading as if towards Mars in the first instant. A course change after they were out of the Earth/Lunar system would start a move above the ecliptic so as to limit the danger offered by the asteroid belt before completing a loop back to a more direct routing towards Saturn.

Shortly after leaving orbit the crew received a series of good wishes from world leaders and their families and the support teams in NASA and Geneva. Personal messages from not only Earth but the Lunar and Mars settlements also arrived. Ellen's included fun videos sent by Judy and Molly as well as a private message from Megan and Alan with an invitation to visit upon her return in a year's time.

* * *   * * *   * * *

Three days into their voyage Jean-Paul found himself in a question and answer session with the Monitor's senior officers. Despite having been briefed before departure about their mission they found that they still had many more questions before feeling able to deal with the star probe's warp launch with confidence.

"Knowing if the warp drives have operated successfully may be the easiest part." he answered, "Very simply the craft should vanish from visual sight. We believe that instruments should be able to identify the distortion in the spacetime continuum for a period. One of your tasks as you know will be to send four sensor probes ahead of the planned route towards Proxima Centauri. If we are correct, they will also be able to track the movement of the probe for a time."

"As I understand it, the operation of the warp drives will impact more than the immediate vicinity of the craft?" was Fran's question.

Jean-Paul smiled. "We don't really know how far the side effects might stretch. My best estimate is probably no more than five hundred kilometres but equally we should be cautious. I can't emphasise enough to you all that this really is at the very edge of our current knowledge. All the theory says that the warp drives will work. The truth is that until the probe vanishes from our view, we cannot be certain of success."

"I am ordered to move the Monitor to a distance of twice your suggested danger area," said the Captain, "before the AI starts the process. Too far?"

"I suspect your orders are being made on the basis of "better safe than sorry"," responded Jean-Paul, "and I wouldn't argue with them."

"I believe that it was you who identified the risk and landed us with this task." Ellen grinned.

"I'm not sure I should take all the credit, or all the blame, for that. It was a team that carried out the calculations that led to that conclusion." was the modest response.

"That's not what I heard!" Ellen's chuckle was infectious.

"Jean-Paul, you should know that Ellen has the inside track on the whole process. She is Megan Piper's cousin!" Fran laughed.

There would be many more discussions over the following weeks including all the crew in turn. As Gerald had pointed out everyone formed part of a relatively small operations team with the numbers topped up with various science disciplines looking into areas such as the impact of long-range journeys on the human being. This trip would be the first direct journey to Saturn and the longest undertaken as a single mission. More importantly they would be responsible for the greatest step taken by mankind - a trip to another solar system and back by a human built probe in less than a year!

Ten days into the mission came the news they had been waiting for. The star probe had left Earth orbit and had started its long chase to catch them. Escorted by the interplanetary craft, the IP Ganymede, and taking a slightly shorter route, the two craft would rendezvous with the Monitor as they crossed the asteroid belt region but, as planned, only at its "northern" edge. The research teams included two astronomers who were eager to film the belt from a viewpoint not previously available to the various unmanned probes from the previous fifty years or so. Those members of the crew off-duty found themselves being co-opted into the process with an opportunity to learn more about the solar system within which they worked. On such a long journey such diversions were, naturally, welcome, even if other projects had to be delayed.

Crossing Jupiter's orbit did not provide a diversion, in itself, as the planet was not on that side of the sun. There was cause for celebration though, as the first humans to reach that point. Only unmanned missions had gone further from Earth. The Monitor and the Titan station were crossing into new territory. It was not that Jupiter was being ignored by mankind. Robots were already building a research station on Ganymede ready for a second research team but scientists still considered Titan and Enceladus the real mystery moons in the solar system and had lobbied, successfully, to have that as the first priority after Mars. In the event that success had fitted in well with the need for the star probe to only engage its drive a long way out from the sun.

"Why so far?" asked Gerald. "After all we are already over five AU from the sun and Saturn is twice as far as Jupiter."

Jean-Paul had to admit that caution was again the watchword. "It is all about the depth of the sun's gravity well and how it shapes the space time continuum. In truth there is limited difference between the two planets in terms of risk. Whereas, trying from Mars at less than two AU, requires the warp drive to handle a steep climb out of the well. It is my belief that, with experience, we will find that we can operate nearer the sun. If not with current technology then with future developments which will also allow faster trips."

"Faster?!" the ship's engineer, Scott, was in place for this session and could not hide his astonishment. "The probe will cover a bit over four light years in less than six weeks and you are thinking that's slow?"

"Well not really slow, but the AI has been programmed to stay within quite strict guidelines with the drives. We do calculate that even the current warp drives could generate fields capable of covering that distance in under a week. In theory the only limit to the velocity of a warp ship is the power of its drives and its fuel reserves. I don't need to remind you that the ship itself is not moving faster than light. It's just that warping space in the way we plan bends the rules about the light speed limit. Warp one will produce a rate of movement of roughly a light year a week."

"I'm quite happy to be reminded," smiled Scott, "I've studied everything I can find about the warp drives and still find it difficult to handle the energies involved. I'm also amazed that NASA had designs for warp drives as far back as they did."

Gerald's comment caused a stir. "I'm more surprised that they funded the continuing research when there was no possible energy source available to power them. Budget constraints back around the turn of the century should have had such research put on the back burner in favour of renewable energy and ships capable of moving within the system."

"Then Megan and Alan came up with the first exotic fuel. Suddenly we have international cooperation on a scale never seen before and increased funding for a space programme that is providing an explosion of development – the Moon and Mars within a matter of a few years. It really is amazing! Not that I'm complaining," said Ellen., "but I still wonder at how such cooperation between nations that have almost been at war with each other, economically if not physically, was possible."

"We shouldn't forget that that fuel has also enabled climate change to be tackled in ways we never thought possible," added Fran, "removing oil, in particular, from the geopolitical arena must have helped."

***   ***   ***

Time passed and three months later Saturn and its rings began to dominate the view from the bridge of the Monitor. Five million kilometres from the planet, Monitor and the probe parted company for a time. The probe's AI moved it further away from the planet backwards along the orbital path.

Monitor slowly manoeuvred into orbit around Titan. Close up the moon looked even more amazing than had been shown by the earlier unmanned probes. Before the two parts of the larger craft separated the Gerry held a dinner for the station's officers at the end of which there were a number of toasts.

Commander Tian, who would be responsible for the running of the Titan station, led the way. "Captain Pasternak, may I and my colleagues wish you all bon voyage and hope the mission is a total success. To the stars!"

"Commander, we hope that your own mission will also prove successful. We will keep in contact. As you know we will be remaining on station for the whole time that the probe is away. So, you haven't seen the last of us." Gerald responded.

Later the separation of the two craft took place and the station moved into its planned orbit around Titan.

Shortly after Gerald gave the order to leave orbit. The Monitor duly moved out of the Saturnian system and started a swift transfer away and toward the probe's standby position.

As they approached the probe the captain authorised the release of the four unmanned craft that would seek to measure the impact of the warp drives as they pushed the probe towards interstellar space. Acting on an impulse he also released a fifth smaller sensor pack and sent it into a holding pattern exactly five hundred kilometres from the probe.

"It occurs to me that understanding the side effects of the drive from a closer point may be of use in gauging the impact for future missions." He explained to Jean-Paul, who was sharing the first officer's station on the bridge.

The next day, everyone was at their stations on the Monitor as the two craft exchanged data before the AI was sent the final "Go" signal and Monitor moved away to a distance of a thousand kilometres.

Thirty minutes later the probe's AI sent a final message confirming systems all clear and engaged the warp drives.

For a few moments the watchers held their breaths as nothing seemed to be happening then, with an abruptness that was almost shocking, the probe vanished.

Large volumes of data were transmitted from all five of the unmanned craft, despite the fact that the probe had vanished within seconds, providing the team on board with many days of analysis and adding to the workload back on Earth once the data had been consolidated and sent home. At the first meeting of the scientific team Gerald was able to show a series of stunning images. These, captured by the fifth sensor pack, recorded an unexpected effect of the warp engines.

The first image showed the probe before launch with the star field behind it, a typical view. As the warp engines were activated the probe's image dimmed while the star field shimmered and started to change colour. In the next image the probe was not visible. All that was left was the starfield shimmering in a bright silver blue. In further images this effect became more pronounced but more localised.

"It seems that the probe's front viewers will show a significant blue shift with the rear ones showing a red shift. We had not expected the blue shift to be visible from outside the probe's spacetime bubble and we may have to review the theoretical studies." commented Jean-Paul.

"That might not be necessary." said one of the astronomers on board, "Might I suggest that the "bubble" is acting as a lens and leaving a traceable signature for the sensor probes to pick up on its return?"

"Hmm. That's not a bad idea. It'll give us something to think while we are waiting for the probe to return."

The next four months passed slowly. Even though the crew and scientists had plenty to occupy them the state of the probe was never far from their thoughts. Although it could return within that time it was not expected for at least a further two to three weeks as its mission included a normal-space, n-space as it was beginning to be referred to as, pass through the Centauri system gathering as much data as possible before again engaging the warp drive to return home. The AI's programming gave it quite wide-ranging freedom to adjust course to examine objects of interest and its only material constraint would be the base fuel for its interplanetary engines.

By the end of the fifth month the general atmosphere on Monitor was of depression. With the probe now seemingly overdue everyone was starting to worry that the mission had failed in some way. Gerald Pasternak relaunched the unmanned sensor arrays to try and find evidence of the probe's track beyond the intended return point.

One set of data reported back caused a degree of bemusement. In space there is no sound but gravitational distortions in the spacetime continuum, it seemed, could cause matter to be pulled into a dense mass heating it to thousands of degrees. The kinetic impact of the particles involved must generate a noise at some level and a sensor array had recorded such noise.

A million kilometres away alarms went off as the message was received. Crew members raced to their posts even before their captain could confirm that the probe had returned from its mission.

"Tracking – do we have a fix yet?" asked Gerald.

"Five minutes, Captain. Second sensor report incoming."

Gerald switched to ship-wide communications. "All stations prepare for thrust. Better make sure everything is secure people, we've waited long enough for this day. Let's not spoil it by getting soup in the network!"

"Fix confirmed Captain. The probe is now operating on standard drives at sub-light. Captain, it is travelling much faster than when it left. Intrinsic velocity almost ten thousand klicks per hour. It is slowing but we are still going to need go to maximum thrust if we are to reach it within a day."

"Helm, maximum thrust."

"Aye, Captain"

Later, as Monitor accelerated towards the rendez-vous, they got their first view of the robotic craft that had travelled to the stars - and returned in less than six months.

*** *** ***

Back on Earth the time during which the star probe was away had dragged even more than aboard Monitor. Megan and her friends and colleagues had regular nightmares in which the probe had suffered various failures or misadventures. Perhaps it had caused a hole in the spacetime continuum and fallen out of our universe completely or perhaps it had reached Centauri but misjudged its arrival and been caught by one of the three stars in the system. As the probe's return was delayed the theories as to why became more and more extreme including destruction by an alien civilisation at Proxima Centauri.

Then came the transmission from Monitor.

"It's back! It's back!" Megan's excited yells woke her family as the message arrived during the night in Houston.

"Mom, does that mean we will see Ellen soon?" Judy's question driving home a more important thought for a teenager.

"Maybe, Judy. But they still have to travel back from Saturn so it's going to be a few more months."

Those months were very full as the probe's databanks were downloaded by Monitor and transferred to Earth. Databanks which were full of information that provided scientists with their first close up look at another star system.

Surprisingly the probe had recorded evidence of three planets, one small and rocky in close orbit around Proxima and a second Mars sized planet whose orbit, around Centauri B, placed it in the habitable zone.

The third planet was something of an enigma. A gas giant which appeared to be orbiting the entire Centauri system placing it almost a quarter of a light year from Alpha when spotted. Early judgement was that it would probably have been missed entirely except that it happened to be on the side of the system close to the probe's emergence from warp space.

At that point the reason for the delay in the probe's return had been assumed to be linked to course changes in its survey of the system. Then it was realised that the probe's sensors had identified the planet's gravitational field as it approached the system. Safety protocols had cut in and the AI had dropped the probe out of warp early – one hundred thousand klicks short of the planet. The fly-by had lasted four days before the AI returned to warp drive for the last run towards Proxima.

Alan was ecstatic when this became clear. "That means that we have managed to create sensors that really work. We couldn't have known for sure and there was no reason to expect that planet between Sol and any of the Centauri stars."

"I wonder why Kepler didn't spot it, the planet I mean," said Megan.

"I think I may have the answer to that," said one of the team. "Sorry, I should introduce myself first, Alejandro Alvarez. Given the distance from any of its possible primaries I doubt that the planet is actually in orbit. We, astronomers, have wondered if there might be rogue planets but to find one on our doorstep so to speak is surprising to say the least."

"What is a rogue planet, exactly?" asked Alan.

"Wanderer might be a better term but rogue fits just as well. Such planets do not orbit a sun and drift through interstellar space. There are various theories as to how they end up there but that's all they are. But it would explain how the Kepler telescope missed it. When it looked at the Centauri system that planet would simply not have been there."

"Well that's one for you to look at and Alan's right it does show that interstellar travel can be lower risk. An unexpected large object has always been a worry. How would the impact effect the warp bubble? A planet clearly would be a disaster but would lesser objects simply be pushed aside? We don't know even now but the sensors at the front of the probe were designed to measure changes in gravitational stress and it seems they do work." Megan's smile warmed the room as she looked towards her husband. "Do you think they will build a manned starship now?"

"Let's hope so, just think what we might find." replied Alan.

Despite this clear success in design the probe proved to have been damaged in several places. At least three micrometeorites or similar objects had struck the forward shielding but of more concern was that the forward elements of the probe, in particular the warp drive torus, appeared to have effectively been sand blasted.

Since the craft travelled in its own "bubble" of space-time while in warp, this latter damage must have occurred while traversing the normal space of the Centauri system.

The team checked with their astronomical colleagues but no-one was aware of a dust cloud around the system.

On-board systems were checked but the cause of the "sanding" remained a mystery. The concern for the probe designers was that the damage had hit the torus of the lead warp engine. The torus had not been in danger of failure on this occasion but, the question was, what if the probe had been moving faster on contact? It was not difficult to decide that additional protection would be needed on any future starship, manned or unmanned.

In due course the probe and Monitor slid into orbit close to the International Space Station. The crew received a rapturous welcome home on transferring across to the station before taking the shuttles to return either planet-side or to the lunar settlement.

To Judy and Molly's delight their cousin was able to start her leave in Houston while she went through multiple exercises to strengthen her muscles after over a year under limited gravity. When she arrived at their home, they were even more excited as two more astronauts were with her – Gerald Pasternak and Fran Hawkins. Both had asked if they could meet Alan and Megan and spend time with the two team leaders as well as succumbing to a pile of questions from the two girls including how could they become astronauts. It was Fran who summed up at the end. "Hard work at school, keep yourself as fit as you can and, if you haven't already, join the Astronaut Cadet Corp."

"Will you both go to the stars?" asked Molly.

"We all three hope that we will but the decision as to whether a manned spacecraft will be built hasn't been made yet. So, we have to wait and see." answered Gerald.

11. Now for the Stars

Two days later, Megan received a message requesting that she and Alan attend a meeting in New York at the UN Headquarters. Leaving the two girls in Ellen's care, school was out on holiday, they caught a flight the next day. Arriving at the UN building they were amazed to find Grigor, Jean-Paul and Scott Bailey there to join the same meeting.

Before that meeting however, they were asked to a side room where they were greeted by, of all people, Gordon Drake. Only Megan and Alan had met the "President's man" as Megan could not help calling him so there were some lengthy introductions before Gordon explained his presence.

"I felt that you should be made aware that the meeting you have been asked to attend is being held under the auspices of the UN Security Council but with representatives of a number of other countries attending. Unusually it will be held in private, no press or media in attendance, and you need to know that whatever happens you will be required not to tell anyone what goes on. Your job will be to answer any questions as well as you can. It is likely that the meeting will continue after your inquisition is finished, not that they will be other than supportive of all you have done, but there will undoubtedly be some sharp and incisive questions."

Grigor asked the question all of them were thinking about. "If we are simply here to answer questions, why are we under a duty of secrecy?"

"It may be that parts of the session will touch on areas where the UN may want to manage any press briefings and they, and we for that matter, do not want leakage which might result in information being spread out of context as it were. Truthfully, the outcome will be in the public domain within a few days. The delay will be to allow the ambassadors to report back to their heads of state first."

"You speak as if the outcome has already been agreed." commented Alan.

"It is never wise to anticipate the outcome of such a meeting. I will see you afterwards."

At that point they were politely asked to follow a UN representative into a large conference room with around a hundred people already in place.

As they sat in a group of seats in the front of the room, a silence fell as the final attendee entered the room – UN Secretary General Chahine.

"Honoured Representatives, we are pleased to have present today the leaders of the star probe project Drs Alan & Megan Piper, Professor Grigor Sokolov and Mr Scott Bailey. Madam, gentlemen thank you for coming. May I remind everyone that we are meeting "in camera" without media or other on-lookers. Please keep your questions specific as far as possible. First question? I recognise the representative for Japan."

"Madam Secretary. Before questions I believe we should formally acknowledge the work of our honoured guests. They have been the drivers of incredible advances in human knowledge and ability. Not only in developing the star probe but finding a form of energy which has allowed mankind to reduce our effect on the planet's climate. Already we see the adverse effects of climate change reducing and with almost no fossil fuel usage in the future it is reasonable to hope that that will continue."

"Honoured representatives – are we in agreement with the representative for Japan?"

There was unanimous agreement and, to Megan's embarrassment, the entire room rose in a standing ovation. After that, as she said afterwards, the questions were easy to handle. Not to their surprise the main questions centred on the damage caused to the probe. Could this be minimised? Was it possible to provide a future starship with better protection? In the end it was Alan who summed up the various answers.

"Can we add protection? Yes. There are three elements. Firstly, we have already identified a substance that could be added to the skin of the ship - palladium micro-alloy glass. Secondly, we believe that fitting automatic lasers could minimise the risk from micro-meteorites. Finally, and as a scientist not my ideal choice, but a set of, call them torpedo tubes, to launch small missiles to handle larger objects."

At length the questions did come to an end and the quartet left with the thanks of the UN Secretary General.

As they sat down to coffees and a rest it was Alan who made the statement. "Those extra countries, who aren't the UN Security Council members, I think they were all members of the G20 Group. They make up the strongest economies in the world. That was about money not security. I think the world is about to commit to building a starship!"

"Keep that thought under your hats, please." Gordon Drake appeared at their table. "Now then. I am instructed that you are all invited to the White House for dinner tomorrow. The President wishes to meet the people that are going to cost him a lot of money!"

Not being able to talk about the reasons for their trip north was not easy, especially from Ellen, although the fact that they had met the President was exciting enough for the two girls. Eventually, however, there was a press conference held in New York at which the UN Secretary General announced that the countries of the G20 and others, Alan was proved correct in his thoughts, had agreed to jointly fund the building of an initial two starships and, assuming the problems of building such craft in orbit proved solvable, a further three ships would also be built. The project was planned to take ten years. The planning of the project and the responsibility of achieving successful designs would be led by the team who had produced the star probe.

The cost of the project was estimated at an eye wateringly high sum of US$20 trillion, a figure that brought gasps from the media at the press conference and, with climate change still a major issue in many countries around the world, some protests at what was seen by many as a waste of money. Nevertheless, over the following months, the various governments were able to point to enough economic benefits from the development and production of the ships to placate pro-testors for the most part.

When the news broke there was plenty of excitement within the Piper household. Even without knowing the size of the proposed ships Judy and Molly were certain that they would be able to become interstellar astronauts.

Their mother, in particular, had to restrain herself, knowing that any objections she might raise would fall on deaf ears.

* * *   * * *   * * *

Within a very short time the sheer size of their task was brought home to them when they met with representatives of the G20 countries to discuss what the latter were expecting.

Gordon Drake started the discussion with a summary of an agreement made, but not published, at the G20 meeting at the UN.

"The countries will be guided by what the experts leading the project consider feasible. However, they anticipate that the first starship to be completed should have a capacity of a thousand crew and support scientists with the following ships larger at each stage. The size of the first ship, excluding its warp drive tori, should be not less than ten kilometres long and its other measurements should be in proportion. Given that size, construction should take place outside of Earth orbit and a second international space station has already been commissioned for priority build in Lunar orbit."

"Ten kilometres!" gasped Alan.

"Over a thousand people?" Megan's stunned voice replicated her husband's shock.

"That's an engineering project to beat them all." was Scott's slightly more considered response, which did not hide his excitement at the idea. "Do they really think that they could be built for that price?"

"That's an awful lot of fuel as well." Grigor being quite practical.

"More than you might think." said one of the Russians. "The ship design should include a hangar capable of holding at least four interplanetary craft."

"How long are you thinking each mission might take?" asked Alan.

"We do not know but wish to plan in such a way that the ships will have plenty of flexibility in their search for planets."

Gordon answered the question the team had not yet asked. "You will have great freedom to select and recruit such experts, from around the world, that you decide that you need. Each country will provide a specific contact to expedite that process if needed."

"This is going to take some time to set up a viable team and identify where and how the different elements can be built before transfer to orbit. The sheer size of the ships will produce some intricate design points just to get the parts into space either with space planes or some heavy lifting vehicles. You can expect to hear from us often over the coming weeks." Scott finished the meeting.

***   ***   ***

And time it certainly did take. Even with seemingly no limits on whom they could recruit and how much they spent there was one simple constraint – designs and the building of the space station simply took time to complete.

It took three but eventually the new space station was operational and the first elements of the first starship began to be lifted into Earth orbit for onward transfer to Lunar orbit. The following year the outside structure of the ship started to take shape and work started to move forward.

By this time Judy had celebrated her eighteenth birthday and was starting a degree in astrophysics while keeping up her membership of the astronaut cadet corp. Molly had also joined the cadets on her sixteenth birthday.

After the star probe mission Gerald, Fran and Ellen had returned to their previous roles with regular missions between Earth, the Moon, Mars and now Saturn. All had hopes of the interstellar missions in one role or another. With the first starship making good progress it was decided to start work on the second as planned.

Although they had been warned that it would be larger than the first ship the team were amazed to find that it would be twice as long. At twenty kilometres long it soon started to catch the first ship up in size before passing it, albeit still as a shell.

Gerald and Fran were recalled to Earth towards the end of the fourth year. Both were offered command of the two ships, Gerald that of the second ship, to be called ISS Einstein while Fran would captain ISS Anticipation, the smaller ship. Both accepted without any doubts. Gerald asked simply that he be allowed to choose his First Officer whom he identified, when requested, as Ellen.

All three were reassigned to the starship project to enable them to start working on fully understanding their new ships and also to start the lengthy crew selection made more difficult as there was an unexpected difficulty that they had not anticipated. The constraint was summarised by their commanding officer.

"Where possible we want to choose crew members whose partners also have astronaut experience or have qualifications in science or engineering. Such people will be first choice as a pair. There will be scope for those with children to still be selected and the ships will be equipped accordingly."

Gerald's response was thoughtful. "Do you mean we are planning for the possibility that the ships may not be able to return?"

"In essence – yes. I should add that the same circumstances will apply to the research staff and other support personnel. Focus on Anticipation which will be ready for trials this time next year. Einstein will follow around twelve months later."

"Are the plans for more ships to go ahead?" asked Fran.

"Yes, though I believe that they will be more the size of the Anticipation. In any case the first missions will be expected to leave on schedule."

From that time, they set to work to build their teams. Prospective crew members were their first priority with the selection of the research teams handled by the UN team with input from Alan and Megan. Gradually the structure of the crew began to take shape and they were able to turn their minds back to the operational side of the ships.

Six months later, a decision was made to see if the warp drives of the star probe could be activated closer to the sun without risk. Given their direct interest Gerald and Fran both elected to join the mission out to a point close to Jupiter but matters back in the Lunar construction station changed their approach. The news was broken to them just before they left. A structural failure in Einstein's rear torus meant that completion of the ship might be delayed by at least a year if not longer. The decision had been made to change the command structure. Gerald would now captain Anticipation with Fran as his first officer.

It was Gerald's task to tell Ellen that she would not be part of that team and that she was being reassigned to the Mars settlement as its Deputy Commander. It was not an easy meeting for the two who had become friends. Despite the promotion, Ellen made it clear that she considered it no substitute for being on an interstellar mission. They did not part on the best of terms.

Two days later Gerald and Fran left for Jupiter. Ellen would not see either of them again. She, herself, left for Mars a week later.

The news broke a month afterwards. The interplanetary craft carrying the support team including Gerald and Fran had suffered a critical systems failure which had led to it being caught by Jupiter's gravitational pull. Helpless and with no power the ship had been pulled into the giant planet's atmosphere – there were no survivors.

"How? How could that happen? No such craft has had a total power failure." Alan's amazement was not unique but as the designer of the power systems on the craft he was desperate to understand what messages had been sent from the craft. What information was available? None of any consequence he was told.

A few days later, Gordon Drake made an appearance in Houston. To their surprise he asked them to confirm that Anticipation could leave for the Saturnian system and complete its internal work on the way.

"I am sure that we could manage that but why such urgency?" said Alan.

"I would tell you, if I could. Or, to be more precise, if I knew." was Gordon's surprising answer.

"You don't know?!" Megan was possibly more astonished by that fact, than by the wish to despatch Anticipation before completion.

"It might surprise you but I am not always fully in the picture."

That evening the Pipers hosted a dinner for Gordon, Grigor and Scott, who was back on Earth for a brief break. Judy and Molly were present for the meal but Megan had then gently suggested that they had better things to do than listen to their seniors. Judy reluctantly agreed, though Molly made it clear she was disappointed.

Not surprisingly the after-dinner conversation moved on to the starship programme and how progress was being made on the three remaining ships whose construction had been commenced. Scott was confident that despite the difficulties with the warp drive housing on Einstein there was no reason why all three shouldn't actually be completed within the original eight to nine-year schedule. "In fact," he said, "that issue with the Einstein has given us ideas on how we might be able to beat the current timetable. We are working on a slightly different build process which will accelerate the process overall. Just don't tell anyone before we can confirm this will work."

The conversation moved on to other things and finally it was time for the guests to depart. As Grigor and Scott left for their taxi, Gordon stopped and turned back.

"If you have a moment, Megan?" he asked. "I need a private word. Won't take a moment."

"Of course. Alan!" she called her husband back to the lounge.

"This is rather delicate. Have you considered that you would be excellent choices for joining the Einstein? In particular there will be a need for someone to head up the research teams.

Before you answer, one point. Given their existing training your daughters would be easy to find places for, as well."

Megan frowned. "I had always thought that I would be faced with the girls telling me that they had been selected and having to grit my teeth and wish them well. But I don't believe I ever considered going with any of the starships. After all we're in our late forties now and I still have so much to do with my research here. Alan?"

"My thoughts mirror Megan's, Gordon. I'm still having to try and understand how there could have been a total power failure in a plasma fuelled interplanetary craft."

"Please will you both consider the idea. The suggestion has come from other parties and, in this case, though I am acting as a messenger, I do think it would be a good idea. Oh, and Alan, I have been told one thing about Gerry and Fran's accident. The power failure was nothing to do with the plasma engine – that much they did manage to transmit before the crash."

"Then what did cause it? Are we being expected to work in the blind?"

"I guess that there must be a good reason for restricting information but I don't know what it is, I'm sorry."

"I have one question, Gordon." said Megan, "If we don't decide to go will that count against the girls being selected?"

"I don't see why it should but it could delay them, given Molly is only just seventeen."

"We will think about it." said Alan. "Safe trip back, Gordon."

Clearing up before retiring the two parents were left to muse over Gordon's "message". Unclear as to why it had been suggested or why they had been given the choice they decided to sleep on it and discuss again over the coming days.

Their deliberations were interrupted forty-eight hours later with a stunning announcement from Oslo. The Nobel Prize for Physics had been awarded to Dr Megan Newcombe, Professor Grigor Sokolov and to Dr Alan Piper for their work on exotic fuels.

Amongst the congratulatory messages that flooded in, were two of particular import. They were from the US President and from the British Royal Family. Both suggested strongly that they should take the opportunity to join Einstein.

12. A Change of Plan

In due course, three months later and six months ahead of schedule Anticipation slipped out of Lunar orbit heading for Saturn on a course that would avoid the Jovian system although it would stop around Saturn for final systems checks before finally engaging the warp drives and heading for the stars.

There was a little surprise that the planned mission routing was not published in detail. Only that the first stage would be to Alpha Centauri and then to other stars that had been identified as having planetary systems.

On Mars, Ellen looked on at the news with little humour. With her expected role as first officer on Einstein gone and the loss of her friends in that crazy accident, she was not the happiest person in Schiaparelli Town. With no choice but to bury herself in the affairs of the settlement she worked hard to improve things.

Unknown to her, her commanding officer, Siobhan, had been flying a flag for her and pushing her own commanders back on Earth with recommendations that Ellen should be re-assigned back to the interstellar project. Her efforts had not seen any success until after Anticipation had left for Saturn and a few months later the Einstein also left Lunar orbit.

Then came news. Siobhan summoned Ellen to her office to tell her that she was invited to command

Einstein. If she accepted, she would be expected to be ready to leave on an intra-system ship which would be ordered to leave for the Saturn system to rendezvous with Einstein.

"Invited?" was her response. "Are they joking?"

Her commander smiled and displayed her sense of understanding and how well she had come to know her Deputy. "Ellen, I am going to miss you. Best get packing now."

"That quickly? Einstein isn't even due to be completed for, what, six months?"

"Those are the instructions I received. I understand that Einstein has already left Lunar orbit but its course will be away from Mars. With the current planetary positions, you will effectively be chasing the starship. I estimate that, given your transport will not actually arrive at the Deimos station until the end of the week, that chase will mean that you will only catch up on the Einstein when it is already at or near to Saturn. Now get off and pack."

"Can I tell my cousins back in Houston? The girls are going to be over the moon."

"I see no reason why you can't. Wish them well, I knew Alan back in England so please remember me to them."

Ellen duly recorded and sent a video message back to Earth and waited for a response. A little to her concern she had still not received a return message when her transport signalled its arrival at Deimos station and she left to board the shuttle that would lift her to the station.

Still not used to her new position as a starship captain, she was startled to be addressed with great respect as she boarded the interplanetary craft, the IP Phoebe whose crew had a simple order – safe delivery to the Einstein of its new commanding officer. Ellen, although now a ship's captain in her own right, was greeted, in time honoured tradition, to avoid there being two captains aboard, with a nominal promotion.

"Admiral, welcome aboard. Please let us know if you want to join us up front."

"Thank you, Captain Jordon, I suspect that I will be spending more time studying the data and other information on the Einstein I've now got. If you need me to take a share of the duty work please do tell me. Oh, and its Ellen while we're on board."

"Thanks, Ellen. Its Rob and Jenny, and somewhere round the back is Hidecki. Just to add to your workload, there's a private message memory stick for you in the middle cabin. We are just completing the offload of supplies for the station. Once that's done, we will be looking to head out. In case you're wondering we have been given enough supplies for the four of us to reach Saturn!"

Ellen moved back into the centre cabin, slightly bemused to be the only passenger in a craft capable of transporting as many as a couple of dozen. Inserting the memory stick into her tablet and running a security scan she settled into her seat. Then she switched from a relaxed stance almost to attention while still sitting. The message was from Megan and her daughters congratulating her on her appointment. The two teenagers were in the background and she could see that both were in astronaut uniforms. As Megan's message continued it became clear why there had been no response to Ellen's earlier message.

"Ellen, by the time you see this message we will already be on our way on board Einstein. Alan and I will be leading the on-board research teams. Judy and Molly have been appointed as Ensigns. I don't know what their roles will be but, no doubt, your command team will be handling that. We didn't tell you in advance as we didn't want to affect your decision as to whether or not to take on the captaincy. Safe journey."

Ellen grinned and thought how unnecessary that concern had been. To use an old adage she thought, wild horses wouldn't have stopped her accepting. Turning to her briefing papers she set to work. There might be several weeks before they reached Saturn but the sheer volume of study would occupy her for much of that time.

13. *And a Change of Course*

The ships were close to the target system. As the radio signals became clearer it became apparent that a secondary source was orbiting one of the gas giants. Instructions flowed once more and the fleet started to adapt. Half cut their deceleration and six changed their course towards the outer system planet.

14. This is Why

Two months later.

"Permission to come aboard, Sir?"

"Permission granted, Captain."

With those words of calming tradition Ellen stepped through the airlock and onto the Einstein for the first time.

"Welcome aboard, Captain" John Lees, the Einstein's First Officer and a former member of the original star probe mission, greeted her. "Would you like a few minutes in your quarters to freshen up after the last part of the journey?"

"No, Commander. There has been enough delay – first the Bridge."

"As you wish, Ma'am. It's good to see you again, Ellen." He continued dropping briefly from formalities.

"And to see you, my friend. Now we need to get on."

"Captain on the Bridge." The ship's computer, recognising her insignia's transmission as she followed her first officer on to the bridge, announced her. The crew members started to come to attention from their various work stations.

"As you were everyone." Ellen stalled the movement quickly as she stopped to study her surroundings in real life for the first time. Although she had spent many hours in simulator practice during the journey from Mars to Titan station and her new command, the actual reality was, as she knew it would be, subtly different and indeed quite amazing.

As she scanned the bridge, she could not but help recall the 20th century television science fiction series that still could be found on digital recordings in most electronic libraries and which, though she might not easily admit it, had been one of her favourite shows during her childhood. Encouraged by her grandparents she had spent many a weekend evening watching the various versions of Star Trek. Here in this modern day was a bridge that was not significantly different from that of the USS Enterprise Mark 2. It was the second slightly unnerving experience of the last couple of hours.

Earlier her first sight of the ISS Einstein had had a similar effect. As had every astronaut, she had seen films of the ship and also simulations but none had really prepared her for the experience of seeing the actual ship that would be powered by the Alcubierre Drive, first suggested just over 60 years ago. She often found it difficult to believe that less than a hundred years after Apollo 11's historical trip and with all the difficulties facing mankind back on Earth it had still proved possible to develop and build the Einstein. It's size at nearly twenty kilometres long dwarfed the original interstellar probe she had, as a junior officer, had the joy of welcoming back home.

She smiled to herself as she compared her thoughts of the Enterprise bridge so similar to the ship she was to command and those of the fictional starship's shape so totally different from the Einstein. The twin-engine nacelles of Enterprise had been replaced by the two Alcubierre drive tori. With the ship itself nestling within its drive structure and ready to be protected from the warping of space time generated by the immense power of the drives it was easily the largest mobile structure built in space. Despite her science degree and later training, she admitted that the means by which the ship would be able travel across space at up to around five light years every week, when at full power, while not actually exceeding the speed of light still mystified her.

The next few hours were taken up with introductions to her bridge officers and with a few heads of department both within her direct command and the research teams before she made the decision to retire to her quarters. There she found a secure message from fleet command on Earth which had been transmitted to match her arrival on the Einstein.

* * *   * * *   * * *

As she accessed the message her thoughts went back to her second deep-space mission - the recovery of the first star probe as it returned from Alpha Centauri. The data they had recovered and analysed showed that conditions within the space time bubble should allow humans to work normally and manage a ship in the warp drive status.

She remembered being surprised that there had been such rapid agreement between the world's governments to fund the building of not just an interstellar capable spaceship but one the size of the Anticipation and that there would be not just a larger second ship built in tandem but plans for three more ships to follow. While Anticipation was ten kilometres long, Einstein, her own command, was even bigger at over twenty kilometres. Only now was it clear why and why both ships carried armament as well as significant cargo space.

Contained in her new orders was a detailed background to the history of the project. It also explained how the first-choice commander of the Anticipation had died. Ellen had admired Gerald Pasternak since he had been her commanding officer on the star probe mission. He had been first her mentor and later they had become good friends. She remembered fondly the last time she had seen him and Fran Hawkins in Houston before the, at the time, terrible news that she was no longer to be a part of the first interstellar voyages.

News of the "accident" which had killed both her friends and their crew had always seemed, to her, a little forced. It had been scant help to keep reminding herself as the grief enfolded her, that mankind had been a space faring species for less than a hundred years and accidents could and did happen. Even then she had been overlooked for the command team of the Anticipation.

Now she sat, still struggling to assimilate the facts that she had just been made privy to.

Gerry and Fran had been killed not in an accident but by an explosion. En route to test the possibility of triggering the original probe's warp engines between Jupiter's orbit and that of Saturn, they had swung past the Jovian system. In this process their sensors found an anomaly. The object spotted was emitting a signal and clearly was not of human origin. Unsurprisingly the team decided to change their course slightly to get closer.

For the first time the rules of First Contact were being brought to mind. As they approached the object, they started transmitting to the unmanned Jupiter orbiter for onward transmission to Earth. Their transmission lasted under an hour. As they approached slowly to within a hundred kilometres the object exploded destroying itself and their ship. We believe, said the report, that there was a matter-antimatter reaction.

The emissions might have been towards a group of objects approaching the solar system, although there was no evidence that that assumption was correct. This formation had been spotted some seventy years before by the Hubble telescope and to the amazement of the small number of astronomers, tasked with understanding what they were looking at, it was moving at almost three quarters of the speed of light towards the solar system. Frantic efforts had finally confirmed that the objects must be around forty light years away. Making the only reasonable assumption that the formation would have to slow on its approach they calculated that they would arrive at Sol in about seventy to eighty years.

Once it had been confirmed that the "sighting" was not of a naturally occurring event and although there was nothing that could have been done at that time the World's governments came together in an unprecedented manner and had agreed, in secret, to fund any research that might provide an escape route or viable defence should the alien fleet prove unfriendly. Indirectly CERN and its sister research locations had benefitted from additional funding as a result. Ellen wondered if her cousin, Megan, had any idea of the real reason why her research had been so lavishly funded over the twenty-five odd years that it taken to achieve the star drive.

When the potential for powering the Alcubierre drives and developing spacecraft capable of effectively travelling faster than light speed had been discovered it was not surprising that the funds had been found to complete and launch the starships.

After the event with the "probe" explosion Earth's governments had agreed that they should continue to prepare for the worst while hoping for the best. One "ship" approaching might be friendly but a large fleet seemed less so.

At the time of writing the report, for Ellen and her fellow captains, the fleet was still about six light months away and slowing on their approach to the solar system. The best estimate was that the alien fleet would now arrive in about nine months' time.

Ellen now learnt that the Einstein was actually fully equipped to carry a small element of humanity in a search for a new home. She was also amazed to learn that a system ship loaded with laboratory equipment and various animal embryos and incubators was due to arrive within the next few days.

When it reached the starship Ellen was to evacuate Titan base and move out of orbit before engaging the star drive. Two light years out they should deviate from the course towards the Centauri system and head out towards one of the stars already identified as having planets.

There was no mention of Anticipation or the later ships but her orders were clear enough – her task was to ensure the survival of her species, should First Contact prove hostile as feared.

For some time, Ellen sat in her quarters gazing at, but no longer seeing, the visage of Titan below. Her entire world had been turned upside down. "Why me?" she thought. "Captain of a starship, yes. But responsible for the survival of our species?"

Slowly she started to collect her thoughts. She knew she would need to involve her ship's officers without delay but, she realised, it might also be necessary to brief the commander of Titan base.

Commander Tian would have received instructions to place herself and her team under Ellen's command. That she knew, but had she been given the background as to the reasons for this? Being ordered to abandon the only manned research station in the Saturnian system would have raised questions, if not objections, from the team of scientists currently dedicated to expanding their knowledge of Titan and the other moons orbiting in and around the rings.

Ellen swiftly reviewed her orders and realised that the only reference to the Titan base was that she must evacuate it and that Commander Tian had been instructed to place herself at her disposal. There was no suggestion that the station commander had in fact been given any information beyond that.

She made a decision. "Computer – connect me to Titan Base. Secure line direct to Commander Tian."

"Acknowledged."

A few moments passed then her screen cleared to show the face of the Titan commander. Their conversation was formal.

"Captain Bayman. It is good to see you and not only because I hope you can expand on why I am to place my command at your orders."

"And to see you Commander! I will be happy to brief you but we have limited time. How soon can you be aboard the Einstein?"

"About 45 minutes, Captain. I have had a shuttle prepped and ready to go since my orders came in."

"Then please make haste – I wish to brief you at the same time as my senior officers. Einstein out."

Ellen tapped her communicator again and instructed the Einstein's computer to pass instructions to her first officer and the heads of the different sections to be in the briefing/conference room in two hours.

A further thought came to mind and she checked that the Phoebe had not yet departed for its trip back to Earth. She then contacted Captain Jordan and asked him to attend the officers' meeting.

Realising that she had not eaten for several hours she requested some food and then settled down to organise her approach to the briefing.

Recalling her own shock a few hours before, when reading the message sent from Earth and the reasons behind the massive change in the interstellar project, she decided that her first approach would be to tell her team the truth about the deaths of Gerry and Fran.

The alien fleet approaching the inner system would come next as the reason for the changes and the abrupt acceleration in the timing of the Einstein's interstellar mission – originally planned to follow several trial runs of a few light seconds over another three months.

Before the main briefing she called her First Officer in.

"Captain?"

"Let's get things straight, as a general rule and certainly in private, first names please, John."

"Ma'am. Sorry. Ellen."

"Firstly, to warn you, the briefing is going to provide a number of shocks which I suspect you will not have been prepared for, I certainly was not. Having said that its probably best that I leave it at that for the minute."

"As you wish."

"Right, practical things. Not everything was detailed in the reports I reviewed on my way to join you. I know that we have four interplanetary ships on board but how many could we take? And could we bring the Titan station into the hold without compromising our capacity for moving ships around? Also, we have another ship inbound which will need to be landed and, in the circumstances, we need to add the ship I arrived on."

"Wow." John Lees gasped. "Let me think. I'm not sure about the station but we certainly could cope with three or even four additional shuttles and all the landers. It's possible we could handle three interplanetary ships. I'll need to check with the chief engineer – on the station issue. I guess not before the briefing?"

"You guess right but immediately after the briefing I will need to know. Now Commander Tian is due imminently, perhaps you would do the honours and greet her."

"Yes. Ellen." John was still struggling with the informality expected of him.

"One last point, will Alan or Megan Piper be at the briefing?"

"Both should be, Ellen, as the overall heads of research."

"Thank you. I will see you at the briefing later."

As she worked on her final outline there was a chime from her workstation – warning of an incoming message.

The message was from fleet command. The latest tracking of the incoming fleet had found that half a dozen objects had changed course and were now moving directly towards Saturn! Their apparent deceleration had reduced and their ETA was now only a month away. Einstein needed to be moving out of the system within the next week to enable it to reach a safe point to engage the warp drives in time.

As a last moment decision, she put out a call asking Megan to attend the captain's quarters. It was an emotional reunion but gave Ellen the chance to warn Megan that shocking news was to be expected.

***   ***   ***

As Ellen approached the conference room, she could hear a buzz of conversation. No doubt, she smiled without humour, various theories were being put forward for her calling such a meeting even before making the tour of the ship that every new captain would normally undertake. As she entered the room a silence fell and her officers were quick to stand followed by the various heads of the science community.

"At ease everyone, please be seated." She paused for a moment. "Firstly, my apologies, to those I haven't met yet, I would have preferred to meet all of you each face to face before now. However, as you will learn, I have good reasons for the urgency attached to this meeting. Now while I have had the chance to review your files on the trip here it would help me if you could go around the table and introduce yourselves."

Her officers went first followed by the science heads. To Ellen's surprise she found that she had met more of the latter than she had her own direct subordinates.

With that process complete she began her briefing with an immediate caveat that questions should be kept until the end. At the end of her presentation there was initially complete silence as the room took in the import of their mission. There had been varying degrees of shock expressed non-verbally as initial disbelief changed to concerns about how this message could be passed on to the rest of the ship's personnel. Not everyone had family members aboard but it was now apparent why so many of those selected did have personal relations of one sort or another onboard. Equally very few did not have family and friends back on Earth.

In the end the quality of her people was underlined in that the questions raised were almost entirely technical and business-like. The one framed in emotional terms was whether or not personal messages could be sent to family members back home. Ellen's response was as they might have expected.

"I believe that they can be sent but they will need to be consolidated and sent via Houston. It may well be that they will wish to delay them until the existence of the aliens is better known. I do not mean that they will read them but simply hold them. I can promise no more than that."

The final part of the meeting centred on how the news would be disseminated to the rest of those on the ship. At the end of the discussion part of the meeting Ellen dismissed everyone with the exception of Commander Tian, her first officer, her chief engineer and Alan Piper whom she asked to attend her in her quarters.

"Jing, Gentlemen, initial comments please. No wait. Jing, you need to brief your teams and get them ready to transfer to Einstein. You go first."

Commander Tian, who still looked shocked, responded. "How do we know that these aliens are a danger?"

"We don't but the powers that be back home feel that being wary is the safe option. As was pointed out a single ship or even a few ships might be friendly. But this group of objects, which are clearly moving under intelligent control, numbers over a hundred. We would be wise, therefore, to hope for the best but prepare for the worst."

"I know. I just wish we didn't have to run. I will get back to the station and brief my people. Who should they liaise with, Captain?"

"John, would you let the Commander have the names of the right people. We should look to shift as much equipment and supplies across as possible. Did you manage to work out if we could just take the station whole?"

"Unfortunately, we can't – it is just too big."

"Wait a minute." Alan interrupted. "I understand about the station being too large to load onto Einstein but, there may be another way."

"And?" Ellen raised her eyebrows in question.

"If we move the station alongside the ship it should stay within the warp bubble. The only problem would be when we want to move in normal space. I'm not sure if that could be solved but we would at least not leave it as a derelict orbiting Titan."

"Do it. But no-one remains on board it. Understand. Jing you had better get moving. You have 24 hours to evacuate the station and transfer to Einstein. That includes all the people, all the independent spacecraft, fuel stores and other supplies."

"Aye. Captain. On my way."

Ellen turned to her own officers. "You had better all get back to your people and spread the word. As we discussed, best keep numbers in each briefing as small as is sensible. Alan, Scott. Once you have covered your people please report back here – I have a task for you once we are moving."

Once alone Ellen sat back, the first doubts hitting home. "Why me?" she thought. "Captain of a starship, yes. But responsible for the survival of our species?"

Fortunately, she would later admit, she did not have much time to ponder her situation.

Her personal communicator bleeped.

"Yes?"

"Message from IP Deimos, Captain. They advise that they will be entering the Saturn system in two days. ETA Einstein half a day later."

"Ask Commander Lees to provide the Deimos with our planned routing away from Saturn. Deimos should divert their course so that they can rendezvous without our delaying for their approach to Titan."

"Aye, Captain."

"And ask Doctor Carden to join me as soon as is convenient. Thank you."

Ellen cut the link and decided she needed to update her Captain's log. She was able to work on this for half an hour before the Doctor arrived.

"Apologies for not arriving sooner, Captain. Needed to set a broken arm first."

"No apology needed Doctor, but first name terms in private please, Will or William?"

"Either's fine, Ellen, I believe."

"Yes, this won't keep you long but I wanted you to be the first to know about the incoming ship, the IP Deimos, and its cargo."

"Sounds intriguing."

"In short then. The Deimos has a crew of three plus a medical team of four. Three nurses and an orderly. So, your team will be growing! The cargo includes an incubator/artificial womb plus, I gather, a stock of frozen embryos both human and animal. My apologies, if my vocabulary isn't quite right."

"Captain, someone has been planning on this for some time then?"

"My guess is ten years or more while the original star probe and then the starship fleet was being built, certainly. You've around three days to prepare anyway as that is their ETA for rendezvous. Talking of people. How did yours react to the news?"

"On the surface, a mix of shock and concern. I sense that they will have more questions in the coming days but will recognise that they may be some of the lucky ones. The main concern will be for family left behind. If we can find a way to understand what does happen, when that fleet arrives, you would have a winner."

"I have some thoughts on how but the design guys will need to see if they can convert them into reality. Thanks, Will. I'll let you get back to your surgery."

With that meeting over Ellen decided that it was time she moved on from her quarters and join her bridge officers for an update on the ship's current situation.

"Captain on the bridge." Einstein's computer voice rang out as it recognised her insignia's coding. Everyone started to come to attention but Ellen quickly stopped them.

"As you were. Just be aware if you hear that in future. We can't have everyone stopping what they are doing – it's going to be more important than formal courtesy."

A chorus of "Yes ma'am" and "Yes, Captain" acknowledged Ellen's instruction as her bridge team returned to their tasks readying the ship for departure.

Turning to her first officer Ellen asked how progress on the evacuation of Titan base was proceeding.

"Better than I expected, Captain. I gather there have been a lot of expressions of annoyance but they are dealing with the situation, as you might expect, and we should have everything and everyone transferred within forty-eight hours."

"Then we need to focus on the essentials, Commander. Einstein will be leaving within twenty-four hours. We will have to leave the station behind. These incoming objects may be weeks away but I do not want to take any risk that they may spot us and be able to track us before we can engage the warp drives."

"Captain, how do we know that they can't follow us into warp space?" The question was raised by a young Lieutenant sitting at the helm.

"Good question, it's Lieutenant Cheung, yes?" Ellen responded.

"Yes, ma'am." There was obvious pleasure from the young woman.

Ellen smiled to herself, this was one to watch but still too young to spot that an important part of a Captain's job was to fit names and faces together quickly.

"The simple answer is that we don't but the fleet of which they form a part was seen travelling in normal space, albeit at almost unbelievable speed. If they had warp drive it is likely we would have had no warning of their arrival around Sol. But let's not take chances. It's our job to avoid any contact if we can. So, people, let's get ready to run."

"Captain, Lieutenant Cheung was off-duty when you arrived, there is one other member of the bridge team also off-duty then. The junior member of our tracking team – Ensign Piper."

"Judy Piper. A member of the bridge team?"

"She had already shown promise before being assigned to the Einstein and has proved to have just the type of approach to tracking that we needed. Judy, I think you know the Captain?"

Judy stood and crossed to her cousin. "Captain Bayman, it is good to see you."

"And to see you, Judy. Well done on gaining your position. Commander, I will let you get on with the preparations for departure but, if you can provide me with someone to show me round, I wish to undertake a brief tour of the ship, at least the major sections after I have eaten. I have studied the schematics but they do not replace the feeling from seeing the real thing."

"Leave it with me, Captain."

Ellen returned to her quarters. Half an hour later there was a hesitant tap on the door. She opened the door remotely and a nervous young ensign entered.

"Captain, Commander Lees has ordered me to escort you around the Einstein."

"Ensign Piper." Ellen grinned. "No need for formality in private, Molly, how are you?"

"I'm well but, Captain Ellen, is it all right to admit I'm scared?"

"Oh, Molly. Of course, it is. Though maybe to your Mom & Pop as well as to me. It is natural to be scared. We are going into the unknown. Being scared is fine as long as it doesn't stop you doing your job. Now, show me round our new home please."

"There's a lot to see. It can take more than an hour just to get from the bridge area to the stern, and that doesn't include the engines."

"True, but take me to the main areas."

Over the next couple of hours Molly led her captain and cousin from section to section of the vast craft. Finally, they arrived at the centre of the research teams' quarters and operation rooms.

"Mom, Pop" Molly called over to a side room with a series of computer screens. Alan and Megan appeared at the door.

"Ellen!" Megan smiled. "With a young ensign." Her face fell. "Molly's not in trouble, is she?"

"Of course not. She was just assigned to show me over the Einstein. You are both well? I couldn't really ask you at the presentation."

"We're fine. But not much different to everyone. Still getting over the shock, I guess." Alan replied.

"That's good. Now I need to finish the tour. Then I want to have a session with you, both, and my Chief Engineer." Ellen checked the time. "Nineteen hundred hours please."

She and Molly completed that first tour of the ship shortly after and she returned to her quarters dismissing the young ensign with a thank you and a quick hug.

A short message to Scott Bailey giving him the time she wanted to meet before having a quick snack and getting her thoughts in order.

The Pipers and Scott duly arrived to meet with Ellen and John Lees at 19.00hrs.

"Thank you for coming, I will try to keep this short. First a question. When Gerry Pasternak and Fran were killed, they were en-route escorting the original star probe, which would have attempted to engage its warp drives just outside Jupiter's orbit. What happened to the probe? There was nothing in the papers explaining the background to my orders."

"I don't know," replied Alan, "there was such a fuss at the time that I'm not sure if the probe actually survived."

"How could we find it if it kept on its course? It won't have gone into warp without a "go" signal would it?"

"No, it shouldn't have," commented Scott, "but I suspect we have the wrong members of the Piper family here, Commander?"

"I agree, Captain. We should set that task for Judy Piper. She will be able to handle that."

"John, please track her down if she's off duty and make that a priority. Ideally I would like to be able to send the probe a go-signal to warp out to the Centauri system – before we warp out ourselves."

"On my way."

Turning to the others Ellen raised the ante. "We may or may not be able to find and activate the original star probe and it is, in any case, a large craft easily spotted when in normal space. My real task for the three of you, and whoever you may need to involve, is this. How small a warp capable craft could you design and build while on the Einstein?"

Megan asked, "Why do you want a small probe, Ellen?"

"The news of the alien fleet and our mission has affected everyone on board and the most common question or fear is that they may never find out what actually happens when the aliens arrive. It is possible that they will not be hostile in which case we could return home. Problem is that any signals from Earth will take over four years to reach Centauri and we aren't supposed to stay there in any case. If we can send a probe through warp space, and it is small enough to avoid detection, we can hope that we will at least know the outcome."

Scott looked at Alan. "We must be able to get smaller than the original probe – that was designed to be strong and built accordingly. Is there a physical constraint on producing the power in a small craft?"

"I need to look into that. The answer is smaller than the original but how small I don't know. To be truthful it's not something I've ever really thought about. We need to be sure that anything small enough to be built within the machine shops of the Einstein could carry warp engines and the fuel for a round trip of tens of light years. Ellen, you are going to have to give us a little time. How long before we engage warp drive?"

John Lees responded. "We will be leaving orbit in a little under twenty-four hours. Allowing for a little margin of safety it will take a further four days before we can warp out of the system. The incoming aliens are still around three weeks away from Saturn but tracking will be watching them closely in case anything changes."

"Right everyone, keep me in the loop. Thank you all." Ellen ended the meeting with a sigh. "I suggest that you get what rest you can. Things are going to get busy."

The Einstein kept an artificial 24-hour day and as it moved into evening ship time the lighting dimmed and most of the people on board were off-duty and relaxing in their quarters or the various community locations around the ship.

Ellen decided that she would leave her quarters and take a stroll via the nearest crew's dining area and the exercise areas nearby and take the opportunity to chat with some of her people.

Meanwhile Megan and Alan were with their daughters having a quick supper. Normally a chance for an easy family time the conversation was centred on tracking and warp drives and Judy had to leave early so as to carry on with her task of finding the star probe's current position, if it was still following its original course. Molly, too, was on duty in the engine room as a Junior Ensign and Megan and Alan were soon left to their own devices.

"Do you think we can really build a "baby" warp drive? Do we have the equipment on board Einstein?" Megan was clearly doubtful but admitted to not being an engineer.

"If we can design one that can sustain warp drive then the machine shops should be able to construct it. The issue will be, can we get it small enough to be built onboard. You should visit them – they are next to the ship's landing airlocks."

"I think I should look into how small the warp engines can be and still work. That is going to be the underpin to your design. Tomorrow is going to be busy for all of us. Best to get an early night." Megan led the way back to their personal quarters. "You know, Alan, I still find it amazing that everyone has their own quarters it's like a giant hotel with multiple restaurants. At least in that sense."

"For the moment that's not far from the truth but there will come a time when movement around the ship will have to be restricted, I suspect. Especially if we find ourselves having to handle contact with other species."

"Do you think that we will have to assume alien species will always be hostile?"

"No, but we should be ready to come across other intelligent life. After all we already know that there is at least one intelligent species out there and indications are that it is not friendly."

"Alan, I think that there must be at least two in the local stellar area."

"Why?"

"The Mars anomaly implies alien intelligence. That one species left a fuel source for us to find but only when we were already a space faring species. Then there was the Jupiter anomaly. I know that it exploded when approached but we don't know that it was broadcasting to that fleet. That transmission may have been a warning to the aliens who left it and perhaps the Mars deposit."

"Megan, that sounds so logical I wonder why it hasn't been discussed before. Perhaps you should find the time to tell our Captain."

15. *Urgency*

The lead ship's sensors identified an enormous ship close to one of the gas giant's moons near to a smaller object. It decided that it was important that that ship should be intercepted and destroyed. The group's deceleration was reversed and the six started to quicken their pace. A few hours later it was decided that each ship should launch two missiles which could be programmed to accelerate more rapidly.

16. On the Way

A day later Ellen sat in her command chair as the Einstein's various department heads reported their readiness for departure. The evacuation of the Titan space station had been a classic case of time pressures pushing through the necessary effort and had been completed within the last hour. Lengthy discussions as to the sustainability of pulling the station into the warp bubble zone had ended with the decision to scuttle it and as a final move it was being towed into an unstable orbit which would decay and end with the station falling into Saturn's atmosphere. The IP craft towing it would then chase Einstein catching the starship after a few hours.

Commander Lees turned to Ellen. "Captain, we are ready."

"Thank you, Commander. Helm, take us out."

The great ship started to move away from Titan, slowly at first but gradually its momentum increased. Ellen could visualise that everyone, who could, would be taking a last look at Saturn and its rings. Before giving the order for departure she had instructed her communications officer to ensure that the rear view was being broadcast to all video screens.

A few moments later there was a gasp of delight from a young woman. "That's it, we've got it."

Ellen turned her head towards the sound. "Might I know what we have got?"

"Sorry, Captain. We have located the star probe. It's exactly where Ensign Piper calculated it should be. It is still under power, albeit at quarter speed, and has crossed Saturn's orbit."

"Excellent, well done tracking. Communications, its Lieutenant Jaeger isn't it? Do we have the codes ready to signal the probe?"

"Yes, Captain. I'm not sure why but they were sent to me at the same time as your last message from command."

"Send an instruction to the probe to align itself with Proxima Centauri and then to engage its warp drives. Message should include an instruction to await further instructions at its destination. Can that be done?"

"It can Captain, I will need to check exact positioning with tracking to allow for transmission time. I assume that we will want the transmission to be on as narrow a beam as possible."

"Do it. Let me know when the probe acknowledges. Commander, would you join me in the ready room, please." Turning to the officer who had announced the probe find, "Lieutenant, please join us once comms has the data they need."

"Yes Captain." Both Lees and the lieutenant responded together, the commander continuing. "Lieutenant Cheung you have the com."

"Yes, sir"

Cheung moved to the command chair and a second officer took her place at the helm as Ellen led the way into her command room just off the bridge.

Before she and John were joined by the Lieutenant, Ellen spoke, "John, please make sure Miss Piper gets the plaudits she deserves. I would do so but given she is a relative I feel I should keep a little distance. I don't want to hear mumblings of favouritism.

Her first officer smiled. "Not to worry, I can manage that. I can say, already, that Judy has the makings of a good officer. In better times I believe she would have completed her degree at the same time as she completed officer training at Lunar base. She is modest and well liked. I have already been working with the rest of the command team on a way in which we could put in place a formal officer-training process in place for those Ensigns with promise. We planned to put it forward to you once we have it drafted."

"Excellent. Once we are out of immediate danger, I will be eager to contribute. Now where is Lieutenant Smythe?"

At that moment the door opened and the young officer entered. "Sorry, Captain, it took a few minutes to provide communications with the information they needed."

"Not a problem. Now we are underway I need you and your team on full alert watching those alien ships as they approach Saturn and I want to know if anything happens to change their current ETA of around three weeks. You must contact both me and the Commander if there is any change – whatever the time and whoever is on-duty. Understood?"

"Yes, ma'am."

"Now. Do we have enough trained personnel available to ensure tracking is fully manned at all times including during the twilight shifts, from now until we can engage warp?"

"I believe so, Captain. The lieutenant and I will check current duty rotas to ensure that is done. Come on Smythe, let's get on that."

The two officers left her ready room and Ellen settled back in her seat to go over their position. Had she managed to cover everything she could? In the event she could think of nothing she might have missed and in due course took over from her first officer in the command seat.

Ship routine settled down on the bridge as the Einstein cruised out towards the safe warp zone.

17. To Warp

The next day Ellen was working out in one of the gyms. Thank the Lord for the artificial gravity she thought, an excellent side effect of the warp drives, even when on standby. They still needed to ensure a minimum amount of exercise but it was much easier.

"Captain and First Officer to the bridge. Captain and First Officer to the bridge."

Ellen dropped her exercise and raced to the bridge grabbing her uniform and carrying it over her shoulder.

"Captain on the bridge."

Commander Lees turned to her. There was a level of concern in his face that she had not seen before.

"Captain, tracking has identified twelve high velocity objects emanating from the alien ships."

"And?"

"Four appear to be targeting the space station, the other eight are on a track that will intercept Einstein's projected position in about 20 hours."

"When will they hit the space station?"

"In about 45 minutes."

"How fast are they moving?" Ellen's amazement tempered her racing thoughts.

"About forty percent of light speed and accelerating. They appear to be relativistic missiles."

Commander Lees, his voice reflecting his own astonishment asked a different question. "Is there any evidence that they can react to a change in our course?"

"We don't know, Commander."

"I suggest, Captain, that we make a material course change now. If they can react to that, we have a different problem."

"Helm, starboard 45 degrees, up 45 degrees. Increase speed by 25%"

"Aye, Captain."

"Tracking, I want to know if there is any reaction as soon as our projected position has changed."

"Comms, please find Dr Alan Piper and Chief Engineer Bailey and have them meet me in the briefing room urgently. Then contact the Deimos, give them our new course and tell them to maximise their velocity and forget about protecting the ship's engines. They must rendezvous within 24 hours."

It took ten minutes but Alan and Scott rushed into the briefing room to find Ellen and John in deep discussion.

"Captain? We came as fast as we could."

"Sit down and we will brief you on our situation."

After bringing the two men up to speed, Ellen came straight to the point. "If we need to engage warp drive within the next few hours can we do so safely?"

"How far out from Saturn are we?" asked Alan. "We suggested four days with a safety margin, so we can say less than that but I would say that we should try and get half that distance at least."

"We will be right on the margin then. If those missiles can track the Einstein and correct for our course change, we can only get to about 40% or 45% of the four-day margin before we would have to take action." Commander Lees' tone radiated concern.

"If we assume..." Scott's response was interrupted by a call from the bridge.

"Captain, the first of the missiles have hit the Titan station. As far as we can tell they simply struck the station. It has broken into three larger parts with smaller debris. The energy output suggests a simple conversion of momentum – there does not seem to be any form of explosives involved."

"Thank you, I'm guessing that the other missiles have not yet had time to alter their course yet."

"Not yet, Captain."

"Thank you. Keep me informed. Scott go on."

"Captain, we have our own missiles. They weren't originally intended to be used for offensive purposes when we designed the protective systems for Anticipation and Einstein, but that was before we knew about the alien fleet. I haven't had reason to check but I suspect their quality and capability will have been upgraded significantly from a purely defensive mode."

Before Ellen could respond there was another interruption from the bridge.

"Captain, I think you should see this."

"On my way. Scott look into the missile capability that we have."

Ellen led the way back on to the bridge. "What should I be looking at?"

"This is a gravitational scan looking back towards Saturn, Captain."

"Put it on the main screen."

A schematic of the gravity well of the Saturn system appeared. Although a deep dip in the spacetime continuum the slopes around the system looked shallow and the Einstein appeared to be moving over the crest of the slopes into the solar well alone.

"Explain this, if I understand it, we are further out of the immediate gravitational field of Saturn then possible in the time since we left orbit." Ellen took a second look and saw three things she did not understand.

"Captain, we think the field has shrunk but we don't know how or why. Then there are dips we believe may be associated with the alien missiles."

Commander Lees interrupted. "You are saying that they have enough mass to have a measurable impact on spacetime? How much?"

"Sir, if we are right, enough impact to threaten Einstein's ability to engage warp if they close to within a million kilometres. The third dip, and the largest, seems to be three of the missiles we thought had hit Titan station. They must have missed and have looped around Saturn gaining a gravity assisted boost to their velocity and are heading back toward the aliens."

"Has there been any reaction from them?"

"A few hours ago, they must have completed their turnover and are decelerating at close to seven g. At about that time they would have picked up a sight of the missiles and they also appear to have started evasive movements."

Alan, who had followed the command team back to the bridge, asked. "When can we expect the missiles to reach the alien ships? And will that deceleration be enough to bring them to a halt relative to Saturn or will they need to use the planet to complete a braking manoeuvre."

Lieutenant Cheung responded. "It may depend on how far they have to change course. It looks as if the missiles have limited manoeuvrability or they would not be able to avoid them. That is good news as it means we should be able to stay out of that million-klick range."

"Unless they are trying to confuse the missile's tracking systems. With six targets it might give them the opportunity to dodge or target the missiles with onboard weapons." Ellen thinking rapidly made a decision. "Prepare to engage warp."

Even as she spoke there as a cry from the tracking team. "The aliens must have just made a turnover they are accelerating again."

"That confirms it. John where is the Deimos?"

"Captain, they've done a great job and will rendezvous in around ninety minutes."

"Right, get everything ready I want them on board in two hours maximum, ship and all."

"Alan, we are going to have to take the risk or we may not be able to get away. If you want to get back to Megan best shift now. Comms give me ship-wide."

"You have it, Captain."

"This is the Captain. We are going to engage the warp drives in two hours please prepare. Bear in mind that we do not know if there will be any initial side effects so please ensure you are secured. You will get a five-minute warning."

Two hours later, with the Deimos landed in the launch bay, the bridge team, including Ellen, moved to their positions securing themselves in position.

"Right team, all the information is that we will be fine operating in warp but we do not have any certainty that there won't be any transitional effects. So, we play it safe. We will also change course thirty degrees before engaging warp. Helm, after that set the autopilot to kick in five minutes after full warp insertion and then to drop us out of warp one light year from Sol."

"Only one light year, Captain?"

"Yes, Commander. Our original orders were to travel two light years before we change course but they also assumed that we would have been able to complete at least two short test runs. One light year out there is little chance of finding anything adverse. We can then take the time for a systems' check. In any case, if there are no side effects, we can countermand that instruction and retain manual control."

"Understood."

"Engine rooms, are we ready for warp?"

"Ready, Captain."

"Computer ship-wide please. Everyone, this is your five-minute warning."

Five minutes passed.

"Helm, engage warp drives."

As the drives came on-line there was a subtle change in the ship's sounds as the normal space engines died and the Alcubierre tori started to vibrate as the engines started them spinning. To the bridge team however there was a more startling change. Helm had, as order-ed, set up the main view screens to show camera views forward and astern.

As the Einstein entered warp the forward view changed subtly with the starfield seeming to shrink and then evidence of blue shift occurred. The rear-view screen darkened, red shift affected the starfield briefly, and then the light simply died.

Ellen breathed a sigh of relief as the change occurred without any apparent impact on the ship's humans. We are on our way, she thought, out into the interstellar void.

* * *   * * *   * * *

18. *Alarm*

Two of the ships had had to be sacrificed to their own missiles as the other four managed to divert course enough to avoid similar calamities. But their own systems signalled alarm as the moving target of the other eight missiles appeared to vanish from sensor contact in only a matter of seconds.

There was little time to decide on the next actions but signals from the remaining fleet overrode the initial plan to try and track the ship. The override was not to be questioned but, even though they knew the message would take more than four hundred years to arrive, the ships began broadcasting to the parent fleet that another intelligence appeared to have faster than light capability in its ships.

19. Onward

The next week was tiring for the crew and officers as they maintained a higher than normal state of alertness. Constant checks were scheduled so that any malfunction would be spotted quickly but these required long hours for everyone. The bridge was manned at its normal status but changes of personnel involved time in handovers that was much higher than usual.

Ellen, at an early stage, had ensured that the view from the forward cameras and sensors was broadcast across the Einstein so that all who wished to could watch the starfield change. The changes were quite subtle as Alan told his family.

"We aren't really moving that quickly compared with what the drives could handle. Our position in space will only have changed by a single light year and in the overall scale of things that means limited change in how the stars look."

"Pop, how fast can we move?" Molly was intrigued by the "not very quickly" aspect of her father's words.

"If you mean how fast can we move through warp space then I'm not sure. We're moving at around fifty times light speed but we know that we could manage five times that figure. Remember though that we aren't actually moving that fast, that would be impossible. The Alcubierre engines work by distorting space-time. We expand the space behind the ship and contract the space in front of it to create a 'warp bubble'. We move space and time around the Einstein and that movement allows us to sidestep the normal limit of light speed."

"That is very clever Pop, did you design it?"

"I helped build it but the original designer was a scientist called Alcubierre who did the work back in the 1990s. He was very clever because he did it even though he knew it couldn't be powered in those days."

"And then Mom found a way?"

"Yes, she's the clever one!"

20. In the Void

A week after the Einstein went supra-light the warp engines died as planned and the ship resumed its intrinsic normal space velocity coasting steadily to a relative stop between the stars.

"Helm, half speed ahead." Ellen deciding that some movement was safer than being a sitting target. Not likely, she thought to herself, but better safe than sorry.

Having made that decision, she took a moment to look at the views forward and aft. That was the moment when she first felt, emotionally, the immensity of the space between the stars. The forward view of the stars was much the same but the aft view showed a vision no humans, apart from those on the Anticipation, had ever seen for real. There was a star in the centre of the field but it took a few seconds for it to sink in that that was Sol. Far from being the sun that they were used to, even when in orbit around Saturn, it was now an average star, brighter only because it was just a light year away.

"Commander, you have the com."

John Lees moved to the command seat as Ellen left the bridge for her side room. "Comms, please ask all senior officers to be in the briefing room in half an hour, thank you."

Thirty minutes later Ellen entered the briefing room to find all her officers standing. The chatter she heard as she approached died when she entered. Signalling everyone to sit, she first asked if there were any urgent problems. Following a chorus of "No's" she asked each of her officers in turn for a status report.

Most of the reports were positive and no more than she would have expected. Only in two areas did the officers raise what they termed non-urgent issues.

Scott confirmed that the first remote checks on the warp engines confirmed these were in fine condition but he needed to emphasise that he and his team would need some time in order to complete a full physical check.

"At least three days, Captain, and preferably four. We'll also need to look at the Deimos in more depth, they pushed their engines beyond their normal limits in catching us."

"Right, best to get on with it, Scott."

The second officer to raise an issue was Angelique Rouse.

"Captain, we have a problem with manpower in hydroponics and in the park habitats. We need extra help on an almost constant basis. I have talked to Commander Lees about this."

"John?"

"Ellen, Angelique is right. The amount of work is far more than her team can cope with sensibly. We have discussed how we can utilise other people to assist but there wasn't time to raise this before we entered warp. I feel we should produce a rota involving everyone for an hour or two a week."

"That is a good idea. One thing. No one is to be exempt. That rota should include all bridge officers and I mean all. That means me too. I suspect that the Doctor will be totally supportive – gardening is a therapeutic exercise."

"Thanks, Captain."

As the meeting broke up Ellen called Scott back.

"Scott, I will be talking to the research heads later today. One thing, any progress with the mini-probes yet?"

"Not really, Ellen, I know Alan and his colleagues have been working on the theoretical modelling to see how small we can go but it's only been a week and they have not yet pulled my team into the work."

"OK. Finally, if you need anyone to carry out external work let the bridge know. We are still underway and I would prefer to cut the engines to reduce any risk to anyone undertaking an EVA."

"Noted, ma'am."

That afternoon the research heads congregated in the briefing room for a shorter meeting than Ellen's morning session. Again, though, the discussions centred on two areas. The Head of Astronomy asked for extra time before they returned to warp.

"I assume that your observations relate to our surroundings here because we are a light year from the nearest star? Not just to see how the constellations have changed?" asked Ellen.

"You are quite correct, Captain. This is a unique opportunity to study and measure the surrounding space. It may help us to confirm so many ideas as to what might be found in interstellar space."

"Or maybe disprove some ideas, Professor?"

"True."

"I am afraid you have four days and no more. This stop is to check over the ship after its maiden warp immersion. If it helps you can be provided with one of the IP craft to collect samples outside of the Einstein but any delay to our departure will only be because of engine problems and we don't expect, or want those, as you can imagine."

The astronomer looked glum but acknowledged the help offered.

Turning to Alan, Ellen raised a questioning eyebrow. "Mini-probe?"

"We're getting there. The problem is balancing size against fuel capacity, both for warp and normal space. We can go very small but then the probe won't be able to manoeuvre when it drops out of warp. If we make it larger it becomes more visible." Alan responded.

"Could we not target Saturn's orbit but on the other side of the sun from the planet? Close enough to see what is happening but far enough from any planet and so minimise the risk of it being spotted?"

"We can try but you must understand that we are assuming that they won't be watching for any intrusion and they clearly have excellent sensory systems. Remember that they spotted our activities around Saturn from at least ten light hours out."

"There is a difference." John Lees interrupted, "When we were at Saturn we weren't trying to hide and would have been visible to a variety of active media. If we make the probe act passively it should only be visible as it exits warp space and when it re-enters warp."

"Up to a point that is true. We do know, however, that it is possible to track a ship in warp or at least its direction, if you are in line. We don't know how far that tracking will last. From the probe we reckon its only for a few hours but we might want to make a deliberate   .

change of course a light week out." Scott Bailey had joined the meeting and felt it appropriate to intercede.

"Suggestions then." Ellen answered him.

"We could use one of the "landers" from Titan station's craft. Using one as a starting point would mean that we will only need to add warp tori to an existing structure. Small but able to carry enough fuel."

The discussion continued for some time but the decision was effectively already made. They would adapt a lander and add warp engines, a high-grade AI and an upgrade in passive sensors. It was agreed that its course would be considered in greater depth.

At the end Ellen raised one final question.

"Alan, how long will it take to complete the probe?"

"With the resources available we should be able to launch in around fifteen days. You will need to decide what course it should follow."

"Right. Leave that with me and the Commander."

Four days later Einstein re-oriented itself with the Centauri system and entered warp space for the second time. Again, Ellen ordered that they should only maintain warp for a period of just ten days at the same speed. A second period would be spent in normal space readying the probe for warp insertion back towards Sol.

During this time Ellen and John spent some time with the head astronomer discussing the relative placement of the planets back in the solar system.

Finally, the decision was made. The probe would be sent on a seemingly random course. Its mission programming took some time to plan but in the end the routing was a complex loop made up of short warp bursts combined with brief spells in normal space to re-align its course to arrive in Saturn's orbit. In that orbit but on the far side from the planet adjusted to ensure that it could observe the Earth/Lunar system directly. Unless its own sensors indicated that it had been seen it would remain simply observing with passive sensors for up to a month.

On the ninth day preparations were almost complete when Jing Tian asked to talk with Ellen.

"Jing, you look well. It seems some while since we were able to talk one-to-one."

"Inevitable, Ellen, despite everything, we remain extremely busy and on a ship this size. But I do need to talk to you about the probe situation."

"I have a briefing due later this morning from the team leaders. What problem is there that I am not aware of?" Ellen's voice underlined her concern.

"It's not a direct problem but two of my team have expressed the concern that using a lander in these circumstances carries a higher risk of failure. The lander was not designed to be operated by an autopilot in such complex manoeuvres even with an upgrade. Both are pilots trained to fly the lander and both have volunteered to travel back with the probe – to act as backup. I believe that it would be wise to accept their offer."

Ellen took a moment to respond. "I understand. I will consider your advice at the briefing later. Thanks, Jing."

Later at the briefing Ellen allowed the team to take her through the full story of the probe preparation, the addition of the warp tori and how the in-built autopilot had been upgraded to handle the planned mission.

"How happy are you that the autopilot can carry out the planned routing?" Ellen's question drew a startled murmur from around the table.

It was John Lees who responded. "Reasonably happy. It is a complex piece of programming and we aren't dealing with a full AI. There is a small risk that it will be affected by local conditions when it drops out of warp and as a result the next move will be wrong. In effect it is possible that it could get lost. We've programmed some back up auto checks so that minor discrepancies can be handled but we can't give you a cast iron guarantee of success."

"What if the backup involved human pilots?"

"Human? We haven't thought about that. You would be asking a pilot to handle the craft with little room for some four months or more. The lander was designed for short two/three-day manned trips not for trips of that length."

Having finished the briefing Ellen and John sat down to discuss the outcome. In the end they asked Jing Tian to join them. Ellen asked the question first.

"Do your two people understand what they will be letting themselves in for? Perhaps four months with minimal room, limited facilities and who knows what they will see back home."

Jing considered her response carefully before saying. "Why not speak to them both yourselves? Unless there is a real technical block on manning the craft."

Ellen looked to John Lees.

"There isn't a technical reason. We can load adequate supplies and load factor is well within safety parameters. They need to understand the physical constraints they will face and the length of time involved. Jing is right we should hear their side before we decide. I would like to review their past experience though, before we talk, Ellen."

"Agreed. Jing let me have their files. We will want to see both of them later." Ellen continued. "I want the probe launched by this time tomorrow. Manned or otherwise."

After the others had left, and while she waited for the later meeting, Ellen considered the timeframes involved and wondered if she could be guilty of ignoring her orders to move only two light years towards Centauri and then to change course. Yet here she was, around two light years out and holding position, as it were, before deciding her next routing when the decisions to trigger the original probe's warp drive towards Centauri and the need to pre-set the return destination of the new probe required that the Einstein must reach that nearest star system first and then wait. The next change of course would have to be delayed by as much as five months to allow for the Sol destined probe to complete its return journey. After some thought she made an entry in her log acknowledging the deviation from her original orders while detailing the background to the reasons. Having faced that issue it occurred to her that if she ever had to face her senior offices the situation would be only the best outcome of the oncoming storm.

It was while considering this that she suddenly activated her communicator and asked for Alan to join her. It was, she thought later, a rather obvious question but not one that had been asked.

"Alan, could the probe craft use a higher warp factor safely?"

"There is no reason why it should be any more dangerous except that there would be less time for the AI to react to an adverse gravitational situation. I would suggest that warp two is easily achievable. Warp three should be OK."

"So, we could reduce the journey time from two months outwards to two or three weeks and the return to the same period."

"Give or take, yes."

"Right. Now for the harder point. What precautions have we taken to ensure data and the warp drives do not fall into the wrong hands?"

"The AI has multiple layers of security and can or will wipe itself if these are breached. As a part of that process it will initiate a self-destruct of the warp engines by releasing their fuel cells. The energy released will rip the engines and the ship itself apart."

With that final piece of the jigsaw in place Ellen and John interviewed the proposed crew. Still somewhat against her own judgement Ellen accepted the proposal and agreed to the craft being manned. Her last decision was to decide that as the probe was to be manned it should be named. As it had come from Titan the name seemed obvious.

The following day the newly named Titan 1 with its crew of two was towed out of the Einstein's landing bay. The two craft powered their n-space engines and rapidly built a distance between them.

Ellen, in the captain's seat on the bridge, opened a tight channel to the probe. "Commander Petlak, Officer Patel. Good luck gentlemen, the gap between us is sufficient now. You are authorised to engage your warp drive. We will see you in Centauri in due course."

A few moments later there was a shimmer of light around the Titan as its warp drive engaged and it disappeared from the Einstein's sensors.

Ellen requested a ship-wide communications circuit. "Captain to all hands. We are about to enter warp space. Next stop the Centauri system. Now let's cut our travel time. Helm, warp two please." Moments later the Einstein itself also vanished from that part of the continuum.

21. Centauri

Eight days later Einstein dropped out of warp about ten astronomical units from Proxima. The red dwarf star glowered in the view screen. It was without doubt an emotional moment for all on board. Once again, apart from the Anticipation, they were the first humans to set eyes close up on a sun that was not Sol.

As they watched a shadow began to pass across the star and the Einstein's sensors recorded a direct view of the planet identified by the original probe. As seen by the probe it had already been recorded that the planet did not match the exoplanet identified back in 2016. The planet, which ought to have been larger, was quite small.

Given the time that they would need to remain in the system, Ellen was happy to authorise the launch of a series of probes to take a closer look, with one proviso. If they were to find a non-natural artefact in orbit they were to back off and not attempt to make any further active examination. In due course the data collected confirmed that the planet was unusually dense with its mass being shown to match that of the original exoplanet measurements.

"It would be fair to say that it is not suitable for humans. Although we could adapt to the higher gravity, its around 1.3G, the atmosphere is toxic. Sadly, it reflects much of the research into how being in the habitable zone does not automatically make a planet suitable for settling." The head astronomer's tone was subdued as he delivered a statement that he knew would not be welcome.

In due course the Einstein slid back into warp drive to manoeuvre closer to Alpha B a quarter of a light year away and settled down to await the original probe's arrival. Now only a few days away.

As they waited Ellen called her officers together for a council of war.

"It occurs to me that we have made some assumptions about the progress back home. Based on the timeframes indicated for arrival of the alien fleet I wonder if our crewed craft might not have arrived too soon."

"That is possible," said John Lees, "but I doubt it. The last arrival timings were at best educated assumptions based on what Earth based observations of the inbound fleet indicated. And we know from the attack on Titan that they are capable of undergoing much higher G forces than previously seen. Given what happened there it would not be a surprise if they changed their approach tactics towards Earth."

"That is a reasonable assumption Captain," Lieutenant Yablon interceded. "I have been reviewing the radio signals being broadcast just as we entered warp space for the first time. I have found one, short, message that reported a change in the velocity of part of the incoming fleet."

"Why did this only come to light now, Lieutenant?" Ellen was startled but her tone was quite stern.

"We were monitoring everything that was going on. Automatic recording but only responding if a message was to the Einstein or to Titan base. There are thousands of items but I only thought to search for "velocity" as a keyword last night. Even that left me with several hundred. I only came across that one this morning. Sorry, ma'am."

"What did it say, Liu?" John asked.

"Half the ships had made a second turnover and were accelerating at about 5G straight towards Earth. The rest were continuing to slow, decelerating at about 3G and spreading out."

"That would make their arrival within the last couple of months. Perhaps four months ahead of the original estimates." commented Alan. "And that means the guys should see first contact."

"Then we must wait. But to return to the reason for this council. We need to plan our next course of action. Specifically, which star systems we should aim for?"

"Professor, your thoughts?" John Lees addressed Alejandro Alvarez, the head astronomer.

"We have two options, which admittedly do overlap. There are the Kepler planets, a small number of which may provide opportunity. We should also look at the other G class stars that fall broadly in line with a routing to match with the Kepler systems."

"Good, please would you and your colleagues draw up a list of potential targets." Ellen looked to move on. "Alan, there is one thing that concerns me about warp drives."

"Captain, what is that? The drives have worked perfectly since we left Sol." Scott interjected a startled response.

Ellen smiled at her engineer's shock. "I know they have but it isn't their operational efficiency that worries me. Until now we have always moved in straight lines and have dropped back into normal space to change course. Why is this? Why is our direction always committed?"

"I don't believe there is any reason why we shouldn't be able to do so. Up until now we haven't used the n-space engines while in warp but after all the ship is sitting in its own bubble of n-space. I guess we are still learning about warp space, Alan?"

"We should try it. Like Scott, I don't see any reason why we can't. But it will be one for the bridge team to manage, Ellen."

"Right. Then we will attempt a change on the next stage of our journey. Now we wait for the probe's return."

John Lees tapped his communicator and listened. "Captain," he said formally, "I can report that we have received a communication from Probe 1. It has just entered n-space on the other side of the system. As ordered helm have set us underway to rendezvous. ETA thirty hours."

"Excellent. Everyone back to your day-jobs."

A day later Ellen was back in the command chair as they closed on the original star probe. As they made their approach, to her surprise there was an interruption.

"Captain, message from Professor Alvarez. He needs to speak with you urgently."

"Can it not wait?"

The ensign on comms duty talked quietly for a moment before turning to Ellen again. "He is very insistent, ma'am, he believes it is imperative that you hear what he needs to tell you." She frowned slightly. "He says it should be in private."

"Tell him to come to my standby room."

"Commander, take over." Ellen left the bridge for her standby room to await the Professor' arrival, wracking her brain to try and work out what the astronomer felt was so important. She had left her door open and only turned when there was a gentle knock.

"Captain, my apologies. I realise that the rendezvous with the probe is important."

"It is, Alejandro, but the Commander can manage that. You said it wouldn't wait."

"Captain, Ellen," he quickly changed his words as Ellen raised a finger to remind him that they were in private, "you ordered that you should be advised immediately if any of the scans found a non-natural artefact."

"You backed the craft away before there could be an adverse reaction?" Ellen was instantly alert.

"Not as such. We haven't found an active alien artefact."

"I don't understand."

"We have found evidence of an advanced civilisation on Alpha's planet."

"Really, and you didn't back off?"

"Sadly, we are a little late. It would seem that the civilisation suffered an extinction level event before they had managed to achieve spaceflight. The ruins, observed from orbit, definitely show a high level of sapience but initial analysis shows no evidence of life."

"You say they suffered an ELE? Can you say how?"

"Not for sure but there is evidence of widespread fire and there is a large crater, almost 200 kilometres across, which appears to be, in relative terms, recent. The problem with that idea, is that we have not yet been able to find any other bodies in the system other than the star and its planet. That in itself is surprising. How the planet could be hit by a meteorite in the circumstances is a real mystery."

"And that is why you wanted to talk to me in private." Ellen had already identified the unpalatable possibility that her chief astronomer was carefully avoiding. "Do you have any ideas as to how long ago this happened?"

"We would have to try for a landing to obtain better data but, best estimate, maybe ten thousand years ago. The crater we have studied is no longer a harsh object but has had time to be weathered and overgrown. You would have to be in orbit to see it. Assuming similar conditions to those on Earth, gravity aside, that is the shortest period we could expect to have elapsed."

"Alejandro, I am struggling to accept that not only was there an alien civilisation on our doorstep, so to speak, but we have to consider that it was destroyed in a deliberate and hostile act. By the same aliens that are approaching Earth?"

"Ellen, we cannot be certain that this was deliberate. And it might not have an external cause. There is a small chance, even, that they destroyed themselves through a nuclear explosion or, in some way released a seismic event that caused the event. It's possible that nuclear war killed them but that doesn't match with a single area of that size and nothing else. We really don't know and even with research over many years might not be able to achieve a definitive answer. I do feel that, while we are waiting for the Titan, we should try to land an unmanned ship near the ruins close to the crater edge."

"Agreed, but liaise with the physicists about what the remotes should be targeted at. I will brief the bridge officers regarding both your finds and the remote running of the craft."

"Captain to the bridge. Captain to the bridge! Urgent."

Ellen and Alejandro headed for the door at a run. As she entered the bridge there was a shout.

"On the screen, what are we looking at and how far?"

"It has just appeared from the other side of the planet. It was apparently in orbit but is now under power and on a course to intercept our current trajectory in 45 minutes."

"How did our probes miss it?"

"My guess is that it was in passive mode and a low orbit." John Lees looked up from his sensor panel and smiled. "It is a human satellite orbiter and is transmitting in code. Captain's code."

"In my room John. Liu, you have command. Comms re-route the message to my terminal."

Once at her desk Ellen entered her identity codes. Usually used only between the Captain and Command Central back on Earth, a coded message from an orbiter was unexpected. As the code was deciphered the terminal changed to a video scene easily recognisable as the bridge of the Anticipation. The starship's Captain started to speak.

"Captain. Apologies that I cannot address you by name. This message can only be accessed by a ship with the relevant codes. That you are seeing this means that the orbiter has identified your ship as human. I assume that you will have already scanned the planet in this system and seen that there was a sentient civilisation. I can also understand that you will be planning an early departure from the Centauri system. This message is therefore short.

Before we leave, we are setting an orbiter to carry out a full sensor scan of the planet and to continue doing so until it identifies another human vessel. Depending how long it has been since we left, that data should allow your research teams to complete extensive analysis of the current state of the planet and, possibly, confirm the cause of the extinction without having to delay any longer than you feel wise. Captain, we wish you and your people all the best in your hunt for a new home. We pray that both our ships are successful. Captain Johannsen signing off."

"That data will allow us to be ready for departure as soon as the probe returns." John was excited by the opportunity given to them. He then went formal for the record.

"Captain, I recommend that we download the data in full. I also suggest that you add a second message and that we then return the craft to its previous orbit with renewed instruction to only contact another human ship."

Ellen also spoke formally. "Agreed, Commander. I will leave it with you to make the arrangements. Please ensure that the Anticipation's message is made available to everyone. There is no need for secrecy now."

"Wait. Ellen, there is a second coded message that requires both our codes." John sounded perplexed by this information. After entering his own identity codes, the second message became clear. Anticipation had left details of their planned routing from Centauri which was towards a system about seventy light years away.

Captain Johannsen's last words being. "Given that I expect our instructions to be similar, this information may eliminate one of the possible targets you are considering. Again, good luck my friends."

"You know, I met Johannsen some years back. Thought he would make a good first officer but at that time he didn't come across as captain material. I guess he proves the old adage. In the right place at the right time." Ellen mused. "And it looks as if he is doing a good job."

"He was to be Fran's first officer on Anticipation originally, wasn't he?"

"He was, John. I think they were lucky to have a good officer available. Now let's look at what we should be doing while we wait for the guys to return."

With no apparent risk arising from the planet, Ellen moved the Einstein into orbit close enough to assist all the research teams to collect added data regarding the make-up of the atmosphere. That orbit also facilitated the landing of an unmanned vehicle to take samples and to release a robotic mobile vehicle with the aim of searching the nearby ruins for indications as to what the inhabitants had looked like.

The question as to what might have caused the extinction continued to perplex the various scientists as there were two things missing. With no apparent meteor remnants in the centre of the crater and no residual radiation it seemed as if there could be no external reason for the event. Yet the sheer size of the crater area argued against a naturally occurring event.

After a week of sampling the theories had been reduced to two. The meltdown of a nuclear power station seemed possible despite the lack of radiation. As had been indicated the event might have happened several thousand years before, leading to a fall in radiation to that of mere background levels. If that were not the case then some natural event must have occurred.

In the meantime, the mobile unit had reached the ruins and started to film the area. To no-one's surprise there were no bodies – the time elapsed had meant that any remains had turned to dust. One building appeared to have survived almost intact and the mobile's controllers carefully attempted an entrance. At the last moment it occurred to them that such a building might have additional hardening and could cause them to lose signal. It was decided that the risk outweighed the benefit until Judy, on duty in tracking, made the suggestion that the mobile attach its tow cable to a fixed point outside and then unwind it as it entered the building.

"Even if the building does block a direct signal you should be able to pull the mobile out using a signal via the towrope. Shouldn't you?" she ended with a mix of nervous confidence.

The trick worked and a few minutes later there were gasps from the bridge officers as the mobile's camera, backlit by its own lights showed the first images of the people who, it appeared, had occupied the planet before the disaster had struck. As the team agreed it was not difficult to refer to them as people since the pictures showed a species that was very humanoid. Stocky and short, based on their surroundings, which as the exo-biologists acknowledged would match how they expected life forms living on a planet with a much higher gravity than Earth.

There was little else in the first room, other than dust, but the second room deeper in the building had clearly been used for the local equivalent of an office or communications centre. There was little discussion as the controllers used the mobile's claw to gently pick up what appeared to be a computer screen and the box nearby. At that moment two things happened. The signal from the mobile flickered and tracking team spotted movement from outside the area.

"There is something moving towards the area at high speed, Captain."

"Get the mobile out of that building and start it back to the lander – NOW. Tracking, how long before it reaches the building?"

"If we assume it is aiming for the building then 25-30 minutes. There appear to be flashing lights on it, looks like purple. We seem to have triggered a burglar alarm, though how it could still be operational, I don't know."

"Show it on screen. Commander, is there any sign it is more than an automated response? Can we tell if there is any lifeform in the vehicle?"

"Scanning now. No heat signature in the vehicle other than from what I believe is the engine. Nothing to suggest that it is anything more than a remarkably capable system to have retained the energy to operate after such a time."

The following half hour was tense as the mobile was extracted from the building, taking longer than it had taken to reach the inner room. In the end it was able to start back with 15 minutes to spare but with a trip of over an hour to reach the lander the tension on the Einstein's bridge was high. Would the quarter hour start be enough if the robotic vehicle's system was able to decide to chase the "absconding villain"? If it stopped at the building, tracking had calculated that the mobile would reach the lander with time to spare but if it simply continued to track the mobile there would only be a few minutes to spare. As the clock ticked down Ellen ordered the team to start prepping the lander for an immediate take-off using a low launch trajectory.

"Captain, may I suggest that the lander transmits all its data now? Just in case there is any other opposition and we lose it. I find it difficult to see how but I feel we should plan for the worst." Her first officer flagged a sensible point and Ellen was happy to concur.

"Make it so. Tracking keep watching that vehicle and let me know if its arrival at the lander starts to overlap that of the mobile."

"Yes, Captain." There was a pause and the Lieutenant on duty suddenly sat upright almost at attention in his seat. "Captain, there is a second vehicle approaching from the other side of the crater!"

"How far?"

"Closer, but it is not crossing the crater itself. It seems to be avoiding it. Unless it changes course, it will not be an issue."

"Captain, we should re-route the lander's take-off. If the locals avoid crossing the crater then, perhaps, we should too." John's words sounded surprising until Ellen's quick thoughts recognised the realism in them.

"Agreed."

As John turned back to his panel, he decided to contact the geology team. After a brief conversation he turned back to Ellen.

"The crater has been identified as volcanic and it is slightly active."

"A volcano two-hundred kilometres across?"

"It would have been, or is, a super volcano. We knew of similar back on Earth although even Yellowstone would not be as big. The best estimate is that it erupted in a series of single vents which combined into a single eruption with a combined explosive power of fifty thousand megatons. In effect it would have resulted in the equivalent of a nuclear winter after the initial holocaust.

More importantly it seems that there is some activity in the very centre of the crater. Given the potential power of such an eruption we should move the Einstein into a higher orbit. If the volcano were to erupt then significant amounts of molten rock could reach low orbit."

"Helm move us out into a higher orbit." Ellen did not delay.

Turning back to the screen views they could see the incoming vehicle slow at the building but without a material stop it turned, clearly scanning the local area before accelerating in the direction already followed by the Einstein's mobile. Ellen made a decision. Instructing the lander's controllers to act quickly and move it towards the mobile.

The move was carried out successfully and the mobile recovered with time to spare. The lander launched for orbit taking a shallow climb which should have kept it out of line of sight of the incoming vehicles. In the event a third vehicle which had not been spotted appeared to open fire on the flying machine. Only rapid manoeuvring by the controllers enabled the lander to avoid the worst of the fire - apparently high velocity projectiles. The lander's rate of climb was accelerated and it reached low orbit in fast time. Following a second manoeuvre the Einstein dropped back towards a matching orbit to enable the team to recover the lander and its invaluable load.

As soon as the recovery had been completed the helm officers moved Einstein back into a higher orbit out of range of a large eruption.

Following the recovery of the lander Ellen decided to take a personal look at the mobile and leaving John in command on the bridge travelled down to the landing bays twelve decks below.

"Captain, good to see you." Scott was already in the bay leading his team in extracting the mobile. The job made harder than normal due to the damage suffered by the lander which had not totally avoided the ground fire. One side had been hit by a spray of bullets which had caused the access doors to be jammed. The engineers were working to try and extricate the mobile without causing further irreparable damage to the lander itself.

As Ellen and Scott talked there was a cry of success and the doors were slowly opened. Finally, the mobile was driven out into its own area and the equipment taken from the building was seen by the scientists in its physical state for the first time. The excitement was tangible but at the same time Ellen could hear concern being expressed as to whether they would ever be able to access the contents, if any. Ellen asked what problems were being identified.

One of the information experts summed up the issues succinctly. "Basically, the questions are. Can we manage to power the machinery? If we can, can we access the data storage without damaging it? Will access be password protected in some way?"

Other input included whether or not they could avoid any traps which might wipe the data away. "Even if we solve all those issues, will we be able to understand the information? Will it be digital, in words, or maybe video? The last, Captain, could be the key to extending our knowledge of the civilisation."

Ellen was startled by the voice from behind her. "Ensign Piper?"

Turning she found that it was Molly who was present, dressed in her Ensign uniform as to be expected, but now with the insignia of a science research team.

"I'm doing different roles until they find where I can contribute most, Captain." Molly was careful to be formal. "This is a fun area, ma'am" she couldn't resist adding.

"Take your time everyone, don't lose it. We can be patient."

***   ***   ***

Returning to the bridge Ellen directed the helm to move the Einstein into an orbit around the star far enough out that they could enter warp without delay.

Three more weeks passed and now the probe and its crew were right on their deadline to return. The senior officers met to discuss the situation following which Ellen took time in her bridge room before deciding to wait a further week. Six days later her patience was repaid as tracking picked up the unmistakeable signature of an approaching warp bubble and the probe finally dropped into normal space only a few hundred thousand kilometres from the Einstein.

The pleasure of seeing their colleagues return from their mission was suddenly tempered when communications realised that the message from the probe was a repeating recording. The probe was operating under the command of its autopilot and AI only and there was no apparent response from the crew.

"Commander. Take a craft and intercept the probe. Carry out a boarding, in full suits. John, we need to know why the crew aren't responding before we land them back on the Einstein."

"On my way, Captain. Liu, with me."

"Lieutenant Jaeger, send an instruction to the AI. The probe is to move into a holding position two hundred klicks from us and to prepare to allow a boarding party. Give it Commander Lees' ID codes."

"On it, Captain."

Twenty minutes later the boarding party's lander was launched and after a short period gently moved alongside the lander probe before linking airlocks. Responding to the Commander's ID codes the AI opened the probe's external lock and the team entered. Moving through the small craft they reached the control room in a few minutes where the crew were found to be in their launch seats apparently unconscious.

The Commander had made the decision to add the ship's doctor to the party and Dr. Carden was quick to move to the fore. It was he who spotted that the crew were being kept in induced comas and had IV drips attached. While he examined the men, the Commander interrogated the AI and discovered that the emotional impact of the events back in the solar system had left the two men unable to face the return journey. They had instructed the AI to travel to Centauri by a routing that was already programmed in but at warp three and then to maintain them in a state of deep sleep or suspended animation until they had reached the Einstein.

"Doctor, how are they?"

"In remarkably good physical condition, but I would rather get them to sickbay before they are woken. I suspect that it would be better if they were no longer in the lander."

"Fine. Captain did you hear that?"

Back on the Einstein's bridge Ellen had been listening in.

"Yes, Commander. Best to bring both landers back into the landing bay. The medical staff can then get to work. Transfer the data records to Einstein but ensure that they are locked with access only to you or me. I feel we should review them before a more general release across the ship."

***   ***   ***

Four hours later both of them had to call a break. Ellen was ashen, while John looked leaden faced. "Now we know why the probe's crew were affected the way they were. We need to share this with the team. I think the warp guys should join us and the senior geologist."

"I'll organise it and get some food sent in."

"Thank you, John. I need some time to collect myself together. To get a hold of my thoughts."

He left the room to summon the senior officers to the briefing room in two hours' time. Time to allow Ellen to calm herself. As the Captain, he knew, she would have to appear strong despite the emotional impact of the information they had seen. The analysis by the probe's AI and brought together in a summary of five weeks' worth of data compiled in the solar system.

Having organised food for both of them he also retired to his own quarters to refresh himself and try to grasp the enormity of the events they had seen.

22. Solar System - First Contact

"Ladies, Gentlemen, take your seats." Ellen decided a less formal approach in her introduction was the right way. In this meeting her officers and colleagues were simply humans observing events on their home planet.

"You are going to see a summary of the events in the solar system a month or so ago. I warn you. You are not going to find this a happy story."

With that Ellen instructed the computer to run the video that had been compiled.

As the tracking team, back before the first insertion into warp, had noted some fifty craft of the alien fleet had stopped their deceleration and had even accelerated.

Now facing two waves of spacecraft, Earth had launched what appeared to be its entire stock of missiles into orbital positions. While these were manoeuvred into positions between the Earth and the incoming spacecraft, the remaining starships, apparently not yet complete had been moved, using their n-space engines. One had headed for the moon while a second had settled into a retrograde orbit keeping the planet between them and the incoming fleet. The third was set on an intercept course with the alien ships.

As the alien fleet's lead ships crossed Mars' orbit, they launched several missiles each. Consistent with what the

Einstein had witnessed at Saturn these missiles accelerated rapidly achieving relativistic velocities far higher than their originating ships.

The danger of these weapons had obviously been identified and multiple planetary ships accelerated to meet them trying, not without success, to destroy them while still out of range of the Earth's defence line. While some were destroyed or diverted the majority were untouched and Earth lost almost as many ships.

The missiles ignored the starship accelerating towards the lead spacecraft and continued on towards the planet. Despite the speeds involved Earth's missiles in Lunar orbit started tracking and launched their own attacks and the film showed multiple explosions as the incoming attack was blunted with most of the alien missiles destroyed. The alien fleet then launched a second wave which again ignored the starship but were clearly looking to overwhelm the defences. It was at this point that the aliens appeared to target the starship with smaller missiles and those watching on the Einstein gasped as the starship shimmered as it engaged its warp drives.

There was already significant theoretical evidence that engaging warp inside of the asteroid belt, let alone so close to the Earth's orbit, would almost certainly be fatal for the starship. What had not been realised was that there would be a massive shockwave across n-space. The starship, once the film had been slowed down, could be seen to implode collapsing into itself. The energy release exploded across space in the direction that the starship had been moving right into the lead wave of incoming spacecraft. The result brought cheers from the audience as all, but the four craft furthest away, could be seen to explode, completely destroyed or left disabled by the amazing impact.

The cheers were short lived as a surviving missile from the first wave was seen to strike the lunar surface close to the settlement. The result of the impact was as if a large asteroid had struck and the lunar surface fractured. While it was impossible for the probe's cameras to see the settlement, it was clear that the fractures would have reached the vulnerable domes. At best there would have been significant casualties even if the settlement was not totally destroyed.

The view suddenly switched to the Earth where the remaining missiles were stirring to race to intercept the second wave of incoming targets. Spaceplanes could be seen rising from the Earth in a desperate effort to meet and destroy the last missiles from the first wave. It was apparent to the watchers that the lunar impact had demonstrated how devastating the impact of even one alien missile would be on the Earth's biosphere. One by one the last of the first wave were destroyed or diverted from their path. Attention then switched to the second wave which was a matter of hours behind the first wave.

The video had been edited to reduce the times but the whole scene still seemed to be in slow motion. Once again, the interceptor missiles had significant success. The remaining lunar segment thinned out the wave allowing the Earth orbital interceptors to target survivors. The spaceplanes were the third line of defence but, as they manoeuvred to bring to bear their own weapons, two of the incoming missiles appeared to explode. The resulting shrapnel turned out to be multiple mini-missiles spreading out to overwhelm the defences. Dozens of defensive ships were destroyed and suddenly there was nothing between the Earth and six remaining missiles.

Desperate launches of ground based defensive rockets managed to divert one missile but the remaining five all hit the planet. One hit the circle of fire in the Pacific Ocean while the second hit the Atlantic Ocean. The first generated tsunamis nearly a thousand feet high. Japan was overwhelmed and the wave hardly slowed as it raced across the waters and across Asia. The wave heading eastwards was unaffected by the Hawaiian Islands. which were simply swept clean, and hit the American western seaboard an hour later. Before it did the full extent of the underground shock of the impact reached the San Andreas and its adjacent faults. While the whole of the circle of fire was now erupting the true impact was magnified as the fault released its built up energy and the entire western seaboard started to collapse into the Pacific in a massive line of fire and lava from Alaska in the North all the way down past Seattle, San Francisco and Los Angeles and on towards the Mexican seaboard. All three cities simply vanished. The incoming wave doused the flames but barely slowed as it raced across the continent and the lava generated lethal storms of steam.

The eastern seaboard suffered almost as badly as another immense tsunami struck. Manhattan collapsed under the weight of the water as the wave mounted almost as high as the one that had struck the other side of the continent. The principal difference was a lack of tectonic activity in the east.

South America suffered almost as badly as the tidal waves from both oceans struck sinking the Amazon basin under megatons of seawater.

Across the Atlantic tidal waves struck Northern Africa and Southern Europe with similar effects, even France and Great Britain did not escape although the waves were lower and had less strength than further south. It looked for a short time as if most of Europe would escape relatively unscathed. Then the third missile struck.

Its impact, just to the north of Corsica, only produced minor waves within the Mediterranean but it also triggered earthquakes and eruptions of Stromboli and Vesuvius. Italy fractured and the impact could be seen rocking the Alps, avalanches crushed towns and long extinct fissures opened. As the continent became obscured by the clouds of dust it was apparent that those still alive, if any, following the initial impacts, would be unlikely to survive the nuclear winter that was building. Much of Central Asia would survive the initial onslaught but equally would not escape the aftermath. And then the fourth missile struck.

By some means it hit with even greater energy than its predecessors, smashing into the Arctic ice cap. The impact released incredible amounts of heat and the ice cap seemed to vanish in an eruption of storms of steam blasting out south in an expanding circle. There was a gasp of anger and stunned surprise as the video noted that the temperatures reached almost a thousand degrees. The underlying waters heaved into tsunamis of superheated water chasing the storms and underneath those waters the planet's crust fractured again.

The final missile mirrored the fourth except that it hit close to Antarctica. The result was another series of tsunamis tearing the southern continents to shreds. The Falkland Isles vanished as did New Zealand, Perth and

Sydney. Southern Africa also suffered with Cape Town and Port Elizabeth sinking under massive waves. Again, the impact managed to strike near a tectonic plate edge and again the crust split generating more eruptions.

The helpless anger of the audience was palpable as they realised that the missiles were intended as planet killers. This was not an attack intended to conquer but simply to destroy. Without the desperate defensive action, the planet would have been hit by thirty or forty missiles with the likely result that it would have been split in half.

The scene shifted to watch the last wave of alien spacecraft which was continuing to approach. As it crossed the orbit of Mars one ship suddenly accelerated on a line that was clearly aimed at Mars itself, fortunately at that time on the opposite side of its orbit. Crossing into the area within Mars orbit the ships began looking to spread around the inner solar system. Despite the destruction of most of the first wave the fleet still kept in a fairly close formation.

As they closed to within a couple of light minutes of the Earth slowing at around 5Gs of deceleration there was a move from a few surviving interplanetary craft out of Earth orbit in an apparently suicidal attack. Then, and only as they drew close to the aliens, a larger craft could be seen. The starship previously named Exodus accelerated towards the other ships and then engaged its warp drive. This time the aliens were closer than the first wave and the Exodus closer to the Moon. The resultant energy flux was devastating and the second wave were annihilated. No ships were left capable of doing more than drift in space but a degree of revenge for the loss of Earth might have been claimed.

The one surviving ship continued to race across the system toward Mars. A brief view of the planet showed a flotilla of landers supported by three interplanetary shuttles desperately moving away from the planet though it was not clear where they were planning to hide.

At the same time, Ellen suddenly realised, the secret of warp drive might also have been protected from the aliens that must be turning back from Saturn after their attack on Titan. Except, she thought, what had happened to the Europa, the starship which had dropped into Earth orbit, holding station on the planet's blindside from the primary attack itself?

With the Earth dying in front of them the video came to an end. It wasn't difficult to grasp the emotional state of her officers and their colleagues. There was massive distress but this was also tinged with anger and not a little lack of understanding.

Why? How could an advanced civilisation simply attack others with the sole aim of genocide on a planetary scale? Attacking with the aim of conquering another planet could be understood. Even attacking only to obtain data and knowledge that might be of benefit to the conquerors. A race that, apparently, did not have a faster than light capability would surely have seen gaining access to that ability worth more effort. Yet this fleet had simply attacked in such a way that the Earth would have been doomed unless it had had the technology to form an impenetrable barrier. No communication had been made or, apparently, even tried by the aliens. Now the Einstein and its fellow starship Anticipation must seek a new home for the surviving humans with no hope of help.

Ellen rose to address her officers, speaking in a voice unusually unsteady and quiet for her.

"What you have seen is a brief summary of several weeks of observation. In due course these sights will be made available to everyone who may wish to see them. The full record will be available but, at first, only to the relevant experts. I suggest, rather than order, that you spread the world gently in small groups. I suspect that almost everyone will have lost loved ones. We will need to continue our voyage and seek a new home for the human race."

"Captain, I believe that our experience from being told of the reason for our urgent flight will help. This is the worst case but many will have feared that it would occur. You can rely on us to handle the telling of this news. Ma'am, please know that you have our unquestioning support." Doctor Carden's response on behalf of the assembly was warm and welcoming.

"We should get the research teams involved in examining the full data and observations as soon as we can. The more we can understand about these monsters the better. We cannot be certain we will not come across them again in the future." It was Alan Piper who reminded them, in effect, that only a part of the original fleet had diverted towards the Solar System.

Ellen nodded in agreement and then added her own thought. "The Europa. It was holding station away from the enemy fleet, in Earth's shadow. We need to know what happened to it."

John took the lead, "Everyone, get to it. Please mourn in private at first but do remember you are all part of one family now and you are not alone." He paused. "Ellen, Captain, that applies to you as well."

In the coming hours the news was spread across the ship. The grief was tangible.

After much work an image of the Europa accelerating away from the Earth under full power was found. Amazingly there was also a recording of a radio signal being broadcast from the ship that it was fully manned and equipped and planned a jump to warp as soon as it passed Jupiter's orbit. The message appeared to have been aimed at the survivors from the Mars settlement evacuation and their routing now began to make sense.

The news, that a third starship appeared to have escaped and that the Mars settlement seemed to have been evacuated in time, was broadcast around the Einstein. The sole good news from the Solar System, not home anymore. Their home, now, was the Einstein until such time as they found a new Earth.

Shortly afterwards the ship left Centauri orbit and a day later engaged its warp drives heading outwards into the unknown.

23. Amongst the Stars

Once the ship was underway and Centauri had disappeared from view Ellen held a council of war with her officers and the heads of research departments. First topic was their initial destination and the head astronomer spent some time explaining.

"We are heading toward the constellation Vela as it does not seem to have been covered by the path of the alien fleet as calculated by Earth's observatories when it was first identified seventy odd years ago. Of course, there is no guarantee that that data is accurate since the fleet was moving at relativistic velocities but it does seem to be a reasonable assumption. As they do not appear to have any FTL capability there is some perceived value in starting our search at a distance of around 100 light years. Our target star is HD75289 some ninety-four odd light years from Sol. There are other systems broadly on our planned routing which may allow us to drop out of warp and it might be worth taking a little time to survey the systems. While HD75289 has been recorded as having planets we must recognise that those exoplanets identified will not be habitable. It does not mean that there is not an Earth sized planet in the goldilocks zone but we should not get our hopes up of a hit first time."

"The goldilocks zone?" "Is that where a planet might be habitable?" "Why don't we think there will be an Eden?" the questions came fast.

"Yes, depending on the star in question it is the distance from that star in which a planet could orbit with water and oxygen in free form. As to why no "Eden". Well Earth sized planets are small and difficult to find when working at interstellar distances. Even the Kepler telescope found relatively few and these were always found to be in tight orbits very close to the primary star. It doesn't mean that they aren't there, just harder to find."

"Right, we look to drop out of warp as we pass any promising systems. Or can we survey them from warp first? I would rather not expose us to n-space view until we reach our target." Ellen looked to move on as soon as possible. "Look into it, please."

The meeting went on to look at supply levels. Fuel was not a problem. The warp drives used surprisingly little of their fuel which seemed to replenish itself as had been seen in the particle accelerators. Megan's research team continued to struggle with the apparent breach of the laws of conservation of energy. The n-space fuel for the interplanetary craft was stable as it wasn't in use for the most part.

As long as the hydroponics and the garden sections continued to work food and air replenishment would not be a problem for perhaps 50 years. After that time the oxygen and nitrogen storage tanks would be close to empty unless they could obtain replacement supplies from bodies in the star systems they would visit.

Research into what was known about the aliens was high on the agenda but little new information had been found beyond confirmation that there was no evidence that they had FTL capability. That they could withstand very high levels of acceleration, as much as a sustained seven gravities, which allowed them to reach relativistic velocities of as much as three quarters of light speed. They were also able to launch missiles which were incredibly dense but could still exceed the velocity of the craft from which they originated. The best news was that the missiles themselves appeared to have lacked manoeuvrability. The negative was that they could have multiple warheads to swamp defences.

The final topics had been discussed, before the meeting, by Ellen, her first officer, the ship's head of medicine and a select group of people tasked with helping non-crew members to deal with the emotional impact of the Earth's death.

Ellen pointed out that even though they were travelling at warp three the journey to their target star would take six to seven months even if there were no breaks in their routine. Such a length of time might well have adverse effects even amongst the astronauts who would have been used to spending long periods within a small spacecraft. For those to whom space travel was a new experience it was almost certain that, added to the Earth's loss, there would be bouts of depression. The team had agreed that the ship's exercise facilities and the relaxation areas should be put to use with sports competitions and live performances by those who were ready to perform for an audience whether that was in drama, music, dance or song. All ideas would be welcome. It was hoped that such diversions would provide positive offsets to the quite natural sadness.

Finally, Ellen looked around those present.

"There is one final issue that is not yet a problem but, if we do not address, could become one." she said, continuing "In the early days of spaceflight and, even more recently, with the interplanetary ships, the bases on Mars and the Moon, space command frowned on personal relationships between crew on missions and, in particular, between astronauts of different ranks. Now you know, and I know, and I suspect command knew, that such relationships did develop especially with the two person craft. It was inevitable and, so long as the individuals were discreet, no action was ever taken. Now that space command no longer exists, we must set our own rules. And these rules will need to address all manner of relationships. We are on our own. We are the human race and ultimately we will need those who wish to procreate and can do so to be able to come together with a partner of their mutual choice."

Ellen paused, casting her eyes over the silent gathering. "From now on there will be no reason why such relationships should not be allowed, whether within the crew or wider.

It is my belief that none of you will seek to take advantage of your rank. However, it is essential, and this is for the good of all and the protection of many. Any member of the crew who wishes to enter a relationship with another crew member who is junior to them is going to have to be careful and such a situation will need to be monitored. Not by me or John directly but by the medical team. Their brief will be to ensure, possibly by interviewing the junior person, that there is no coercion.

In terms of the people on the ship, we plan to make it clear that, while we are not trying to be the older generation stopping our kids from meeting the opposite sex, or even the same sex, there must be rules to protect especially the youngsters already here. Broadly the same exclusions that applied in the western world, age of consent, those who are acting in parentis loco, teachers or anyone training young people. Any questions?"

"How do we handle those issues where cultural differences would have different exclusions?"

"That is a good question and, while we aim to take into account such differences in many ways, this will not be one. The vast majority of people onboard were either born in western civilisation countries or brought up and exposed to their ways of life. I will happily meet with any group that feels that they are being discriminated against to explain in person why they will need to work within those rules. We are not in a place that will allow us to have multiple "laws" according to cultural views."

There were a few more questions but Ellen felt, correctly she was told later, that the general view was that the rules were sensible.

***   ***   ***

The Einstein continued through space pushing its warp bubble to the limit, at least as far as the engineering team and the theorists deemed safe. As the weeks passed by, the crew and passengers, as the crew light heartedly referred to the non-crew research teams, settled into a routine.

Regular exercise was mandated. Although the artificial gravity was good it was still only three quarters of a G. The need to ensure bodies remained fit should they find a new Earth similar to their old home. In fact, the medical teams were pushing the envelope and trying hard to get everyone to work harder to strengthen themselves. When asked why, they were always ready.

"If the world we find is habitable we will want to settle there. We do not want to have to pass it by just because its gravity is 1.2 or 1.3G. Best that we work as if that is what we find."

The other, and less desired, was the mandatory sessions in hydroponics and the horticultural areas. Only the fact that Ellen and her senior officers did their own stints carried the issue with minimal excuses being made to avoid the work.

It was when she was undertaking one of those chores that Ellen was interrupted, briefly, by Dr Carden.

"Doctor, you're on this shift as well?"

"No, Captain. I came looking for you, away from the bridge for once." He replied. "Ellen, if I may be informal? You are late for your medical. I don't want to force the issue but I do need to complete a full process for you."

"I have so little time, Will, and I feel perfectly OK." Ellen was a little apologetic but her grimace indicated she wasn't happy about the need to visit the medical section.

"My first, medical input, is that you are overworking. Long hours on the bridge, double sessions in the gym and, I suspect, additional work down here. Ellen, you need to find some way of relaxing. Take advantage of the entertainment that was set up at your suggestion. Read a book."

"But…"

"No buts. If I didn't know you and your record, I would say that you were hiding from yourself. And I do know about Command. It is a very lonely place at times and the fact that you have a great team supporting you doesn't always help. Are you sleeping?"

"I...."

"Ellen, you are like many of the other people. They are either not sleeping or they are having nightmares. My teams are spending a lot of time trying to manage these symptoms. After all, this is wholly reasonable we have seen our homes destroyed, we've lost friends and family. Look, Ellen, this is not the place to go into this. I have checked and you will finish your next period on the bridge at midday tomorrow. Your medical exam will follow then. It's in your calendar and diary and your first officer is aware that you will need to attend my section at 1pm. No excuses."

Ellen bowed to the inevitable and meekly nodded her acceptance.

"Tomorrow then."

That evening, Ellen did try to relax and, instead of eating alone, joined other crew members and researchers in one of the communal dining rooms. Her presence was acknowledged by different people but, in line with an unwritten rule, there was no formality and she was allowed to effectively ignore her teams without causing offence. A few welcomes from some who knew her best was the limit but it was clear she could join any table without question should she so wish.

It was a better time than she had had for some weeks and, to her delight, she found Alan, Megan and their daughters in the same place. There was a happy few hours as they swapped stories and updates on their various roles while enjoying the food that tasted much better than that served in her own quarters. What did surprise her was that she had difficulty sensing any underlying effects of the loss of the Earth despite the fact that it must have still been raw in everyone's minds. She flagged a mental note to ask the Doctor about this.

Right at the end of the evening, Megan asked Ellen for a private chat.

"Ellen, it's about Judy."

"Is there a problem, Megan? I ought to have heard if there is. She's proving to be an invaluable member of the bridge team and fits in really well. Officer material if I ever saw it, though I keep some distance from decisions made by my senior people as to how she develops. They know she is my cousin and, I believe, find it easier to handle decisions knowing that I prefer to avoid any suggestion of nepotism. So, she will make her way on her own merit."

"Sorry, not a problem as such. It's just that she has told me that she likes John Lees a lot. And she thinks he is also attracted to her. The issue is, he is the first officer and she is only an ensign. We know about the rules for your crew, and other teams, to avoid the risks attendant with the senior junior status. If he isn't interested, Judy would rather gently break away, emotionally as it were, without damaging their professional relationship. She doesn't know how to approach it."

"Megan, leave it with me."

"Oh lord, I just thought, you and he? You aren't, are you? I mean…"

Ellen laughed, for the first time in a long time, with genuine enjoyment.

"Megs I don't think I have ever heard you mix your words like that. No, there is nothing between us. Captains need to be free from such a relationship. I like and have the utmost respect for John, in other circumstances, he might have been the Captain, but that is the extent of our relationship. I will handle this."

"Thank you. You know that you have respect and not a little love by everyone on board. And no-one envies you. Many do feel that they couldn't handle the responsibilities you have, even the heads of the research teams who have their own issues." Megan's voice was much calmer. "So, don't forget that support is at your back."

Having made their farewells for the night, Ellen headed back to her quarters more relaxed than she had been for longer than she could remember.

The next morning as she returned to her bridge and the command chair, she decided to address the problem, she had been set by Megan, head on.

"John, in my ready room please. Liu, you have the com."

"Ellen?" John Lees was concerned at the unusual command. And raised his eyebrows in question as Ellen closed the door behind them.

"John, excuse my enquiry. I need to know whether you have found a partner or if you are in a relationship."

"Ellen, no there is no-one special at the moment. You should know. At our command level we have to be seen to be above question. A relationship might cause a blurring in how our actions are perceived. Even if they are 100% correct. Why do you ask?"

"This is the delicate piece. Is there someone in the bridge team you might wish to be involved with in other circumstances?"

"Well. I mean maybe but she is a junior and 10 years younger and…." John responded rather nervously.

"And she's related to your senior officer?" Ellen smiled. "John, she likes you and I believe she would go further but for the same reason you hesitated."

"She came to you?" John stuttered.

"Not directly, but she talked to someone else who asked me for help. Judy wants to progress it but she needed to know if you liked her in the way she thought. She's bright, you know, and didn't want to interfere with the professional relationship if you didn't feel the same way. That is as professional as you can ask. Now, she's due off-duty in an hour, I suggest a coffee might be a good starter!" Ellen smiled and finished. "Good luck to you both."

As her first officer left the room in something of a daze, Ellen suddenly had a thought. "John, I'll deal with the review process. No need for you two to go through that." She followed him out back on to the bridge and returned to the command chair settling in for the next four hours in the best frame of mind she had been in for some time.

*** *** ***

The weeks passed by with a degree of monotony. In the end, the sole star system they passed was a binary pair of two red dwarfs with no identifiable planets. The astronomy team working with the engineering team had extended the range and accuracy of their instruments. In addition, they were able to compensate for the distortion caused by the warp bubble which was the most difficult of the problems set by Ellen. As a result, the system allowed for a first test of the improved equipment even though the outcome was disappointing.

*** *** ***

One area where the research was limited to theory involved exotic particles and Megan had buried herself in that field largely to the exclusion of everything else.

To Alan's distress he found that she was not sleeping and her resulting exhaustion was affecting her entire outlook. As he explained to Ellen.

"She is mourning her family. She could cope, just about, with the loss of her parents but losing her sister has hit her really hard. Add to that, she feels that she is just self-pitying. She knows that others, of course, have lost family as well. I wish she would talk to the Doc. but she claims it will be a waste of time."

"There's nothing to stop you from talking to Will direct. I'd do that first, better if he can find a solution. I could order her to see the doctor but I'd rather avoid that if I can."

Alan took Ellen's advice and asked the doctor how it would be best to approach this. Will Carden studied Megan's file for a few minutes then with a startled look at Alan.

"I hadn't realised Megan's maiden name was Newcombe. "The Newcombe", of course, how stupid of me." Continuing he explained, "I don't follow science issues that closely, there is or was enough medical stuff to keep me occupied. I managed to unlink Newcombe and Piper in my mind. Tell me, her sister, was she in medicine?"

"She was head of the medical section on Mars before she was reassigned to Space Command back on Earth."

"Good Lord! Dr. Marion Newcombe, I feel more stupid by the moment. We need to talk to the Captain."

In a short time, they were in Ellen's ready room.

"Ellen, do you have the postings for the Europa?"

"Will, sorry?"

"Just the officers. There is a good reason for asking. Can you confirm who was to be head of the medical unit?"

Ellen opened up her personal computer access and spent a few minutes looking through the information sent to her after she was aboard the Einstein.

"I only have the provisional listing. Head of Medical was a Dr. Jacob Brandt."

"I thought as much, you don't have any updated information? I knew Jacob well. An ideal choice until he was diagnosed with an inoperable brain tumour just before we left. I rather suspect that your sister-in-law, Alan, would have been next in line but I can't guarantee it."

Ellen suddenly stared at her keyboard. "But I may be able to. The Europa's last broadcast was quite long and may have carried some personnel data which I never looked at. I had no reason to before. It seemed a bit of a waste of time then."

It took a few minutes and Ellen's command codes to access the full message but there, in a list of senior officers, was the one she wanted. Marion had been appointed to the Europa and was aboard their sister ship! Alan left the room almost at a run to find his wife. Her sister was safe and, even if they might never be able to meet again, that was the best news.

***　　***　　***

In an effort to break the monotony and resultant boredom, Ellen and John arranged a variety of emergency scenarios for the bridge crew without warning. As they discussed after each successful outcome their concern was that the real thing would, of course, not be one for which they had practised.

"I guess that is facing the inevitable," said Ellen. "The best we can do is make sure the teams can work well under stress. Then whatever the universe throws at us they can handle as best as they can. Speaking of which how are you doing?"

"Fine and yes, Judy is great." John's smile reflected his feelings for the young woman.

Despite the lack of external stimulation, the various research teams found plenty of work to do. The volumes of data already collected in the Saturn system and of the attack on Earth itself was enough to ensure that there would be no lack of work for some time and, of course, there was the data that flowed into the Einstein constantly covering the warp bubble and surrounding interstellar medium through which they were moving.

The personnel team had recruited a number of non-crew members to act as reporters and writers for a regular electronic magazine, it would have been a combination of blog and vlog back on Earth and fulfilled a similar purpose on the ship's web. This helped everyone keep in touch with what was going on in the ship which given its size often meant that some parts were a complete mystery to those in other parts.

*** *** ***

Three months into their voyage Cesare Bianchi, responsible for much of the work analysing the attack on the solar system, messaged Ellen with a request for a meeting to discuss the results of their initial research. Ellen, who had been keeping a quiet eye on progress, decided that her senior officers should attend that meeting.

Despite her oversight of the operation she was surprised to find that Alan and Scott were to lead the presentation but as Cesare explained it was input from engineering and the power experts that had enabled them to understand data that, at first sight, did not seem to add up.

Alan led the way explaining that closeup footage of the alien ships, relayed from unmanned probes which had been launched to carry out passive sensor watch showed that the aliens did not appear to use rocket-based engines but highly efficient ion jets. Titan was able to tap into the data feeds from the human probes monitoring the aliens, he explained.

"Wait a minute, they were able to accelerate/decelerate by as much as seven gravities. What sort of ion jet produces that sort of power?" John was stunned by the statement.

Alan was quick to respond. "We did say that the initial data did not seem to add up and it doesn't until you measure the size of the motors compared with the size of the ships and add in an extra source of power. Firstly, the ships must be mostly engine plus missile capacity with almost no other space on board. Secondly, we think that they are using an anti-matter source of energy. Although the ion motors are big and provide excellent manoeuvring, you are right, by themselves they couldn't manage seven gravities but if you add a secondary booster then it seems the ships can handle it. We have analysed the booster output and it is an ultrahigh energy blast. Short and sharp but not unlike the way the energy balls acted back when we first produced them in the particle accelerators. We can't manage anti-matter or produce it for that matter, in any safe way. Even so our calculations suggested that these blasts were still not strong enough to provide enough g-force until we realised that we had assumed that the ship tonnage was in line with what human ships of the same size would be."

Scott intervened. "We were lucky. One of the close-range sensor units was near to the first wave of ships when they were destroyed by the side effects of a warp drive imploding. The data transmitted, and accessed by Titan, before the probe itself was destroyed was enough to allow us to analyse the spectra of the ships. They were or, I should probably say, are made mostly of lithium and beryllium. There is some carbon and aluminium but we are still baffled as to how you could make a spacecraft with that mix of elements."

"What about the missiles? They contained extremely dense warheads, planet crackers."

It was Cesare's turn. "At launch they did not appear have that density but the warhead was very large. We think that they held a container of energy which, once launched, triggered an internal implosion to produce a miniature neutron core."

"They seem to have technology far in advance of us. Why not FTL?" Ellen was also bemused.

"We don't know but I wonder if there are elements of that development they simply never found?" Cesare continued. "However, there is a more frightening development in our knowledge of them."

"Which is?"

"Our understanding of their structure combined with analysis of the destroyed ships, albeit at a distance. Put simply, these ships are either entirely robotic or operated by AIs. We can find no evidence of any organic lifeforms." Cesare paused as she saw the shock on Ellen's and her officers' faces. "Nor could we find any evidence of a central ship that might be acting as a master control running the other ships by remote. Unless such a craft was being run by a master AI, that is."

Ellen took a deep breath. "That means, unless fresh evidence contradicts this analysis, there are two possibilities. Either a race of paranoid beings who have set out to destroy any sentient civilisation that might challenge them and use robots/AIs to carry out exterminations. Worse, we have a group of AIs that have revolted against their founders and now are also on the genocidal route against all organic life. I say worse because I do not believe that it would be possible to negotiate with such beings."

"There is a third possibility, Captain." Lieutenant Yablon, one of the quieter members of the bridge team spoke up.

"Liu, go on." Ellen made a mental note to have John remind the youngster that formality was not necessary in officers' meetings.

"The alien race which started this may not have meant for it to happen. Might they not have sent out automated ships to seek out other intelligent life and make contact."

"Contact and destroy?" Scott's response was harsh and Liu stuttered to a halt. Ellen's voice cut in. "Liu, go on, what are you thinking might have happened?"

"Without FTL they might have decided, that to make contact they needed to send a fleet with an AI in control. Fitting the ships with defensive capacity and an ability to repair and replace. Something like von

Neumann probes. Perhaps they made a first contact and were attacked, forced to defend themselves. After that perhaps the AIs' programming was corrupted and they now believe their only defence is to attack first."

Alan commented. "I think that that is at least feasible. Good thinking Liu. Von Neumann machines would explain why they could accept the losses of the first wave and not pull the second wave from the attack. From our point of view our approach can't change. We will need to work on systems that will allow us to resist another attack should we come across the same aliens. With von Neumann machines we can't assume that the ships, spotted back in the 1990s, are the only ones."

"I hadn't thought about it before but could they hit us from outside the warp bubble?" John's concern was apparent. "As far as I know we have to drop out of warp to do anything with n-space?"

"I think I can answer that one. We know that there is a barrier at the edge of the bubble caused by the warping effect. At warp three the bubble expands into a globe roughly 1,000 kilometres in diameter. To an external observer it and its contents, the ship, are invisible. Having said that, when the original star probe engaged warp drive the Monitor was able to sense the distortion of the spacetime continuum for a short while. If that distortion could be tracked then we have one vulnerability. A salvo of their missiles could force us to drop out of warp due to their gravitational effects." Ellen had, of course, been on the Monitor and seen this for herself.

"I am not sure that I agree." Alan responded. "While you are right about the effect of a salvo of missiles they would need to know, in advance, where to fire them.

We are moving at close to half a light year a day. As far as we can tell they have to work at less than light speed and, even if they spotted the distortion, we would be out of their range in seconds. And they can't warn other fleets because their messages are limited by light speed."

"In warp we are relatively safe as long as we can avoid any massive objects. We will be most at risk when in n-space and too near a star's gravity well to be able to jump to warp again." Cesare's comments settled some of the nerves present.

Ellen decided to move the meeting on apart from indicating one area that the development teams needed to focus on. The work on sensors to allow detailed scans of star systems while still in warp had made significant progress. Now she decided that the close-range sensors, already good, also should be worked on to improve their performance. She finished with an instruction.

"I want to know that there is nothing likely to damage us before we drop into n-space. At the moment, I have a doubt that we can be that certain. To work everyone."

24. Personal Concerns

The weeks passed by and much research was carried out amongst all the different disciplines and throughout the Einstein there was little idle time.

Those not directly involved in research or the running of the ship found their time absorbed in producing the entertainment. Crew members when off-duty were informally tasked with training those who wished to learn more about the crew's tasks. Of course, part of the time on-duty was also dedicated to providing training to junior members of the crew.

Almost everyone was too busy to dwell on the past even in the medical centres. With over 4,000 people on board it was inevitable that there would be accidents from time to time and the medics also had a schedule of examinations not only for the crew but also the rest of the people.

It was Ellen who found occupying her time hardest. With the Einstein moving at warp three and on a course that would not pass near to any other systems, her time in the command chair was unexciting. The rest of her time, officially, on-duty involved inspections of the ship and re-viewing reports on her crew. Despite every effort to keep busy she found all too much time to spend looking back at the events in the solar system and worrying about the prospects of coming across the same aliens again. Sleep was becoming a short and restless time at best. It was apparent to her bridge team and to others that she was feeling the pressures as her demeanour and temper worsened. Finally, her first officer sought out Megan for help.

"It's my job to make sure my Captain is OK. That's aside from my personal concerns. My problem is that she's tending to shut me out and the rest of the bridge team as well. It's not good for her nor for the general morale." John's feelings were clear.

Megan asked the first question that occurred to her or rather answered it. "She's still doing everything well that she should be. So, this is about her own mental health. You're worried that the stress of leading us to a new home is weighing on her."

"Exactly. The trouble is that she's stopped taking in the entertainment or even dining in the mess. Spending too much time on her own when off-duty."

"She has no-one to share that time with?"

"No. It was hard enough for me as the number two. Very difficult for the Captain. She must be seen to be impartial."

"You'd like me and Alan to try and draw her out?"

"Yes, but try and not involve me or Judy?"

"Understood. How is our daughter doing?" Megan smiled. "We don't see as much of her these days. She seems happily busy all the time."

"That's my fault. Apart from her duty hours I've encouraged her to study for her officer exams. That doesn't leave much time for her to relax but I will suggest she should spend some time with you and Molly."

"Thanks. Perhaps we could all have a meal together? You said Judy was studying for her officer exams, can they be taken on board?"

"Ellen organised it – we do need to provide more backup and the process never did need to be on Earth although in practice it was. Judy has all it takes and the desire – so suggesting she do them was pushing on an open door. Dinner is a date."

They parted company and Megan was left to muse on how she could help her Captain and cousin. That evening she and Alan spent time in thoughtful discussion.

"It seems to me that Ellen is lonely. As captain she needs to keep some distance from her team but that means personal relationships must have something of a barrier beyond which she feels she cannot pass." Alan's voice was grim.

"I can understand that if it involved one of her crew, whether in the bridge crew or else. That shouldn't stop her joining in the various activities and mixing with others." Megan was no happier. "We need more time to come up with an answer. I think I will speak to some of the other team leaders, on the quiet of course."

"At least it sounds as if Judy is doing OK. It'd be nice to see her more often but I guess that's what happens when they grow. At least Molly's around when she's not on duty."

Megan grinned at her husband. "I'm not sure how long that will last. She seems to have found a friend that she wants to spend a lot more time with."

"Well, I shouldn't be surprised, given that she could be your younger twin." Alan laughed.

Megan's chats came up with one solution and a few days later Ellen was approached by the informal entertainments committee with a request. Please would she act as the question master over a series of tough quizzes that the team had been working on.

"John, why do they think I would be a good choice? Have you had anything to do with it?"

"Ellen, beyond the fact that they are seeking entrants for a quiz, I know nothing about it, but I can guess why they think that way. You are seen to be above any petty rivalries that might arise and," he paused carefully, "most people would like to see more of their captain."

"Are you saying I'm not doing enough for the ship?" Ellen responded with a hint of anger.

"No, Ellen. No-one questions that. They do worry about the time you spend "locked" away on your own though. Ellen, you need to feel the support and emotional backing you have throughout the Einstein. You need to have less time to worry about things you can't do anything about and to realise that you really aren't alone."

"I hear you." she paused then, "Alright I'll do it."

"And get out more, not just on inspection tours, but to meet people around the ship." John smiled. "They can't all come to you. Remember we still have around four months before we are due to drop out of warp. So, there is plenty of time to look in on all the various teams. Now you are due off duty and I can leave the bridge in the hands of Liu. Let's go have a meal in the deck restaurant."

"If you insist."

"I do, Captain!"

***   ***   ***

In due course Ellen did take the role of question-master and, as expected, was an immediate success. She also started to visit the various research teams in their areas rather than only hosting meetings with the team leaders or even restricting contact to reports via Alan and Megan as the overall senior managers. As John had intimated, she found these meetings uplifting even where there was little or no progress to report. Combined with a programme of visits to the various relaxation areas scattered around the ship Ellen had less time to be alone musing.

Less time, of course, didn't mean no time and she still found herself feeling alone and close to tears before she slept. Nevertheless, her schedule of operational visits helped to remind her that there were many people whom she could call on for support.

*** *** ***

A month later, one team leader made a call on her while she was on duty and asked for a private conversation. Leaving the bridge under the command of her helmsman, Ellen led the way into her standby room. Her visitor cut straight to the reason for asking for Ellen's time.

"Ellen, have I, or my team upset you? It is four weeks since you set up your process for visiting the different teams. Some have had two, if not three visits. Only one team has not seen you." Commander Tian sounded confused and rather angry. "I thought we got on back at Titan when you visited and I can't work out how I might have gone wrong."

Ellen stared at her friend and suddenly felt more emotional than ever before. "Oh, Jing, I am so sorry. Of course, you haven't done anything wrong. It's my fault, I have been avoiding you just because of how we were back when we were waiting for the probe to return.

That was the best of times, since I left Earth for space operations. Now it's different. I can't be in a relationship not while I am the Captain. Even seeing you in the department heads' meeting is hard."

"Ellen, that makes no sense. I'm not a crew member and my team doesn't even overlap the command structure. Are you my Captain? Of course, you are and I can tell you there are few who envy you and your responsibilities. Oh, I report to you in an administrative role, yes. But that doesn't mean you should miss out on the personal side of your life. And, my love, I don't want to miss out either. Remember, most of the rules were set when we were expected, eventually, to retire from the services and return home. Now that that is not an option, we must be able to solve this our way."

Her emotions brimming over Ellen moved towards her friend. Their embrace was hard but their kiss was cut short as Ellen's coms-link buzzed with the call of "Captain to the bridge - urgent." At the same time, her first officer opened the door. "Ellen, we have a problem..." his voice dying as he took in the scene before his face broke into a genuine smile. "Sorry you are needed now."

Leaving Jing behind and with only a swift flick of a hand through her hair Ellen moved quickly to her command seat. "Right. What is this problem?"

Lieutenant Yablon turned to her. "Sensors have identified a fast-moving object crossing our path. The safeties dropped us out of warp."

"Change course 45 degrees to move us aft of the object's trajectory. Will that be enough?"

"Diverting 45 degrees captain. We can't avoid its effects completely. Ma'am its fast but not that fast and it is large."

The first officer looked up from his board. "It is only about 15 klicks in diameter. Its relative velocity is around a hundred thousand klicks an hour. That is fast. Astronomy team has been alerted."

Ellen made a decision. "Full acceleration on n-space drive. Change course a further 15 degrees. Let's get as far from whatever it is as fast as we can. But I want a look at what it is. Have we no visual yet?"

"Only electronic imaging as yet. We are still a billion klicks away from it but it is very dense. Hence its gravitational drag. I project the nearest we will get is about one hundred million klicks. Captain, to trigger the alarms at this range it must be almost as dense as a neutron star!"

"Captain, I have Stephan Kolaski for you."

"Put him on speaker, Lieutenant."

"Captain, the object must be a neutron star. You need to get us away from it as fast as you can."

"One moment, Stephan. Helm, can we go to warp safely?"

"For a few seconds, Captain, but only a few. And it would be risky."

"Do it, warp one, three seconds. Current heading, now."

"Warp one, three seconds, ma'am."

Silence fell on the bridge as the seconds passed and the ship shuddered with the sudden changes in engine power. To an obvious sense of relief, the screen, after flickering, stabilised back showing an n-space sight.

"Distance to star now about five hundred and seventy million klicks, close point three hundred and fifty million. Is that good enough Stephan?" John's voice was a little edgy.

"It should be, commander. The mass of the star is around twice that of the sun. Before we went back to warp there was a chance that we would be pulled into orbit and I am not sure that we would have had the power to reach escape velocity. Bravely done, captain. And thanks for acting without doubting my advice." Stephan's voice reflected the warmth of having his recommendation acted on without question. There was applause in his background as the rest of his team listened in.

"Stephan, thank you for the warning. I guess you and your team will look to make the most of being in close up with that star. When you have a moment, I'd appreciate your view on how such an object might have cut across our course. We were no longer expecting to pass by any system before our target."

"Certainly, Captain."

"John, while we are still in n-space either you or I should be on the bridge at all times. Get some rest. We'll rearrange shifts – six hours on, six hours off. Normal spells for everyone else."

"Aye, Captain."

In the event Ellen's caution proved unnecessary and three days later, following a course change to bring the Einstein back on to its target bearing, warp drives were engaged and the neutron star vanished into the rear.

***   ***   ***

From that time their captain's approach and spirit could be seen to have improved and life on the bridge and for its officers was easier.

25. Horror in the sky

Seven months after leaving Centauri the Einstein approached its initial target system, HD75289. Five light years out, Ellen ordered a reduction in their velocity to warp one to allow the various research teams to get a view of the system before it was necessary to risk dropping into n-space.

She had researched the limited information available on the system before deciding that she needed a detailed briefing by Alejandro, Stephan and their team.

That meeting started with more information about the neutron star which, Stephan explained, was not something new in itself. There had been several spotted by the larger telescopes back on Earth and it had been postulated that these wanderers were remnants from supernovae events involving binary systems. As the supernovae collapsed the companion star might strip enough matter away to avoid a black hole forming. The resultant neutron star could then be "thrown" out of the system. Difficult to spot, their encounter had been a chance event.

"In summary then we should be alert, as we were, but repeating the meeting is not that likely." Stephan concluded.

"Thanks, Stephan. Any questions?" Ellen turned to her team of specialists and there being none, then asked

Alejandro to talk about the system they were finally closing in on.

He explained that the star had been identified as having an exoplanet early in the twenty first century although this was a gas giant orbiting so close that it completed an orbit in less than four days. Initially studies had indicated that the system had no other planets. Later analysis of the data then suggested the possibility of earth sized planets further out and this had led to the choice recommended when en-route to Centauri.

"How soon will we know if that later research was right?" Alan could not help but jump in.

"We are studying the system now. No success yet but it is early in the process. The team are scanning a large volume of space and, of course, any planets might be on the far side of the star. I should add that we have found the gas giant orbiting close in. It is a little smaller than originally calculated but would appear to have a larger solid core than usual for a gas giant. As soon as we find any other planet or planets you people will be the first to hear."

Three weeks later, with the Einstein now less than a light year out, came the news all were hoping for. Two planets had been found, both in the goldilocks zone and both with atmospheres. The good news was tempered a short while later with the added information that the atmosphere of the smaller one contained fatal levels of cyanide gas. However, the other planet was hopeful. Although larger than the Earth with a gravity level of 1.1G, the atmosphere appeared to be a close match with Earth's being 24% oxygen and 74% nitrogen with only minor levels of trace elements. The bonus was that there was evidence of significant amounts of water present and no apparent sentient life. Certainly, the surveys had found no evidence of industrialisation nor had comms picked up any radio noise.

While the astronomers and exo-biologists had been hard at work, the bridge team had also been active looking for any evidence of alien life off-planet. Their surveys had proved positive in that they could find nothing to suggest that the system had been visited by aliens either in the past or present.

Having listened to the various reports, Ellen took the decision she had hoped would be possible and as they reached what had become known as the warp perimeter of the system.

"Helm, cut warp drives. Switch to n-space drive at six tenths. Course to intercept planet 3."

As her helm officers acknowledged the order, Ellen went to a ship wide channel to announce the proposed plan. She finished with a warning.

"We know very little about the system, despite the excellent work carried out by our various teams. Therefore, we will be taking it steady as we close into the orbit of planet 3. You will need some patience as arrival will not be for another month. Captain out."

Ellen and her team could almost hear the muted sigh from around the ship but patience had become an essential for everyone and there were no negative comments made. At least not anywhere that a crew member might overhear!

Despite that, the month passed quickly, with data flowing in from the sensors and a number of fast probes authorised by the command team, many of the research teams were fully occupied and volunteers from non-specialist areas were gratefully given opportunities to help.

Typically, it was one of those volunteers that spotted the big news. Planet 3 was inhabited by different lifeforms. Herds of animals were found on the larger landmasses and flocks of bird like creatures could also be found.

Einstein slowly spiralled into orbit and the sensors went into overdrive. Two days later Ellen authorised a flight into the atmosphere to collect air samples. Carrying a biologist and a chemist she agreed that Lieutenant Yablon should pilot the lander.

"No risks, Liu. Stay above 3,000 metres until we have the chance to analyse what you collect. And full protective space suits to be worn."

"Aye, captain. We'll play it safe."

An hour later the lander slipped out of the docking area and dropped towards the planet. Following a shallow descent, the vehicle took an orbit to reach the outermost layers of the atmosphere. The regular radio checks were then breaking up as the ship heated up with air resistance. The signal blackout lasted a short while before Liu's voice came on-line again.

"We're in clear air. There is a little turbulence here. We are at 15,000 metres and starting our descent to 3,000. Beginning data collection and transmission. The guys are working on collecting air samples every 1,000 metres. Over the water at present heading for the major landmass. Should cross the coastline in 15 minutes. All systems nominal."

"Carry on, Liu. We are listening in."

As the lander continued its descent, the first samples were being analysed on board and confirmed the initial orbital studies. The air was mostly as expected except that there was a surprisingly high level of carbon monoxide amongst the trace compounds and elements, amounting to almost 2% of the total mix. The biologists and their colleagues were mystified by this as there appeared no reason for its presence.

The lander's descent continued steadily down to 4,500 metres when Liu's deadpan reporting changed to reflect a level of excitement.

"Now dropping towards 4,000 metres. There is a flight of birds coming in from behind us. They are amazing. Clearly birds but shaped more like pterodactyls, long necks and totally black. Some of them are even higher than we are!"

"Birds at that height? There was nothing on Earth that could have got near that height unless they were in the major mountain ranges. They must be predators of some form." The head biologist sounded stunned and concerned.

"Liu, watch out for those birds. How big are they?" John reacted to the concern heard from the biologist.

"Very large. Oh my god, they're huge!" Liu's voice echoed her amazement. "They weren't as near as we thought. Somehow the radar didn't give us accurate measurements. They must have been," she hesitated as she made a mental estimate, "two or three kilometres back instead of a few hundred metres. They're fast as well. Closing on us. I'm slowing our descent."

Ellen suddenly interrupted. "Get out of there, maximum thrust! Now!"

"Climbing now." There was a sudden thud over in the background. "Two of the birds have landed on us! My god they've broken through the roof! I don't believe it. Their beaks! They've got Dennis! They are ripping us apart. We're going down!" Liu's terror could be heard even as she fought to fly her damaged craft. "Sorry,

Captain I can't keep control! They cut Dennis in two. Oh god, Mo!" Mohammed's scream was cut off instantly and the Einstein's sensors could see the lander in a crash dive. Liu's voice then came back on with surprising calmness.

"Tell Rich I loved him. Hitting self-destruct before they get me. Maybe I'll take a few with us."

The bridge crew watched on, in horror, as the lander exploded, releasing all the power of its fuel cell. The expanding ball of heat and lightning engulfed dozens of the "birds". Most were destroyed but to the surprise of the on-lookers some simply spiralled away trailing smoke and gliding towards the land.

"How could any survive the effect of the fuel's heat? Get Megan Piper and her team working on it." Ellen's shock could be felt across the bridge.

"Captain, one of the earlier probes is in range of the area where the damaged birds are landing. There is a herd of animals nearby. They are stampeding towards the birds! That's incredible they're more like pterosaurs and they are feeding on the hurt birds."

The feeding was not one way. As the probe was remotely brought to a hover and the scene unfolded. Even the injured birds gave a good account of themselves and in short order another flight of fit birds took advantage of the distraction to attack land creatures, picking them up with claws that could rip through even the apparently thick skins with little resistance. Then, to add to the carnage, a second species of flighted creature was seen flying from the opposite direction. A fraction of the size of the first group they were clearly able to cause significant damage with large numbers swarming on the larger birds bringing them down while apparently eating them in mid-flight.

The bridge team continued to stare with undisguised awe, the emotional impact of the loss of the lander and their colleagues suppressed for the moment. As they watched the picture shuddered. Ellen reacted quickest.

"Full power to the probe now! Get it into orbit!"

"It's reacting slowly, captain. It must have creatures gripping it. Or they've damaged it already." The helm officers were struggling with their controls.

"I don't care, get them into vacuum. Let's see what they are made of." Ellen's temper showed in her tone.

"Doing our best, ma'am. Maximum thrust, climb rate increasing. Altitude 4,000 metres, 5,000. Leaving atmosphere. Adjusting course to orbital stability."

"Keep it at least 500 kilometres from us until we know more about these killers. Long range sensor analysis as soon as the probe gets close enough."

An hour later as the probe came into range of the Einstein's cameras the sight on the main screen showed that there was a single bird still locked to the vehicle. A bird as large as the probe itself. Other damage confirmed that a second creature must have been attached but had either lost its grip or deliberately let go. As they watched the bird appeared to try and detach itself even as its body started to distend in the vacuum. It failed in its efforts although the probe was suffering more damage as the creature's death throes caused gouges in the outer skin. Finally, the stomach could be seen to split and the innards spilled out across the probe and into the space around.

"I need two volunteers for an EVA in hardened suits." Ellen's voice delivered her concern that the risk to the Einstein was not yet over and a decision not to allow the probe to dock until they were happy that any risk had been totally removed. Then her careful approach was endorsed as their attention was drawn back to the screen in time to see the external skin of the probe start to dissolve. "What the hell could cause that?" she continued.

John's order overrode her question. "Helm, full power to the probe, get it further away. Send it back into the atmosphere." Turning to Ellen. "Whatever that substance is, it looks as if the fuel cell is at risk. We can't take a hit of that power this close, even if those creatures could."

As the probe started to enter the atmosphere it started to break up and, with a suddenness that left those watching breathless, it exploded as the fuel cell's containment fields failed. Ellen instinctively flinched but the probe was now a quarter of the way around the planet and the Einstein was protected from a direct hit.

The remaining probes were safely retrieved as the planet continued to revolve beneath them. With the urgent activities now over, the bridge crew could release the overriding feelings of loss. Ellen called in the standby crew to take over and allow those on-duty to take time to recover. For her there was the sad work of talking to those linked with the lander's team. Liu's boyfriend Richard was known to Ellen and that made the process more of a struggle than the same conversation with Mohammed's parents, who were members of the bio team. Dennis Tyler was one of the few people on board the Einstein to have no relatives and no known relationships, beyond those of his professional colleagues.

The following day a service was held in memory of the three lost. Ellen spoke at length about each of them but her summary was simple.

"We are all in a strange place and the loss of our friends reminds us that there are dangers all about us. In our hunt for a new home there will be the need to take risks. Our colleagues knew this and we should remember them with pride."

∗ ∗ ∗   ∗ ∗ ∗   ∗ ∗ ∗

The research teams worked flat out in an effort to understand the planet below them. Much of their findings were inconclusive but the overriding recommendations confirmed the expected outcome. HD75289d was not the planet for humans.

With disappointment the major feeling on board the Einstein headed away from the planet and its star. Now the astronomers suggested that a binary system some thirty light years away would be worth investigating.

"The two stars orbit each other every 140 odd years and while the larger star would not support any planets in habitable orbits the smaller is similar to Sol and is worth a look."

Five days later they engaged the warp drive and the Einstein set out on its two-month journey.

Routine again settled onto the crew while the physicists continued to muse over the apparent impossibilities of creatures with the power to rip a spacecraft to shreds and to withstand the heat of a fuel cell explosion. The only explanation was a subtle development of all the species from a reptile base to a further state of the dinosaur model, developing defensive abilities against other animals but how remained imponderable.

∗ ∗ ∗   ∗ ∗ ∗   ∗ ∗ ∗

As time passed the development of crew and associated people continued with the junior crew members preparing to be tested in various aspects of their abilities to make the next step.

In the second week John found himself woken by repeated sobs from Judy.

"Judy, what is it?"

She turned towards him. "I'm sorry, John. I didn't mean to wake you. It's Liu. She was such a good friend to me and she's gone." The tears returned. "She's gone and all for nothing."

"Judy, my love, let it out. She was a friend to all of us and we lost her but not for nothing. We didn't know what was going to happen but that saved us all. So, it wasn't for nothing. Without that loss we might have dropped many more people down before we found out about the wildlife. Liu would have gone even if she had known of the risk, that is what we do. What you might have to do. What I might need to do."

"But I'm only an ensign, I won't have to lead the way, like you."

"You won't be an ensign for much longer though, will you? You're ready for the final stage now." John's confidence could be heard in his voice.

"Oh, John. What is the use of it all? We're never going to find a new home." Judy's despair brought her to more tears.

"Judy, of course we will find a new home. Only three systems and we have already found two planets capable of sustaining human life. That the second wasn't suitable for mere humans, well it just shows that not all planets will be available to us. The first, in Centauri, was too close to Earth. Even the aliens might reach it in seven or eight years. We will need as much time as possible to settle our new home and build the defences to ensure that another Earth doesn't happen again."

"You really believe that, don't you?"

"Yes, it's just a matter of time. Now come here, let's dry those tears away and, well ...." Judy rolled over and the current situation was forgotten for a little time.

The next morning, as they prepared to take over their bridge roles, Judy suddenly asked. "John, what did you mean, "I'm ready for the final stage"?"

"I meant that you have been put forward for promotion. It won't be my decision nor directly Ellen's though she will have to confirm the recommendation. In a few days, I expect. You just need to be a little patient. Oh, and keep this to yourself, Molly will be having her position in engineering confirmed as well. Now we need to move."

They did move after John extricated himself from the hug and kiss planted by a much happier Judy.

Later that day, Ellen on one of her duty tours stopped by the physicists' area. She did not expect to hear any news of positive progress on the analysis of the creatures being shared with the biology section but she had the opportunity to chat to Megan and Alan in a quiet corner and warn them that their girls were both going to receive good news the next day.

"Keep it to yourselves but I wanted you to know and, in case anyone comments, I have deliberately not been directly involved in their progress and the recommendations come from their immediate superiors. Even John has had nothing to do with it. Not that we are surprised but given our relationships it was important that we distance ourselves as far as possible."

Megan's smile was tempered with a slight frown. "You know about Molly? Perhaps not, she had kept it quite private. She had a boyfriend, Dennis. He was on the lander. She has been very low. She blames herself for losing him, it seems she encouraged him to volunteer to be the chemist on board. Will she be able to stay in engineering with this promotion? She has set her heart on finding a way to strengthen the landers to avoid a repeat."

Ellen grimaced. "And Judy's distraught over Liu Yablon. Poor Molly, she will get over it but I know how she must feel. Her promotion will be to Senior Ensign, Engineering. She will not be moving unless she asks for a move, don't worry."

"Damn it, Ellen. It's so easy to forget how you must be feeling over the whole event. Trying to work out how we can avoid such a disaster at the next planet, how we might have avoided it happening anyway. Am I right?" It was Alan's turn to frown.

"Up to a point, they were the first of my people I have lost and it hurts but our training warns us of that pain being a part of command. I just have to do as you say and accept it as a part of our journey, I guess. Jing has been taking the brunt of my emotions though, I don't know what I would do without her."

"I haven't met Jing, other than in the heads of staff meetings and even then, only across the room so to speak. Maybe we can get together after the promotions are confirmed." Megan said. "Now I think Scott wants to talk to you. We will see you later."

***　　***　　***

The following day, six of the Einstein's crew had their promotions announced. The hard part for Ellen was interviewing each of the three candidates who had missed out all for different reasons. Encouraging them to carry on and look to satisfy their seniors in the areas where shortcomings had meant that promotion was not yet appropriate. The easy bit, before the little ceremony to award the relevant insignia to each successful individual, was the meeting, in her ready room, with Judy.

She opened the conversation with a surprise. "Congratulations, Lieutenant Piper."

Judy was startled. "Lieutenant? Surely not. I'm only an Ensign?"

"Are you questioning your Captain's knowledge?" Ellen's smile made it clear that she was not angry at being questioned. "Judy, we need a new Lieutenant and the recommendation came from every section you have worked in. You are ready for that move and no-one else is, at the moment anyway. Just to reassure you, the crew numbers are somewhat unbalanced with too many Ensigns and not enough Senior Ensigns so someone was going to have to make the leap and I am so glad that it is you."

"I, I, thank you, Ellen." Judy stuttered. "Nobody told me this."

"Not even John? No, thinking about it, he would be even more careful. Now you might be less happy about your new role, given recent events. You will be taking over as a member of the helm team. John has told me about your feelings for Liu. It may help to know that it was she who suggested you were ready to take over from her. She was moving over to engineering before the loss of the lander."

"I will make sure she would have been proud."

"Good, now you may want to talk to your sister. I don't think you have had the chance since the loss, have you? I know she has been lost in her own research."

"I haven't seen her. We've texted but that's all. Why?"

"Her boyfriend was on board the lander. Dennis Tyler?"

"Oh no! Mom and Pop didn't tell me. Oh Molly! And I was distraught over the loss of Liu. How must she be?"

"Best to get down to engineering, you've got time before the ceremony and she'll be there too."

Judy made her escape, but not before giving Ellen a smart salute that she returned with another smile.

***   ***   ***

Einstein continued on its way with nothing to break the process of research and development. More effort being put into strengthening the different craft that would be used in planetary operations in the future. Molly led the project team despite her youth. Her knowledge of materials learnt from her father made her the obvious choice and some progress was being made. Their problem was that the attempts to identify what the creatures were made of were still hitting a brick wall.

A second engineering team had made advances, with the aid of Alan's team's, in defensive weaponry. Using exotic fuel in small quantities they had managed to produce warheads capable of significant damage. The main issue centred on producing enough fuel. The development of a particle accelerator small enough to be built on the Einstein with the ability to still manage the velocities required was simple in theory. In practice finding strong enough materials was less so.

Two weeks and seven light years out from their target system the astronomers got very excited. There were two planets orbiting the smaller sun. The possibility was that one might be within the goldilocks zone. The second planet might also be in the zone but was a gas giant somewhat larger than Neptune.

"So, what you are saying is that there is a possibility of a habitable planet?"

"Yes, but we can't be sure yet."

"Right." Ellen continued. "Let's assume that the smaller planet is habitable. The question is, this sun is in orbit around a second star, someone said an orbital period of 142 years. So, how far in AUs are they apart? How close would the planet come to the second sun? What would be the effect on climate and habitability? I need answers as soon as possible."

"We can't be sure without closer examination. It'll take time."

"Find out. I want to know the odds for a sustainable settlement." Ellen's exasperation was clear. "Assume that it is habitable at the present time. Extrapolate if you have to."

"We'll do what we can." Alejandro did his best to placate the captain's mood.

The Einstein continued to close with the system. As they approached the warp barrier, Ellen called a meeting of her officers with the specialists, asking for a report on the planetary structure. It was not good news. The smaller planet's orbit was not circular. It seemed that the gravitational effect of the larger star had distorted the orbit into an exaggerated ellipse. The orbit thus took the planet away from its parent star which meant that, as far as could be confirmed, there would be a severe winter lasting more than half the orbital period. A sustainable settlement although not impossible was not realistic. The current orbital period meant that the winter was now starting and temperatures were already falling to more than 100 degrees below zero.

∗ ∗ ∗   ∗ ∗ ∗   ∗ ∗ ∗

"So, we move on. Where to now?" Ellen's disappointment was tangible.

Alejandro paused before giving an answer. "There are no more known planetary systems within three hundred light years. At least none had been identified from Earth in this direction. I would suggest that we change our current bearing to one toward the galactic centre. I don't mean that we look to reach that but there are possible stars in the Hyades cluster some fifty to seventy light years from here. I cannot guarantee that there will be suitable planets but we will give ourselves multiple chances with only short journey times between the various stars. The cluster itself contains a large number of very young stars but also older ones which would be our best bet."

"Why the older stars?" John asked.

"The younger ones are mostly blue white and hotter. Any planets may be too young to have developed ecosystems capable of sustaining life, apart, perhaps, for bacterial levels." The voice was not immediately recognised by Ellen then she realised that it was Hannah Newton, one of the planetary biologists. Usually a little quiet and reticent individual, the subject was obviously her forte. "It might still be worth having a look if it could be done without using up too much time. But a viable planet would be an exception to the rule."

Having given the order to change course, Ellen started thinking. Then she took two actions, firstly asking Alejandro and Stephan to provide a detailed map of the cluster, including measurements of the individual warp zones, and then making a ship wide announcement which finished.

"The only planet that we might have settled is entering a winter that will last for the equivalent of twenty months or 70% of its year. For half that time the temperature will fall to more than 150 degrees below freezing. A sustainable settlement will sadly not be viable. We are therefore moving on to a star cluster about five months travel time away. That cluster holds a significant number of stars that may have planets. I know that this is not the best news but we must continue to travel in hope. We do know, now, that potentially habitable planets are not uncommon."

Following the receipt of the map, which the astronomy team provided with multiple caveats as to its accuracy, Ellen summoned her tracking and helm teams together and gave them a task.

"I want you to develop a routing that would allow us to pass close by as many of the stars without dropping out of warp. That will limit our search time and reduce the number of systems we need to visit individually. Focus on the older stars and give them priority. I don't need to say that we need a safety margin and some of the stars in the cluster are less than two light years apart. You have two months to come up with an answer."

That task was to occupy the team for most of that time both on and off duty for several weeks before they were able to tell Ellen that they had a reasonable answer. When she questioned the apparently odd start the answer was even more surprising.

John had reviewed progress from time to time and explained. "To get the best overall solution we need to move above the ecliptic of the cluster. It's a bit of a misnomer since we usually use the term to refer to the shape of individual systems rather than the periphery of a globular cluster. But it will allow a high-speed pass around most of the cluster snaking back and forth. In effect we will try to orbit the cluster in a spiral. That covers around half of the stars before we need to slow down and enter the cluster itself."

"How long will it take?"

"Assuming we do not stop at all, around nine months before slowing. Once we are in the cluster it would be unwise to travel much above warp one and we may need a further year to complete the survey."

"How many stars will we be passing on that first sweep?"

"Around eight hundred will be close enough to provide useable data. There are close to three thousand stars in the cluster but more than half are young blue white stars so we have concentrated on a route that allows us to view mostly Sol-type stars. We can't sensibly complete a full orbit of the cluster. That would take six or more years even at warp three."

"Well done, now we have some time before we need to adjust our trajectory. Please have the route checked by the astronomy team and, I suggest, ask for a few volunteers to review it. While I am happy enough, we should take the opportunity to get some outside input. Thank you all."

The added input did lead to minor changes to the routing but as Ellen had expected these were not material.

26. Danger in Hyades

Two weeks out from the cluster they adjusted course to start a spiral sweep around the outer "northern" edges of the cluster. With passive sensors on full alert and telescopes fully operational the ship and its people were on edge hoping for an early result.

Three months later they had passed by no less than twenty planet bearing stars, including five blue white star systems. Two of the latter went against the perceived view that these stars would be too young as there appeared to be super-earth sized planets with oxygen atmospheres in both.

Seven stars turned out to have smaller binary companions which had not shown up in the original surveys both from Earth based observatories in the past nor from the Einstein's own teams. Alejandro had explained that from Earth it was likely that they would have been seen as separate while his own team's examinations had not had enough time in which to find such binaries except for the thirty or so already known systems.

Given the balance between time needed to complete a spiral course and that to switch and examine each system, Ellen decided to carry on with the initial survey and her decision proved right almost immediately when an outlier amongst the stars on the edge of the cluster proved to have a complex system with, at first check, no less than eleven planets. As they could drop out of warp on a course that would take them through the system in good time without significant loss of time overall, she made the decision to carry out a detailed survey of the planets that appeared to be in the goldilocks zone. Two days later Einstein dropped back into n-space for the first time in many months.

Even as the ship started forward on its n-space engines the proximity alarms went off.

"Emergency manoeuvring. Secure yourselves." Judy's voice rang out around the ship as she and her colleague fought to take them clear of a cloud of planetary debris. Despite their best efforts the ship rang to the sound of multiple impacts and for several minutes the ship rocked about. Most of the crew, with their training had reacted to her warning quickly but there were many around the ship who were thrown around before they could grab hold of supporting items.

Gradually the impacts reduced as the Einstein pushed free of the cloud and its movement stabilised.

Ellen had managed to remain in her seat but there were two of the bridge crew who had not been as lucky and colleagues rushed to assist them.

"Medic to the bridge. Damage reports quickly everyone. Helm, why did we not have more warning?"

"Not sure, Captain, but possibly we ran into a meteorite cloud. The cloud's intrinsic velocity must have been high enough that it was not within our sensor range until we dropped out of warp. We have pulled out of the system's ecliptic and are checking for more debris." Neil, Judy's colleague, paused and then gasped. "If sensors are correct the cloud is huge. Ma'am, we have been lucky. Sensors are showing three or four bodies the size of asteroids. If we had collided with one of those, I'm not sure the ship could have survived and I don't know why the lateral sensors didn't trigger a warning before we dropped out of warp."

"Could we have gone straight back into warp?"

"Not on the heading we were on," said Judy, "our evasive turn would have allowed that, if necessary, but we were too close to the warp critical edge of the system before that turn. We may have to allow more room next time we approach a star system."

"I agree, we should drop out of warp at least a light hour further out."

Damage reports flowed into the bridge and Ellen was glad to hear that the main ship had suffered little or no damage with the shields having absorbed most of the impacts. One of the warp tori had been hit by a larger body and had suffered what amounted to a significant dent. Engineering were already getting ready to undertake an EVA to inspect this and ensure that their warp capability had not been impaired.

The medical teams were able to confirm that except for a few broken limbs there had been no serious casualties, though most people were shaken by the event. Internal damage was limited mostly to spilt drinks and food spills in the kitchens.

The surprising news was that the astronomers already had an answer for the existence of the multiple bodies. The cloud actually appeared to encircle the system at roughly the same distance from the star as Saturn was from Sol.

"Captain, we believe it is the local equivalent of the Oort cloud back in the solar system. Only much closer to the primary and much denser. In warp we would have expected to pass through this further out, not enough mass to affect us and then well behind us as we re-entered n-space. This far in is odd but it may simply mean that the system is younger than Sol and the cloud has not yet been pushed further out by the solar wind."

With the engineers wanting time to check the warp torus, Ellen decided to continue towards the inner planets, with her team on full alert for any more unpleasant surprises. She then tasked the astronomers and planetary scientists to look for any other anomalies.

As time passed the Einstein moved carefully inwards passing a gas giant which was much like Jupiter. The planet had four moons, two of which were almost the size of the Earth. Close examination showed no atmospheres.

"That is another surprise," Alejandro told Ellen, "moons of that size ought to have an atmosphere of some sort. Extreme conditions yes but these are also surprisingly large bodies. I am bemused, I must say."

"And the two planets further in?"

"Ellen, they look promising but we must take care to carefully examine them from orbit before landing or risking humans. I still wonder that we didn't see the potential problems last time."

In due course they entered into orbit around the first rocky planet. Even as they cut engines it became apparent that the atmosphere would have been breathable if it had been denser but it proved to be very thin being more like the Martian atmosphere or Earth at 20,000 metres. Sadly, they left orbit and moved on to the second body, orbiting at about 0.9AU out from the star. Two small moons orbited the planet.

"Will it not be too hot?" was the question posed. The answer was again promising. The primary was smaller than Sol and not as hot. The closeness appeared to be offset by the lower energy output of the star. Once again Einstein moved into orbit.

For the second time in their voyage, the planet offered hope that they might have found a new home. Similar to the Earth in many ways with mass such that, although the planet was slightly larger, its gravity at ground level was almost identical at only a little above that of Earth at 1.05G, a difference that humans could easily handle. The atmospheric pressure was also amazingly similar to Earth's and had an oxygen/nitrogen mix readily breathable. There was great excitement growing across the Einstein as everything being observed increased the apparent match for humans. A Shangri La as was suggested. There was one question that was baffling the scientists. Why could they find no evidence of life other than vegetation.

"We have an oxygen-based atmosphere with some level of carbon dioxide. We have oceans or seas and rivers. There are mountains and forests and plains which appear to contain grasses and other elements of vegetation. There should be evidence of birds, mammals or reptiles. There is nothing!" Hannah sounded desperate for an answer. "I am worried," she continued, "this does not match any of our theories on how you can get such an atmosphere mix or such a variety of vegetation – why do we have no animals?"

John turned to Ellen. "Captain, we are missing something. There is no evidence of an extinction level event that might have wiped out any animal lifeforms nor are we finding anything in the atmosphere to suggest a problem. But everyone is shaken by the lack of lifeforms even more so than that those on our last attempt proved so dangerous."

Ellen asked a different question. "No animals or birds that we can see. Hannah, you didn't mention insects?"

"Scans from this height aren't very reliable but you are right we haven't seen anything."

After several hours of discussion Ellen finally decided to send a small un-manned probe into the atmosphere to collect physical samples of the air at high altitude. "If that proves clear we will follow up with a low-level probe. Make sure that the samples are kept in isolation and that the probe is sterilised before being landed in the dock. If there is anything lethal in the atmosphere, we do not want to give it a chance to get loose in the ship. In fact, see what can be done with remote sensors before we bring anything aboard."

"Isn't that a little over the top?" said a voice in the background.

"Maybe, but our job is the safety of the ship and everyone on board. We have an apparent anomaly here. For all we know something caused the extinction of every living thing except vegetation. So, we play it very safe. Right?"

"Aye Captain." The chorus of voices died away as the meeting broke up.

The probe launched a few hours later, carrying an open container, and rapidly dipped into the planet's stratosphere. As soon as the container was filled with air it was closed with a vacuum seal and then enclosed by a second container within the probe's interior. In a fast loop the vehicle climbed back into space moving swiftly into a course parallel to its parent ship.

As it closed with the Einstein several figures could be seen in EVA suits carrying various torches. The flames and also liquids were being poured on to the outer skin. Only after several minutes of this was the probe cleared to be driven into the docking deck. Once its engines had cooled, the container was extracted using remote handling and carefully moved into a secure lab usually used for handling fuel cells. The scientists started work moving samples into separate sealed bottles for extensive examination.

***　　***　***

"First Officer to the bridge. First Officer to the bridge."

John raced through the corridors to reach the bridge in response to the urgent call. Arriving he found Ellen bending over the communications officer looking at a series of texts scrolling across the screen.

"What on Earth?!"

"We have been hailed."

"Sorry Ellen. Did you say hailed?"

"Yes, tracking picked up a small satellite orbiting the closer of the two moons. Within a few moments we received a radio signal from it. When we did not respond it sent a second signal in the form of, well for want of a better description, a text message. Trouble is that there is no base upon which to translate either signal."

"I suggest we do respond with details of the Einstein and then the recorded first contact message."

"What good will that be," asked Ellen, and then realised what John was suggesting. "You think that the satellite might have translation technology? Better than ours, I mean."

253

John thought about it and then carried on. "We are concerned about there being no wildlife on the planet. Let's assume that that is a wise place to be. Could it be that the satellite has been left by another spacefaring race to attempt to keep us, and any other spaceship for that matter, from landing?"

Ellen turned back to her comms officer. "Ray, do that and then send a copy of the junior English dictionary and include the pictures it contains. It may assist the translation programme on board that satellite. John, why do I suddenly feel that the universe is actually crowded with advanced sapient races?"

"I guess that, if you think about it, we shouldn't be surprised at all. The aliens that attacked Earth, the civilisation that had existed on Centauri and now this. And don't forget the find on Mars, we accepted it as a source of the base material for fuel but there was a lot of questions over how it got there and one did centre on it being left by another race of spacefaring creatures. Either for us, if we advanced far enough, or maybe as a fuel dump for other ships."

"Yet none of these came to our solar system." Judy's interruption was almost plaintive.

"They may have, hundreds or even thousands of years ago. Maybe they are avoiding the region now because of that fleet of automatons. We know that the ships that attacked Earth were only a small part of those first seen by Hubble. How long they have been going and how wide their scope is we can only guess." John expressed his initial thoughts although Ellen felt he was holding back on some other more worrying ideas.

"Have we completed the transmission?"

The ensign sitting in on the comms station nodded, "Yes, Captain."

Ellen then asked for any linguists not on the bridge to attend the briefing room where they were shown the transmission and heard the original soundtrack. "Everyone. Ideas, please. What might these mean? I will be on the bridge."

Two hours later, Teri Larding asked to see Ellen privately, rather than on the bridge. A quick check through her background told Ellen that Teri was Irish and a real polyglot, fluent in twelve languages. Ellen called her to the ready room. Teri then explained that she believed that the transmission, which was on a repeating loop, amounted to a very short message in multiple languages.

"I doubt that we will get a response to our transmissions." Teri explained. "If I am right, the message is a warning not to land on the planet. The satellite has been left to provide that warning to any ship in orbit. It is saying something like "Stay away, do not land." and in at least seven languages."

Ellen's response was carefully worded. "Teri, why did you feel the need for a private meeting?"

"I don't think that my colleagues want to believe that this is what it means. All they can see is a home, a Garden of Eden."

"How sure are you?"

"I'm not sure, not one hundred percent anyway. All I have is that the message is very short and the planet lacks any wildlife and no-one knows why. What else can it be? Why would that satellite have been left? If not for that reason."

"I understand. Keep this to yourself for the minute. I want to hear from the analysts before we decide." Ellen rose to shake Teri's hand. "Thank you for your courage. You must be one of the younger members of the team."

* * *　　* * *　　* * *

Returning to the bridge Ellen asked for an update from the labs. The answer was unexpected. There was nothing that could be identified as being dangerous but on the other hand there was nothing positive either. No protective layer of ozone. The air was a mix of pure oxygen and nitrogen with only traces of any other gas. Despite this there were minute amounts of a bacteria which appeared to be dormant and that was a concern as it shouldn't be there.

Ellen asked why that was a problem and learned that a dormant bacterium was a contradiction. It should be either dead or active not asleep. How it could exist was a mystery. The scientists had decided that, if Ellen approved, they should expose a small animal to the atmosphere. A mouse was suggested.

In response to her question they confirmed that this could be achieved without any risk of contamination. Ellen agreed and the experiment proceeded. Thirty minutes later the lab team were in something of a panic. "Captain, we must eject all the air samples, get them off the ship!"

"Ellen, we can use a missile tube to do that," John said thinking quickly.

"Do it. Then I want to know why."

The head scientist came to the bridge in a very subdued mood to explain what had happened.

"We allowed the air sample to mix with air in a container with a mouse. For a few moments nothing happened. Then the mouse started to literally dissolve. It was eaten alive and reduced to a skeleton in less than ten minutes. A few minutes later most of the skeleton went. Whatever the bacteria are they were clearly heavily active and no longer dormant. We wanted no further involvement; it would have been too dangerous."

"I seem to remember that there was a flesh-eating bacterium back on Earth. Related?" Ellen managed to withhold her discomfort only with difficulty.

"Only in the sense that both did the same thing. On earth there were various counter bacterium that restricted the eater and although there were reported deaths, they tended to be one-offs. This appears to have had no predators and to have run wild. Unless someone could find a counteragent, which had a one hundred percent success rate in eliminating the eater and had no side effects the planet will remain uninhabitable for any form of higher life. This looks like someone fought a biological war with total success or worse."

"We were lucky that we were suspicious then. And now the message from the satellite makes sense. It really was a warning. My compliments to Teri Larding, she recognised the import of that message when others did not."

Later that day, Ellen met with John and Alejandro to discuss the way forward. There was no way that the Einstein could accelerate its own survey of the cluster. It had already been demonstrated that that would be unwise and Ellen did not intend to place the ship at more risk than was necessary.

John suggested that they make use of the warp capable probes both the manned and the automated original star probe. By splitting up the cluster into segments a broad survey might be completed in half the time or even less.

"That would allow us to eliminate the majority of the outer stars more quickly. We could reduce the main search for a suitable system by months."

It was not difficult for the astronomers to find a routing for the automated probe spiralling around the outer stars as had been planned for the Einstein which would now move more towards the centre to close with those stars too far to survey at speed. Dropping to warp one they would also launch a manned probe to search on the opposite spiral route.

In the end that initial survey would take nine months by which time over seventy percent of the outer star systems had been surveyed from less than a light year. Of the nearly four hundred stars, the systems with Earth type planets had been limited to less than sixty. Furthermore, half of these were doubtful targets as the planets seemed to fall outside the habitable zone.

Devising the next stage was not a straightforward matter since the targets were not in a simple line. In the end the decision was made to take the nearest stars first. There would be repeated disappointments as the early systems were to prove to have no habitable options. Despite that the Einstein and its associate craft continued the search.

27. Dissension

In the meantime, Ellen and her team had to respond to an increasing element of disturbance within the ship as some doubts about the reasons for not trying the last planet were being spread. It seemed that a few people believed that Ellen and her crew wanted to continue the voyage because being astronauts was their only field of experience.

As the personnel team explained, with four thousand people on board it was inevitable that among those with limited work to do, until a new home was found, there would be time to question decisions made at the top of the chain of command. Such questions were not always a bad thing but there had to be a semblance of justification. Ellen's best approach would be to defuse the concerns directly. Video of the events when they lost the lander and of the demise of the mouse should be shown. It might not stop any conspiracy theorists entirely but it would make it harder for them to obtain any more followers.

"I take it that you feel I would have been better advised to show them immediately after the events." Ellen commented.

"Captain, there was no right or wrong decision on how to handle the release of the videos. Especially the lander's last moments. Clearly many would not have wanted to see their fellows dying in such circumstances. Unfortunately, others have taken that decision as reason to question whether the events really happened. Bear in mind that for many years similar minds argued that man did not land on the moon in 1969 or that the later missions ever took place and they did have film of the events taking place."

"So, I am damned, whatever decision I might have made."

"Maybe but all you can do is to try and remind people as to why we are here."

Ellen started the process of visiting groups and showing the film of the events. She found it interesting that no dissension was shown to her personally even when she sought to get her story challenged.

Three days into the process she rounded a corner to find the two young Pipers in a screaming row with a young man Ellen did not, at first, recognise.

Judy was about to physically attack the man when Ellen interrupted, "Lieutenant Piper! Attention!"

Judy came to her senses and reacted accordingly but Ellen could see that the rage was still in her eyes and both she and her sister, who had also snapped to attention, were on the edge of crying. "My quarters, the three of you. Now."

"You can't order me around, I'm not crew." The young man shouted though he sounded scared rather than tough. "I'm going back to my mates and will tell them how even questioning your actions gets me beaten up."

Ellen calmly took a second look at him. "Your family are involved with hydroponics, aren't they? Its Paul Grey isn't it?"

He looked dismayed that she had recognised him and started to edge away towards a lift door.

"Well Paul. Let's be clear about two things. One: you haven't been beaten up by anyone let alone by a young woman. Secondly, you are on a spaceship and, as Captain, I do have the power to order you about, as you put it." As he hesitated, she continued. "Now you can attend my quarters now, voluntarily as you might wish to put it, or I will arrange for ship security to find you and arrest you. Now they have had very little to do this past year or so and will, no doubt, be delighted to have some real action."

"I'm not coming, I know what happens to those who go against you. They'll have to find me first." As the lift door opened, he jumped past two surprised people coming out and vanished from sight.

Ellen sighed. Activating her comm she contacted engineering first and then security. As she had said they had had little to do. Having to handle nothing more than the very occasional drunk this was new to them. At her instruction engineering had frozen the lift controls until it reached the lower deck. She then despatched a security team to the lift to extract Mr. Grey. After a moment's thought, she also contacted personnel and asked them to get the young man's father to come to her quarters.

On reaching her quarters she found the Pipers now very subdued. She decided to talk to them separately at first. Leaving Judy outside she took Molly through to her private office and asked her to explain as simply as she could exactly what had led to the confrontation.

Molly decided, rightly, that this was not an occasion for informality. "Captain, ma'am. He started it. He came up to us demanding how we could support you and then added that Judy had got her position by "sleeping with the boss". She was going to laugh that off but then he started demanding to know who had shot Liu Yablon."

"Pardon, did you say shot?"

"Yes, ma'am. He said that he had seen her body in the morgue and she had been shot in the head. He reckoned it had to be you or the First Officer. When Judy told him that he was a braindead liar, he said he would have been able prove it except they had moved the body. When I supported Judy, he laughed at me, slapped my face and called me a simpleton. That was too much for Judy and she went for him but you came around the corner and stopped it. I think that might be for the best. I think Judy might have killed him if you hadn't intervened, ma'am."

"Thank you, Molly, sorry, I should say Ensign Piper."

"Ma'am, Ellen. I would have reacted like Judy if he had mentioned Dennis, I really liked him and I wasn't ready to lose him. That man is a nasty person."

"I know Molly, your Mum told me you were very close. Even so I will not be able to ignore this, so you can expect to hear from your line superior in due course."

"Yes, ma'am." The youngster left Ellen looking subdued and more than a little upset.

"Lieutenant Piper, come in." Ellen's voice belied the formality of the summons but Judy was definitely as subdued as her sister, "Captain, ma'am. I am sorry you had to see that." were her first words.

"Apology noted, Lieutenant. Now perhaps you would explain exactly what led to you being about to assault another person."

Judy gulped and then told much the same story as Molly had except that it seemed there had been a part just before Molly had arrived on the scene.

"He first grabbed hold of me as I was leaving the rest rooms demanding the truth about how Dennis, Mohammed and Liu died and why Molly kept ignoring him when he had told her that they had not been on the lander. Then Molly came over. We were going to have some food together, and he started on about me and John and about a body in the morgue."

Her story tallied reasonably with that of Molly. Judy, however, emphasised that the death of Dennis had hurt her sister much more than people realised. As for her ignoring Paul Grey, well he was too ready to attack, verbally, the bridge officers for no reason. Molly would have had more sense than to get involved with him even if Dennis had not already won her heart. It was not the first time he had harassed her but it had to be the last or other crew members might get involved in defence of one of their own.

Ellen asked a few minor questions but knowing the two young women well had little doubt as to the veracity of their stories. Dismissing Judy, she gave a similar warning about discipline.

A short time later, the security team arrived with a dishevelled Paul Grey in handcuffs. "Sorry, Captain, we would have been quicker but Mr Grey was unwilling to come quietly." The lead officer grinned. "He seems to believe that you will have him shot and then dispose of the body with our help!"

"Right, well perhaps with his father here he will feel safe enough to not try running off again. Jorge, thank you for coming so quickly. Gentlemen, I think we can remove the cuffs now."

It was Jorge who spoke next, turning on his son, "Just what have you been doing to involve the Captain and her officers."

Paul, who had turned the same colour as his name, stuttered, "Nothing. I just asked two of them why they wouldn't tell the truth about Liu's death. This rubbish about flying monsters that could eat landers whole! Then the Captain came to arrest me. Just because I had seen enough to blow her story apart."

Ellen decided on a secondary approach. She summoned the ship's senior doctor and when he arrived at her rooms asked him to take them all to the morgue.

"Sorry, Captain, did you say morgue?"

"I did, Doctor. If you would be so good."

"Captain, I don't understand. We don't have a morgue. It has always been a concern for me, with so many people on board it is inevitable that sooner or later we will have a death and may need to carry out an autopsy. I have asked engineering to look into solving this potential problem before it arises and I know they are working on it. But there simply isn't a morgue at the moment."

"So, Lieutenant Liu Yablon's remains couldn't have been lying in it."

"Remains? She triggered the self-destruct on the lander. I doubt we would have found anything at all. Even if we could have accessed the crash site. The fuel cell heat would have destroyed the craft and its inhabitants leaving little more than soot particles."

"Thank you, Doctor. I am sure you have more urgent things to do than wasting more time here." Ellen turned to Paul Grey again. "Now you told my officers that you saw Liu Yablon's body in the morgue. Perhaps you would like to explain."

"Paul, you need to listen to the Captain and tell us what lies you have been spreading and more importantly why." Jorge interceded.

"The crew just want to extend the journey. They know that they would be surplus to requirements in a settlement. They're only good at being astronauts." He paused.

"Go on" said Ellen.

"We've seen three habitable planets and all you can come up with are wild excuses as to why they are no good. Centauri might arguably have been too close. Then we have giant flying birds that can destroy landers, I mean, destroy interplanetary capable craft? They can't expect us to take them seriously. Now we've got an "alien" warning coupled with a "dissolving" mouse when we could all see that the planet was an Eden. Flesh eating bacteria? Whoever heard of such rubbish. If we don't stop you the ship will carry on forever finding habitable planets and then reasons why we can't land on them and stay." Forced to pause for breath he looked indignantly at Ellen, challenging her to reply.

"Paul, believe me when I say that I truly wish that either of the last two planets could have worked for us. The first was, as I think you recognise, always going to be too close to the Solar System. The alien ships may have been able to get a line on our original path away from Sol. Enough anyway to make them follow us to Centauri. It might take them ten years or so but not much more and we would not have been able to mount an adequate defence in that short a time. The other two, do you really think that we would kill three valued people just to make an excuse not to land? I won't waste time on the third except to say that if we had not been so careful you would have died a horrible death alongside everyone else."

"Now you just tell us, no planets, no planets. Why should we believe you?"

"Because it is true, the nearest we have come to, in the last twenty systems, were super Earths. We might be able to handle 1.2G as humans but not 3G or 4G." Ellen paused as she pondered what should be done with the young man. Clearly his poisonous approach needed to be stopped but how? Then a thought occurred to her.

"Paul, how much of your science studies did you complete?"

"Erm, well most of them before Dad decided to take the family into space. It has been agriculture since then. I liked physics and maths most." The tone in his voice told Ellen that she had found a good answer.

"Jorge, your hydroponics team is going to be down one I'm afraid."

"Captain?"

"I am going to reassign Paul to the astronomy section. They are always complaining about the need for more eyes to analyse scans and so on." Turning to Paul, "Perhaps seeing the data for yourself as it comes in will encourage a change of viewpoint."

"If I must, I will give it a go," was the reluctant reply.

"One last thing, you owe two people an apology. Both of the Pipers lost close friends to the "birds" and you attacked them for defending the truth. That was uncalled for and, while I understand their response, you've also led them to both receiving reprimands and appropriate punishments. Now you can expect to hear from the astronomy section later today with your scheduled start time. This is an opportunity for you, don't waste it."

It was a subdued Mr Grey, who left ahead of his father, who stopped to thank Ellen for handling things the way she had. "He's not really a bad lad, just frustrated. I hope he will return your generosity well."

"Jorge, one point. I understand that he has been putting pressure on the younger Miss Piper despite her rejecting him. I would rather he hear a fatherly lesson in how to behave. If he doesn't stop it could have serious repercussions for him, ones I'd prefer to avoid."

In the following weeks it was noticeable that the levels of dissension did, in fact, reduce despite the various craft passing differing systems where the planets proved to be unattractive to human habitation. Too big, not enough atmosphere, too hot, or too cold. Despite the disappointment the dangers of getting things wrong seemed to have permeated through the ship.

28. Eden lost - again

Then came the news. A system that had been surveyed by the automated probe was going to be worth a closer look! The probe had been programmed to return to pre-arranged points to report findings back to its parent ship. System sixty-one was a G-type star with a number of planets including an Earth sized one in the heart of the goldilocks zone.

The planet in the habitable zone appeared to have breathable air and free water and Ellen, having reviewed the initial data, decided to divert the ship to the system in question, reprogramming the probe to take over the Einstein's original survey route.

Einstein dropped out of warp on the very edge of the system taking no chances of another meteorite swarm or an Oort cloud in the wrong place. Safely on the edge of the system and with sensors on full alert the ship eased its way inwards on half power.

The system had seven planets with three gas giants further out from the primary than Jupiter and its closest companions. There was a much larger gap in the system than that seen back in Sol with no apparent asteroid belt.

"You have to wonder what happened to the planet you might have expected to find in that gap." Ellen and John were discussing the data being collected.

"It does seem odd. The asteroid belt was often perceived as having been a planet that never formed or a planet destroyed even though there was no evidence of the latter. How our understanding of the solar system's structure might have worked without the belt is an interesting question."

As they moved closer towards their target the incoming data from the leading probe increased the positive news. A mix of land masses, extensive water, good oxygen/nitrogen mix in the air and no apparent negative elements. There were also some early indications of lifeforms both on land and in the water but no sign of any advanced civilisation.

Interestingly there were also two moons in orbit, both of sizes much like Deimos and Phobos.

"There was no sign of these in the original probe data, I wonder why?" Ellen thinking aloud before then asking the same question of Alejandro. His answer was not what she expected.

"The probe did see one moon but not the other. I don't know why but I have got the team working on that difference in data. There must be a reason and we need to understand it. As soon as we have an answer you will."

The lead probe continued to feed readings back focussing on the two moons and their motions relative to the planet. With the live data flowing in, the astronomy team worked like beavers to complete projections of the full orbits. Not forgetting the fact that one moon was apparently missing from the original data they double checked all the figures.

As their course took them close to one of the gas giants a separate probe was despatched on a close flyby orbiting the planet and its numerous moons. The data received as it skimmed the atmosphere was surprising.

Rather than predominantly hydrogen and helium there was a significant proportion of nitrogen, in fact the data indicated that more than 75% of the gasses at the top of the planet's atmosphere were of that element or nitrous oxide. The astronomy team were left bemused by a breakdown of the upper atmosphere which did not appear to obey the usual rules. It was only data obtained as the probe swung past the other side of the planet that suggested a reason for the inconsistency. Despite the size of the planet indicating a gas giant the atmosphere was less deep than normal. The solid core appeared to be huge, perhaps ten times as big as expected and was covered by liquid seas apparently a mix of water and acidic compounds several thousand metres thick.

"Now we understand how nitrogen could be so high in the atmosphere." Alejandro explained. "The atmosphere itself is surprisingly shallow."

More time passed and the Einstein closed into a distant orbit further out than the moons. At which point there was a further discrepancy in the data. To their surprise the second moon was missing.

"I don't understand, Alejandro. First, we have one moon, then we have two moons. Now we have only one moon?"

"I wish I knew, Ellen. We are trying to work out why."

With the planet's biosphere ticking all the right boxes, two landers were dispatched, one to fly low over the land while the second remained at altitude providing aerial protection.

Their initial mission proved that everything about the planet was as positive as could be hoped for and finally they were given clearance to land and collect samples of soil and water. Dropping down to land on one of the beaches it took just a little time for the teams to collect the samples plus a couple of fish found in the shallows. Finished they returned to their mother ship without mishap.

Ellen sat in her command seat almost holding her breath as did the rest of the bridge team. Finally, the news came in. Everything about the samples said that this was the Eden they had been searching for.

With spirits rising and plans already being made to choose landing sites the sudden warning that all was not well came as a shock. Ellen was forced to call a meeting of her senior team and the various heads of research. She began.

"In summary, all the initial research shows that the planet is suitable for us to settle on. There are no obvious dangers though we should always take precautions against the unknown. Now I am being told there is a significant danger to the planet. One that we cannot ignore. Alejandro, what is our problem?"

Alejandro looked downright miserable. "You know that the original data provided by the probe only showed one moon. The second probe found two moons. But when the ship arrived into orbit there was, again, only one moon and it was not the first moon but the second. I am sorry to say that we now understand why. In simple terms the first probe only saw one moon because there was only one moon to see. The second moon was seen at a specific part of the combined orbital structure of the planet and two moons."

Scott was astounded. "Are you saying that one moon was invisible? Or not there?"

"In a sense, it was not there. I admit I am struggling to understand the orbital mechanics of the planet and its moons but the analysis is definitive. Neither moon is in a stable orbit. In astronomical terms one or the other must be a recent capture by the planet. The trouble is that it has affected the orbit of what must have been the original moon such that both are now actually in orbits that are highly elliptical but also loop the planet in a circle before being slingshotted by the other to and from the planet. Again, this must have happened recently, perhaps as little as a thousand years ago."

"But why does this cause us concern? Erratic tides? Or what?" John demanded.

"As I said the capture of the second moon must have happened recently, at least in astronomical terms. This situation is not stable in the long term. In fact, it isn't even stable in the short term. One of my team has calculated that one of the moons will cross the planet's Roche boundary possibly within the next decade. For sure within a century."

"Roche boundary?" Ellen asked.

"The Roche limit is that point at which a satellite will break up under the gravitational stresses caused as it closes with its primary."

"How would that affect the planet? And the other moon?" John now looked worried as he posed his questions.

"The moon would at best break into smaller pieces forming a ring or rings. There would be significant meteor impacts. We don't know how it would affect the second moon. There seem to be two possibilities. Firstly, if it is at perihelion it could easily break up as well. If it is at aphelion, we aren't sure. We have never seen such a system so we are looking at theory. We have to warn you, though, that the worst-case scenario might see the second moon impact the planet in an ELE."

"And this could happen at any time? Why now? Just as we arrive?" Ellen was struggling with what she was hearing and the disappointment that it seemed to ensure.

Alejandro looked no happier. "We don't know. All we can say is that this will happen and probably in our lifetimes. If I had to give a reason, my best intuition is that the whole system is still relatively young and we know that the solar system in its youth suffered major calamities caused by planetary realignments. Remember one of the gas giants failed to match all that we believed was to be expected. Maybe this is just one of those events. A settlement would be at great risk and unlikely to have enough warning to escape the events we have forecast."

Ellen closed things with a final statement. "I guess that we must look to move on. I think that that means we really should look for systems that appear to be older and possibly more stable. Back to the drawing board everyone."

*** *** ***

As they left the room Alejandro called Ellen back.

"I thought you might like to know that the initial observations and deductions were the individual work of a certain Mr Grey. He has proven an invaluable addition to the team. Of course, we did check his work but it was wholly correct. I think that he was more disappointed than anyone but he may well have grown up in those few hours."

"Tell him I am pleased to hear that he has found a spot where he can contribute and a well done." Ellen may not have liked the message but to find that her earlier decision, on how to handle Paul Grey's issues, had proven well founded was satisfying.

***　　***　　***

As the ship slowly moved out of orbit and away from the primary, Ellen found herself faced with a challenge from a group of people, led by a member of the support teams, who were unhappy at not being involved in the decision to abandon the system as unsafe.

"We know that you convinced Paul Grey that your earlier decisions were correct even if they were questionable. We don't know how. This time it is clear that there was no reason to not land a settlement, all the data proved that the planet was a suitable place to settle. So, you tell us how you justify this decision. Why should you remain as Captain of the ship when your decisions have so clearly been wrong?"

If Ellen was shaken by such a challenge, and she was, she did not allow it to show in her answer. "Senor Parass, my job is to find a safe haven for the people on this ship, all the people, who may well be the only surviving human beings. We cannot be certain that the other starships will be successful, no matter how much we may pray that they are. As to me," she continued, "I will remain as Captain as long as my fellow officers consider that I am fit and able to command them. If you consider that it is right to challenge those decisions, I would suggest you talk to the relevant areas of expertise whose experience and knowledge we all rely on for good advice. In particular talk to the astronomy team about this latest decision to move on and abandon the idea of settling the planet we have just left. If they had not identified the problem and I had cleared a landing, then based on our best understanding of planetary orbital mechanics I would have condemned you or your children or, at best, your grandchildren, to the risk of the entire settlement being wiped out by natural events over which we would have had no control."

Senor Parass replied. "That is not enough. We should have been asked if we wanted to take this hypothetical risk. You can't make such a decision without consulting the people on the ship. We should have been able to vote on it!"

At this point John Lees, who had been an onlooker for the most part, intervened. "Senor, I would have thought that with your experience in the Navy you would have been fully aware that no ship is a democracy. You ask the Captain to consult with everyone and then allow a vote. That is not how things work and I think you know that. What does happen is that the Captain consults with her senior officers and the various heads of department where their expertise is appropriate. In this latter case the lead advisors were the astronomy team. Having taken that advice and input into account the final decision must be that of the Captain, and frankly, Senor, I don't envy Captain Bayman for one minute. She has a responsibility that few are capable of handling well and we should be extremely grateful that we have her as our Captain. Now take your group and think hard about how you can support her rather than undermining her. If you wish to have a briefing from the astronomy team on this last planet, or the biologists and medical teams on the previous decision please let me know and I will arrange it."

It seemed for a minute as if Senor Parass might continue the argument but some of those who had accompanied him interrupted his intention to speak again. One young woman effectively ended matters, for the time being anyway, by saying. "Captain, Commander. Thank you for your time. It is clear now to me, and I feel others here, that our complaints are inappropriate or at least that we should reconsider how we might feel better informed in the future. Despite this meeting and those challenges voiced by our colleague, I believe that we can concur fully with the Commander's comments as to the responsibilities of the Captain. It would be good if we could meet with the astronomy team so that we can better understand why the risks were considered too high."

John answered. "I will arrange for them to contact you, Senorita. We will ensure that any presentation is made available to all on the ship who may wish to participate. Now if we can move on, please. The Captain has been on duty continually for almost sixteen hours and needs some food and rest."

∗ ∗ ∗   ∗ ∗ ∗   ∗ ∗ ∗

The presentation did take place and, for the time being, the majority seemed to accept that the Captain and her crew were acting in their best interests. In private though, Ellen and John both agreed that they would need to keep a watch on things especially if finding a potential planet should be delayed.

* * *   * * *   * * *

The Einstein and her probes continued their journeys, criss-crossing the star cluster with little success.

That was not to say that there were no new discoveries. Binary systems dominated, some with planets but none that could be identified as habitable. The most disturbing scene was a system that involved a binary pair of stars so close that their coronas were linked with stellar matter being exchanged depending on the orbital position.

The astronomers were quick to point out that such pairings were not that rare though they usually involved a larger star feeding off a smaller companion or in reverse, a smaller, often a neutron star extracting matter from a larger companion. For two stars similar in size to orbit so closely suggested that the crowded nature of the cluster was the cause.

Despite the disappointment of another planet not suitable for settlement, there remained optimism that a suitable home was only a matter of patience and time. As the months passed and no such planets were found that optimism lessened.

29. Land Ahoy!

With the outer stars of the cluster finally surveyed and the probes back with the Einstein. Ellen and her team were forced to ask the question. Was it worth moving deeper into the cluster?

Alejandro outlined their position. The nearer to the centre of the cluster the closer together were the stars to each other and generally younger. Einstein would have to move carefully at no more than warp one and inevitably be forced to spend more time in n-space.

"Are you saying that we must leave the cluster to find a viable system then? We had hoped that there would be more than one option. Now it feels as if we are wasting time."

"Ellen, that may be the only answer. We have already carried out close surveys of more than nine hundred systems within the outer regions of the cluster. Long range surveys of the core stars aren't as accurate but there only a few older suns there anyway. A few systems seem to have planets which are possible targets but only a few. And we cannot be sure that they are viable."

"Alejandro, tell us. How long to reach those systems? And, if we decide to leave the cluster, where do we go next? And how long to get there?"

"They are still thirty light years or more away from us. Three months at best if we loop over the nearer stars and route from above the cluster. That would allow part of the journey at maybe warp three."

"Three months, OK. And the next target?"

"A set of stars fairly close to each other. Not a cluster but all are sol-type. They are forty odd light years away, the other side of a nebula. That will slow us as we can't be sure of the gravitational effects. I suggest that we allow six months." Alejandro paused. "Seven months from the other side of the cluster."

"I understand. We will need to consider those options. Thank you all." And Ellen ended the meeting.

Later that day she met with her senior crew to review the choice that they faced. After over an hour of discussion Ellen still did not feel ready to make a decision. Just as she had adjourned the session a voice that had been quiet throughout was heard against the general murmurs of the group as it broke up.

"Ma'am?" Ellen raised a quizzical eyebrow at Judy who reddened. "Sorry, Ellen, why do we assume that we mustn't exceed warp one in the cluster?"

Stopping the exodus from the room, Ellen responded. "How do you mean, Judy?"

"Are the distances so narrow that we can't steer our way at higher warp speeds? After all we can get within 50 AUs of a sol-type star and surely even in the heart of the cluster the stars are more than a light year apart. I am sure that your helm team can follow a route avoiding any stellar gaps less than, say, one light year. At worst we could slow when having to slip through such spaces."

"Let me understand, Judy. You feel you and your colleagues could thread a way at more than warp two?"

"Yes, I know I could and I am sure that they can as well."

The other helm officers agreed that they would be able to do so but warned that they might need spells in n-space to align some of the moves rather than trying sharp manoeuvres in warp.

"Right, thank you everyone. John and I have much to consider. We will get back together in, let's say, six hours."

Ellen and John continued their conversation over some food, focusing on the different time frames.

"We could just head away from the cluster and perhaps find a suitable system in maybe six months. That won't be popular but, if the cluster option fails, we are looking at around nine to ten months should we aim for the cluster systems. And we shouldn't forget that those time lines only cover the time in warp. We will need another week per system, possibly." John decided that he needed to act as devil's advocate to provide a private opportunity for Ellen to fine tune her thought processes. He continued. "On the other hand, we might find a cluster system in a matter of weeks if we are lucky. It's a balance between gaining three or four months or losing the same period."

"The cluster has demonstrated that Terran type planets do exist but viable ones are less so. Thanks, John. I need to think through everything before we decide."

A few hours later Ellen came to a conclusion. As had been said before the "buck stopped with her" and she, not without reluctance, came to a decision. Having freshened herself up she headed for the bridge.

"Captain on the bridge." The computer's voice alerted the bridge crew to her arrival but, as she had laid down from her first day, those present simply acknowledged her presence. John Lees stepped to one side to his station leaving the command chair free but Ellen ignored this for a moment speaking out to her team.

"As you know we are faced with different options at this stage in our search for a new home. Having considered the pros and cons I have decided that we will aim for those systems within the cluster that have been identified as possible targets. I will want us to minimise the time to reach the nearest and that will mean hard concentration on behalf of you all, especially those on the helm. The next few weeks will be exhausting. Given the pressures if you have a doubt as to your capability to complete a duty spell you must flag this to the senior officer on the bridge. Noted?"

A series of acknowledgements came back to her as her words struck home. Sitting down she gave the first of two orders. "Helm, take us to the edge of the cluster and then follow the planned route towards the far side. Warp two then once clear warp four." There were startled gasps from a number of people, the Einstein had never used warp four before. "Aye, Captain." chorused the helm officers as they took the ship into warp.

"Comms, department heads please." Following acknowledgement that she was speaking to all departments and areas within the Einstein, she explained their updated plans. Asking them to brief their own people, she also warned that there might be sharp changes of course which, even in a ship the size of the Einstein, might cause people to lose their balance.

Einstein accelerated on a course taking it away from the cluster at first before making a gentle curve back toward their target zone. Now cruising at warp four they passed by multiple star systems that had already been surveyed, before Judy, on duty as lead helm, suddenly cut their velocity to warp one turning to Ellen, who was in the command seat.

"Captain, there's an anomaly! According to my sensors there is a star, two light years ahead, which is not one of those we surveyed. Given where it is, we should, at least, have recorded its existence but there is nothing showing."

"Maintain course, Lieutenant. Comms, get me Professor Alvarez."

"Alvarez, here. Yes, Captain?"

"The star in front of us. How did we miss it first time around?"

"Captain, I don't understand. We shouldn't have missed any stars on the periphery. Captain, may I suggest we drop out of warp for a closer look?"

"Helm, n-space drive, three quarters power. Hold course. Passive sensors to maximum."

As Einstein dropped out of warp the star became clearer on the main viewing screen. Clearer but not totally so.

"Can we not get that into better focus?" Ellen demanded.

"Sorry, Captain. That is in focus. It would appear that there is a cloud of some sort between us and the star causing a misty effect on our view." John looked up from his own screen which showed a similar picture. "It seems that there is a thin nebula surrounding the star."

Time passed with nothing to break the monotony. Then Alejandro requested access to the bridge.

"Captain, we have reviewed the original data. As you know this region of the cluster was initially covered by the automated probe, before it changed course to enter the cluster itself. As it passed the star, we can see ahead the probe was actually already turning away from it and, we think, that as a result it misread the stellar type as a red dwarf. I believe that the nebula softened the star's brightness sufficiently to make this an understandable error."

"Have we not been reviewing the data collected by the probe?"

"We are doing so, Captain, but hadn't reached the data covering this area. I can only apologise."

"So, Professor, what do we have?"

"A G-type star, similar in size to sol. There appear to be planets though we can't be sure about suitability yet. The probe's data is obviously inconclusive."

"Right. Helm, warp three, hold course until we encounter nebula, then slow to warp one. Drop out of warp at your discretion."

"Aye, Captain."

A day later Einstein reached the nebula. With warning signals flashing the ship dropped out of warp briefly continuing on its n-space engines until the bridge team were satisfied that it would be safe to re-engage the warp engines to cover the remaining light-year and a half to the system.

Challenged to explain the nebula, the astronomical team struggled. As Alejandro explained there was no logical reason why it had formed between the star ahead and the rest of the cluster.

"We would have expected the pressure of the solar winds from those stars on this side of the cluster to have pushed it at least to the far side of the system. The local solar wind seems to have blocked it or maybe caused it."

"Could this affect the system in an adverse way?" asked John.

"I don't see how. The relative motions suggest that the system is orbiting the cluster at a different angle to the nebula which is moving away, slowly."

"Orbiting?" Judy found it hard to understand how the astronomers had discovered this.

"Yes, Lieutenant. We have accessed observations, made by the Hubble telescope, of the cluster. You must remember that the Hyades cluster is the nearest such phenomena to Earth and was the subject of a lot of work back on Earth. My colleagues have identified this star and using the observations over some eighty years, some before Hubble, are convinced that the star is on a path that orbits the cluster. I should add that it will take many thousands of years to complete that orbit! It is some eighty light-years from the cluster's core after all."

Einstein reached the warp boundary of the system and dropped back into n-space moving inwards to the system's star. Three planets were spotted almost immediately with two gas giants at distances similar to Saturn and Neptune back in the solar system, there was no Jupiter apparent at first but two rocky planets did orbit the sun closer in. As the ship approached the inner system two more planets were seen as their orbits brought them from behind the star. One orbiting so close that it could be seen to be transiting the star in only a matter of hours. The second planet in an orbit just under an AU from the star and in the heart of the goldilocks zone. The other two planets seemed uncannily equivalent to Venus and Mars, although both were further from the star than the second planet. The third planet's orbit came closer to that of the asteroid belt back in the solar system.

"Helm, adjust course for planet two."

With care, and an increasing optimism, they moved into orbit around the blue and white vista that reminded them, almost painfully, of Earth in a way none of the previous possible planets had. The sole moon was not as big as lunar but orbited close enough to produce tides.

Once in orbit Ellen authorised unmanned probes into various orbits and high atmosphere approaches seeking to collect as much data as possible before risking lower level flights over the surface.

With her mind very much on the dangers demonstrated by the previous two attempts these were maintained for several days providing increasing data loads for analysis.

The best results were the existence of life both on land and in the seas. The birds that could be seen were feathered rather than otherwise. The most important aspect was the lack, in so far as could be seen, of any sapient species on the land.

Eventually after a week of uneventful surveying Ellen agreed that lower overflights could be undertaken by unmanned probes. With a show of optimism that she feared would be misunderstood she instructed that these surveys should start looking for suitable landing sites that would enable a settlement to build and then expand over time. Asking the advice of Angelique Rouse before outlining her own thoughts.

"Captain, I suggest a coastal location above cliffs but near a river delta. That would allow us to have a fresh water supply but still be within easy reach of a supply of fish. However, we will need land for cultivation as well as for buildings. We should also look to identify any likely areas that might provide us with metals. A nice and easy challenge everyone. Given that the climate could well be very like 19th century Earth, rather than the more extreme weather seen in the 21st century we should be looking at latitudes similar to Northern Spain and California. It would be good if we could find an area where it is springtime."

Jorge Grey had joined Angelique and added.

"Captain, we will need some soil samples. We can check the compatibility with our own soil. If it is compatible then growing earth type crops will be much easier. If it isn't then the sooner, we can look at how viable locally sourced crops will be for the settlement the better. That will make Angelique's comment about springtime even more important."

"Noted thank you both. Any other thoughts people?"

"It might be as well to focus on sites that are on the western side of the two continental landmasses." Unusually it was Megan who spoke up. "On Earth the western sides had milder weather than the eastern sides, places such as Vancouver, Britain, northern California. Sorry." She added as she heard the murmurs of grief.

"No apology needed Megan," Ellen reassured her, "we can't ignore our past. Our memories are still clear and harsh but nor must we forget our origins. Now let's get the probes airborne."

Multiple flights were launched being operated by AIs but with close overview by remote controllers. Ellen and John were playing safe and looking to avoid any unnecessary losses should the unexpected happen.

After a week of hard work by the teams most of the surveys had been completed to the satisfaction of the various research teams who were then given a further week by Ellen to come up with results to be presented at a meeting of senior crew and department heads.

Overall it was good news. The local flora was close enough to Terran plants that the horticulturalists and agronomists were confident that they would be able to feed the settlement or at least grow crops from the seed bank on board. In fact, the compatibility of the local ecology with that of Earth was a surprise to all the specialists in that area. As they advised Ellen.

"All the theory on how we would interface with life on other planets has supported the idea that, for example, alien bacteria would not be a danger to humans as their development would have been very different. It was not hard to expand that idea into other ecological areas. The planet might have been prepared for us, impossible as that might be."

No serious issues had been identified with plenty of wildlife but no unusual predators had been spotted though there were clearly some as the zoologists expected. There were no adverse microbes in the various samples and no apparent sapient lifeforms. All in all, the planet looked to be the ideal location for humans to live and thrive.

"The orbit is quite stable as far as we can tell with a year equivalent to sixteen months, Earth time. The planet's spin is a little slower than we are used to so the days are a little over twenty-six hours long. For the moment we should assume that the seasons are proportionally similar. That is spring/summer would be eight months with autumn/winter similar." Alejandro sounded as positive as Ellen could remember.

"That leaves the choice of landing site." Ellen was trying hard not to sound excited. "John, please would you explain where we are on this."

"Using our original thoughts, we have managed to identify just two possibilities." He started. "There were several more. A number failed on one or more of our requirements. The biggest reason for avoiding other sites turns out to be none of the reasons we considered. The planet, as we should have expected, is still tectonically active and two of the coast lines we looked at are clearly close to the edges of tectonic plates with an attendant risk of earthquakes and, in one case, existing active volcanos. For that reason, we decided to eliminate them from the short list. Of the two, one is a large island just off the coast of the mainland, the other is on a river estuary. Given that our knowledge of the local fauna is still limited, we are recommending the island which is roughly the size of the old Sicily. We may need to cross the strait between it and the mainland when seeking metal deposits but that will not be a problem given that we have more than adequate transport to manage that."

With no-one in disagreement Ellen formally authorised the initial landing of a specialist team in one lander. Very conscious of the unexpected she ordered that a second lander should fly a cover pattern over the surrounding country at all times.

While the first two craft were being prepped, the crew turned their attentions to how the settlement would be housed. Ellen made the point that her original orders had deemed the Einstein to be a settlement ship but she was not aware of any equipment to support the early stages of a planetary landing. "Surely," she said, "there must have been some preparation included. Tents or similar, at least."

Shortly afterwards there was a eureka moment in engineering. Molly decided to search not the physical areas but to ask the ship's computer a simple question. "Computer, what references do you have for colonisation or settlement landings?"

She was not surprised that the computer chose to produce a list of entries rather than a single verbal response. What did give her cause to gasp was a set of references to storage areas deep in the bowels of the ship, areas which to the best of her knowledge and that of Scott, when asked, had never been accessed. Scott reported to Ellen providing her with the details of the references.

"We have these but nothing else and the storage areas appear to have been sealed electronically. There are no codes included in the computer references."

John was bent over his station running an officer search through the data. Then he turned, slightly bemused, to Ellen, "I think these simply need you, Ellen, to insert your command codes. Here."

Ellen crossed to the station and entered her identity codes and a moment later a detailed list of contents and access codes to the relevant storage areas appeared. To their amazement not only were parts for pre-fabricated buildings included but also heavy-lifting gear and a cargo sized lander with its own docking bay. "How could we have missed this?" Ellen asked.

Scott, looking embarrassed, admitted that the sheer size of the Einstein was the answer. With extensive storage freely available and not even full in some cases there had never been any reason to look further from the normal docking bays. There had been full stocks of all the equipment needed on board and the fact was that the additional docking bay was well camouflaged.

Ellen retired to her ready room and studied the detail. Then, half an hour later, she called her first officer in.

"John, this is almost unbelievable. Those holds have everything to build a functioning settlement. Solar powered houses big enough to house four, solar powered communal buildings, heavy lifting gear, construction diggers, farming equipment, even ultralights. You name it, I suspect it's there."

"Ultralights? What about water equipment?"

"Water purifiers, if that's what you mean, but also a few boats, mostly fishing vessels. Someone spent a lot of time thinking about what would be needed. I thought we would have to move our labs from Einstein but there are even a set of prefab buildings with medical and research facilities."

"I am still struggling to understand why this information was not freely available until now. If the question hadn't been phrased correctly, we might never have found out." John was being quite formal given that Molly was Judy's sister.

"That's true but I have to believe that the release of that data must have been programmed in some other way. There would have been no reason to hide it for ever. What it does do is give us a flying start in setting up the first settlement and it will leave the Einstein fully equipped. Nevertheless, Molly's actions deserve recording positively."

"It sounds as if you have plans beyond "New Eden"."

Ellen laughed. "I guess it was always likely that that is what it would be called but yes I can think of a few trips for the ship, post set up."

* * *   * * *   * * *

With that they broke up to arrange the various planning meetings that would allow a full transfer of personnel to the planet. The logistics of the move were eye boggling, as the various teams acknowledged. Assuming the advance party reported no serious difficulties the transfer of materials even with the heavy lifting lander would involve more than a hundred sorties while just moving the four thousand plus non-crew members would involve the three ordinary landers in a total of more than three hundred trips not including those to allow the crew some relaxation planet side.

With an advance team on the surface, Ellen decided that they should study their surroundings and the eco-system they were faced with for several weeks before further people were committed to the planet. While there was a degree of disappointment in the delay most of those still on the ship accepted that an element of care was sensible given past experiences.

The best news from the earlier sample collections was that the local soil was a surprisingly close match to that of Earth and the agricultural team, a combination of the hydroponics and biology teams, had taken advantage by planting a series of test crops. All the initial signs were that these would grow well as the climate was proving to be temperate. To date there were no apparent pests to seriously damage the various plants and crops.

"Though we feel that that is because the local animals haven't yet identified these as edible, yet." Explained one of the team with a grin. "When they do, we may need to be more protective of them!"

While limiting the number of those exposed to the local eco-system, Ellen and her team oversaw repeated excursions by landers and unmanned probes around the planet, searching for metal outcrops and other areas of possible interest.

The biologists took pleasure in overflights of various animal herds and close ups of birds. There were many different specimens but none, that they could identify, more dangerous than similar animals that might have been found on Earth. Occasionally they had managed to spot the local predators. Perhaps not surprisingly, on a planet predominantly of mammals, they did not differ to any great extent to the big cats of Africa. What did appear to be missing was any local equivalent of the monkeys and apes of Earth.

"It is somewhat surprising that the reptile population is much lower than we experienced on Earth." Emica Kichida, one of the biology team, commented to Ellen and her team during a review of the findings of the first weeks. "I find it difficult to believe that there could have been an event equivalent to that which killed the dinosaurs. Our best assumption, for the time being, is that the evolutionary process simply did not produce large reptiles at all. Equally the lack of the big apes and monkeys suggests that this planet might never have produced a high-level civilisation. As far as we have been able to see the most intelligent creatures are the local equivalent of the Earth's cetaceans."

"Given that the first non-human civilisation we found was humanoid in form, why is it that evolution has not managed that here?" Will Carden sounded perplexed.

It was Hannah Newton who responded. "We agree. All our previous computer modelling suggested that the humanoid form was the most logical outcome of how evolution worked. Now we may have to revise all that knowledge and theory."

"Are there any other possibilities for sentience?" Ellen, ever practical, cut to the heart of the question.

"So far, no obvious ones. But we have only been surveying the planet for a short time and I wouldn't like to suggest that we could possibly have seen all there is to see. For the moment, there is no evidence of any beings with an advanced technological civilisation.

The medical team's comments about the planet overlapped that of the biologists. Will Carden outlined a few issues with the insect population.

"You won't be surprised to know that there is a multiplicity of types. Our main concern is that there are a number of fliers that can cause bites and stings. We will need to develop improved anti-histamines in case any generate an allergic reaction. Other than that, I think that we should be reasonably safe from local diseases as there are no commonalities with the human system. We will have to be careful to watch for any developments in the future that might show that local germs are adapting."

Finally, after three months of tests and local examinations, Ellen called together all the Heads of Department and confirmed that they should prepare their people for transfer to the new settlement as fast as the crew could organise the transfer of the settlement equipment and buildings to the surface. This was scheduled to take another six months but as planned the new settlement would begin to grow across the plain chosen from orbit. At that meeting Ellen suggested that the Einstein would be tasked with a further search of the cluster and asked that she be advised of any individuals who wished to volunteer to stay with the ship.

The following days saw the start of the transfer of people down to the planet together with tents for temporary accommodation. The heavy-lifting lander was in immediate use moving the first sections of the buildings and within a matter of a few days the first homes were being assembled by the engineering department supported by all the other groups. With almost a thousand buildings to complete there was a need to spread the workload and for the people transfer to move more quickly. A couple of months later there was a small ceremony to mark completion of the first fifty buildings at which Ellen was present not as the captain, having spent time helping the construction teams, but as one of the helpers.

A year after the first humans landed on the planet Ellen made her first trip planetside in her official role as Captain.

"Everyone. We have spent many months preparing for today and I wish to thank you all for all the work that has been undertaken. It seems appropriate that we should celebrate with a Harvest Festival. Even with all the equipment available the planting of the crops took a great deal of work. That we have had a successful harvest does, for me, provide a great reason for optimism for our future. Nevertheless, to paraphrase a great leader of the past, today is not the end of our task but only the end of the beginning. We must look towards a future which we now know may hold dangers that were once the domain of the science fiction writer. Today we have the people, the technology and a great start here on Eden. We must now work to develop a planet with the defences capable of avoiding the fate of our first home, Earth. This will not be easy but everything I have learned about you tells me that you will set about that task with conviction. I am also delighted to hear that that commitment is supported, by the fact that we have a dozen or more future mothers already, thanks to each, and everyone, of you.

I now have the honour to formally name our new home, here. As an astronaut, I am delighted that you wish to honour the memory of another astronaut. From now on our home will be known as Yablon Town. As we grow our new home, please know that I will be alongside you."

*** *** ***

After the celebrations were complete and most people had left for their new homes, Ellen found herself with a small group of friends, John Lees, the Pipers, Will Carden and, of course, Jing. It was John who asked the question that had occurred to each of them.

"Ellen, you said you will be alongside the settlers. Do you mean that you intend to join the settlement on a permanent basis? What is going to happen to the Einstein?"

"John, is it not obvious? I intend to announce my resignation as Captain tomorrow. It is time for change and yesterday I signed the necessary orders and instructed the computer that as of tomorrow the Einstein will have a new Captain, Captain John Lees. I will leave it to you to choose your first officer, though I suggest that Cheung would be a good choice."

Megan broke in. "Ellen would it be reasonable to assume you have an idea of your role, planetside?"

"I gather that certain suggestions have been made that we will need an Administrator, if it is acceptable to everyone, then it is a job I'd be happy to take on."

"Oh good, one I can avoid then. A few people were trying to nudge me that way but, I think, that it has been generally assumed that you would stay on the Einstein."

* * *　　* * *　　* * *

As the group broke up Ellen called John and Judy back.

"John, you will find a list on board the ship of the crew and other volunteers. There are enough to run the ship and provide good specialist support. My last order for the Einstein and its crew is also detailed but, in short, I am sending you on a search mission around the cluster to see if there is intelligent life on any other planets or, for that matter, any ones that would provide a second home for us. After that, well, you may have to find another role for the ship. We do need to keep Einstein operational and with an adequately trained crew. I propose that we have a formal handover on board tomorrow."

John, who was still a little stunned by Ellen's words, took a deep breath.

"As you wish, Captain. Tomorrow, on the Einstein."

* * *　　* * *　　* * *

30. *A Watcher Awakes*

The skeleton crew still on the Einstein were on a low level of alert but it would have made no difference if they had been at a high state of awareness. Nothing happened to trigger the Einstein's sensors but, on the other side of the system, circling one of the gas giants, a computer, already ancient in Roman times, stirred from its electronic sleep as its sensor array, spread across the system, reacted to the increase in radio traffic arising from the various craft involved in the repeated transfers from Einstein to the planet. With an increasing level of awareness, it began a study of the system, looking to identify the events that had caused it to wake.

***　　　***　　　***

About the Author

David Adams was born in England in 1952 and spent his working life in finance. First as a banker until, as he puts it, he saw the light and switched from poacher to gamekeeper spending most of his career in Corporate Treasury functions as Group Treasurer for a number of multinational companies. Now retired he spends what little free time he has playing golf, walking the family dog and, on occasion, looking after the grandchildren with his wife Marion.

Lightning Source UK Ltd.
Milton Keynes UK
UKHW040845010720
365584UK00006B/107